The Rebel and the Cowboy

The Rebel and the Cowboy

A Carmody Brothers Romance

Sarah Mayberry

TULE
PUBLISHING

Chapter One

*U*H-OH. *THAT'S A bad sign.*

Eva King watched with growing unease as the young receptionist at the Marietta Motel had a hushed, furtive conversation with an older woman Eva guessed was the manager. Both women turned to look at Eva briefly before resuming their consultation.

Eva ran a hand through her short blond hair. She'd been driving since early this morning and all she wanted was a shower and something to eat that didn't come from a fast food window. But instead of handing over the key to her room when she arrived five minutes ago, the receptionist had tapped at her computer briefly, rifled through printouts on her desk, then called her boss out from her office.

Not exactly reassuring.

Finally the older woman patted the receptionist on the shoulder before stepping up to the desk, a mask of polite concern on her face.

Eva braced herself. Experience had taught her people were always at their most polite when they were about to disappoint.

"I'm so sorry to have to tell you this, Ms. King, but we

have no record of your reservation. And unfortunately, we have no vacancies at the moment. June is always a busy time of year for us."

"That's not possible. I have my reservation right here," Eva said, showing her the confirmation she'd printed out three weeks earlier when she made her online booking.

"Unfortunately, there's just nothing in our system. It's incredibly strange—this has never happened to us before and I'll be getting our computer guy to look at it first thing."

"Okay, but where does that leave me?" Eva asked.

"I can give you the number for the Graff Hotel in town, if you like? There's also Bramble House B and B, but I know for a fact they're booked out this week because we got the overflow." The manager's smile was full of professional sympathy.

Eva was tempted to stand her ground and argue harder, but if there were no rooms, there were no rooms. It wasn't like the woman could just magic accommodations out of thin air.

"Thanks, but I've already got their number," Eva said.

"As I said, I'm terribly sorry. I've got your details, though, so if something comes up unexpectedly, I'll call you."

"Great," Eva said. "Awesome."

Lips pressed together to hold back some choice four-letter words, Eva exited to the parking lot. Standing in the afternoon sun, she tried to fight the panicky feeling tightening her chest. Her big meeting was tomorrow. The rest of today was supposed to be about doing reconnaissance, getting a sense of the town, and scouting the location of the old grain elevator that would be her canvas if things went well. She didn't have time to waste finding somewhere to sleep for the night.

Don't freak out. Take a deep breath and THINK.

One thing was certain, she couldn't stay at the fancy hotel the motel manager had recommended. She'd considered it when she first looked at options for accommodations in Marietta, but the moment she saw the high-scoring reviews for the Graff, she'd known Dane and his crew would want to stay there. Despite his reputation as an edgy street artist, Dane was five stars all the way when he traveled.

Eva would rather sleep in her van than stay under the same roof as her ex-employer, who also happened to be her ex-boyfriend. Hell, she'd rather sleep in the woods, with wolves and creepy-crawlies to keep her company.

But hopefully it wouldn't come to that, because any second now, she would come up with a brilliant plan to find somewhere to sleep for the night. This was what she did best, after all—troubleshoot. For five years she'd put out fires and solved problems for her ex. Now it was time to use her skills to help herself.

Any second now.

The panicky band around her chest got tighter as her brain remained stubbornly blank. There was so much riding on the next few days. Everything, really.

Concentrate. Get your shit together. There must be someplace else to stay around here, even if it's not an official motel or hotel.

Hope in her heart, Eva pulled up the Airbnb app on her phone. Sixty seconds later, she shoved it back into the pocket of her skinny jeans. Apparently the sharing economy hadn't reached small-town Montana just yet. Damn it.

Okay, fine. She was going to have to get creative. Crossing the lot to her beaten-up black van, Big Bertha, Eva climbed in and started the engine. The motel was on the outskirts of town and it was only a short drive before she was cruising down the aptly named Main Street, scanning the well-kept, quaint western storefronts, determined to find a place locals frequented. A general store or café, someplace where the staff would have their finger on the pulse of the town.

She found what she was looking for almost immediately—the Main Street Diner looked as though it had been around since the fifties, and Eva could see they were doing a decent trade, even though it was nearly three on a Tuesday afternoon and not exactly rush hour.

She parked the van, then sent up a prayer to the universe. *Running water and a pillow, that's all I need.*

She entered the diner and was immediately enveloped in the homey smell of bacon and coffee, with a base note of waffles. Laughter rang out, the sound loud against the background murmur of people talking. Eva took in the red brick walls, the booths along the wall, and the tables in the window before moving to the counter, where red leather-covered stools were bolted to the wooden floor.

There was a spare seat on the end next to a slim, dark-haired woman who was absorbed in her phone and Eva paused beside it.

"Okay if I take this?" she asked.

The woman glanced across at her with a distracted smile.

"All yours; help yourself."

Eva slid onto the stool and watched the waitress refill coffees at the other end of the counter. An older woman with a genuine beehive hairdo, she looked like exactly the kind of person Eva needed.

Finally the waitress noticed Eva, bustling over with her order pad at the ready.

"Good morning to you. You looking for food or coffee or both?" the woman asked.

The plastic badge on her chest told Eva the woman's name was Flo and Eva offered her a smile.

"Coffee and apple pie, if you've got some."

Flo propped a hip against the counter. "We've got apple pie, cherry crisp, and a peach cobbler that will knock your socks off."

Eva laughed. "Wow. All right, I'll try the cobbler. My socks like to live dangerously."

Flo smiled as she jotted down Eva's order.

"Also, I wonder if you could tell me if there's anyone local who has a room to rent?" Eva asked. "Just for a few nights? I was supposed to stay at the motel, but there was some kind of mix-up with their reservation system and they don't have anything available, and apparently Bramble House is fully booked, too."

"Then your next best bet is the Graff. One block down and over, just turn left," Flo said, sketching directions in the air.

"Unfortunately, my ex is already booked to stay there. So that's not really an option for me," Eva confessed.

"Done you wrong, did he?"

Eva managed a tight smile. "He'd tell you differently. But yeah, he did."

Flo tapped her order pad with her pencil, eyes narrowed in thought. "Let me have a think. There are a couple of people I know with empty rooms now their kids have gone off to college. They might be willing to help out. Let me make a couple of calls. I'll be back in five."

Flo filled a mug with coffee and slid it toward Eva before moving off.

Eva wrapped her hands around the warm mug, silently willing Flo to come through for her, because she really didn't want to sleep in her van.

"Excuse me—sorry, I didn't mean to eavesdrop, but it was kind of unavoidable," the woman next to her said. In her mid-twenties, she had long, dark wavy hair, and an open, attractive face with big green eyes. "You're looking for somewhere to stay in town?"

"That's right," Eva said. "Feel free to make my day and tell me you know some place."

"Don't get too excited yet. We're not talking about the Hilton here."

"What *are* we talking about?" Eva asked.

"Me and my brothers have got a ranch twenty minutes out of town. There's an old Airstream trailer parked behind the barn. It's plumbed and wired in—we use it as a guest room when people come to stay—but it's pretty basic."

Eva sat up straighter, hope fluttering in her chest. "Are you kidding me? It sounds amazing."

The woman offered Eva her hand. "I'm Sierra Carmody, by the way."

"Eva King."

"If you're interested, I'll talk to my brothers and see if they're cool with renting the trailer out. Then you can come check it out and decide if it's for you or not."

"I am about as interested as it's possible for a person to get," Eva said. "In fact, if you're not super careful, I'm going to hug you any minute now."

Sierra laughed again. "Give me a moment and I'll see if I can get Casey or Jed on the phone."

She slid off the stool, and once she was standing, Eva could see she had nearly eight inches on Eva's own five foot three, with long, coltish legs and a slim build. Eva watched Sierra walk outside to make her call, wishing for the second time that day that she could read lips.

Not wanting to appear completely desperate, she swung back to face the counter and drank her coffee. Surely between Flo and Sierra, there had to be a solution to her temporary homelessness.

A couple of minutes later, Sierra slid back onto the stool beside Eva.

"Okay, we're good to go," she said.

"Really? They said yes?"

"They did. But again, wait until you've seen it before you get too excited," Sierra warned.

"Given that plan B was sleeping in my van, it's going to take a lot to un-excite me," Eva said, relief washing through her.

"How do you want to do this? I'm about to head home now if you want to follow me, or I can give you the address and you can swing by later?"

"Now is good for me, if it's good for you."

Flo returned with Eva's cobbler then, a rueful expression on her face.

"Sweetheart, I'm sorry, I tried both people and neither of them was home. But I'll try again before you leave and we'll see what we can do for you."

"I think I've found something—Sierra's going to help me out," Eva said.

"Eva's going to come look at the old Airstream behind the barn," Sierra explained.

"Perfect, I love it. Clearly it's fate—you two were meant to sit next to each other," Flo said, patting Sierra's hand before moving off to greet new customers.

Sierra caught Eva smiling and shrugged. "Small towns. Everyone knows everything about everyone. Hot tip—do not buy condoms from the local drugstore if a woman with red hair is working the cash register."

Eva laughed. "Okay. Duly noted. But I'm pretty sure that's not going to be an issue for me while I'm in town."

"Never say never, right?" Sierra said with a wink.

Eva pushed the cobbler so it sat halfway between herself and her new friend.

"Have some peach cobbler and live dangerously with me, Sierra Carmody."

"Why not?" Sierra said.

Eva scooped up a spoonful of dessert and made happy noises when a party started in her mouth.

"Yeah, the diner has the best desserts in Marietta," Sierra said. "So, are you in town for work or family or something else?"

"Work. Hopefully. I've got a meeting tomorrow. If I get the job, I'll be staying longer, but it's a bit of a long shot."

"So what kind of work do you do?"

"I'm an artist," Eva said matter-of-factly.

"Really? That sounds pretty cool," Sierra said, her face bright with interest.

"Mostly I work outside, on scale. Big murals, that sort of thing."

"So if I Google your name, will your art come up?" Sierra asked, already reaching for her phone.

Eva shifted on the stool. "You probably need to search for Dane Dafoe."

How she hated having to say that. After five years of collaborating with Dane in every way, it still burned that she'd never been given the credit she was due.

"Oh. All right." Sierra tapped away at her phone.

"There should be a few—"

"Oh my God. Did you do this? That's amazing," Sierra said, eyes wide as she stared at the image on her screen.

Eva leaned close to see Sierra was looking at a photo of the ship's hull she and Dane had painted in Norway. A portrait of a Valkyrie warrior painted in shades of gray, black, and blue, it was an epic piece that never failed to move Eva.

"That was a big job. We had two days to paint the hull before the ship was due out again," Eva said. "Coldest I've ever been in my life."

"This is seriously cool. Amazing," Sierra said, her gaze still intent on the screen.

Eva felt a familiar wash of pride tinged with regret as she

watched the other woman's reaction. She'd put so much into the Norway project—months liaising with the ship's captain, its owners, the port authority, the local council. Then there'd been all the research she'd had to do to find out if the aerosol paint brand she and Dane preferred would be suitable for maritime use in cold temperatures. Eva was the one who had discovered the tough top coat they'd used to preserve the mural and ensure it would last for years to come, just as she was the one who had uncovered the local myth about the warrior queen who had led her people to victory hundreds of years ago. She'd roughed out the concept and spent hours suspended from the ship's deck, painting side by side with Dane.

But it was Dane's name in the newspapers, Dane's name in the art review magazines, Dane's career that had shot even higher into the stratosphere, while she didn't even rate a footnote or a casual mention.

"So are you doing something like this in Marietta?" Sierra asked. "I mean, not a ship, obviously. But are we getting something this awesome?"

"That's the plan. The Chamber of Commerce is working with a local builder to transform an old grain elevator near a housing development just out of town."

"You're talking about the old Clarke grain elevator and Heath McGregor's development."

"That's the one," Eva confirmed, recognizing the names.

"I thought they were going to tear that elevator down?" Sierra asked with a frown.

"I think the owner refused, so the next best option was to pretty it up. Which is where the Chamber of Commerce got involved, I believe."

"Of course, because of the aforementioned small-town situation. God forbid anything happen without everyone being all up in everyone else's business and there being a community vote on it," Sierra said with an eloquent eye roll. "So you have to audition for this job, is that the story?"

"Essentially, yeah," Eva agreed, even though it was a little more complicated than that.

"So who are you up against?"

"Dane Dafoe, the guy I worked with on that," Eva said, indicating the image still filling Sierra's phone screen.

Sierra sat up straight, her expression arrested. "Wait, is he the ex you mentioned who is staying at the Graff? The one who did you wrong?"

Eva smiled tightly by way of answer.

"Oh, man, that sucks."

"Not if they give the job to me," Eva said.

"This is true." Sierra brushed her hands together decisively. "Okay, Eva King, let's head out to the ranch so you can cross 'somewhere to sleep' off your to-do list. Then you can concentrate on beating this Dane guy, who I'm sensing is a bit of a douche canoe."

"He's one hundred percent douche canoe, with a sprinkling of asshole on top," Eva said.

"Then let's do this," Sierra said, pulling out her wallet to settle her bill.

Five minutes later, Eva was sitting in Big Bertha, engine running, waiting for it to truly sink in that her accommodation crisis was solved. It had only chewed up an hour of her day, too, which meant she could still scout out the grain elevator and get a feel for the town.

Then she just had to convince McGregor Construction and the Marietta Chamber of Commerce to take a chance on her when she met with them tomorrow afternoon.

Because that was all she needed—just one chance, one opportunity. After all these years of paying her dues, surely that wasn't too much to ask? She had the runs on the board; she'd just never been acknowledged or credited for all her hard work.

She could knock this out of the park—if someone was prepared to let her take a swing.

She realized she was strangling the steering wheel, her knuckles white with the strength of her grip.

It's okay. You've got this. You can do this.

And if she couldn't… Well, that was a rabbit hole to disappear down another day.

Up ahead, Sierra pulled away from the curb, and Eva followed suit. One foot in front of the other. That was the only way she was going to get through the next few days.

CASEY CARMODY WAS in the barn when he heard the sound of cars pulling into the yard. Wiping dusty hands on the seat of his jeans, he adjusted his hat and headed out into the sunlight to meet their prospective houseguest.

It was so Sierra to offer a helping hand to a random stranger she'd met at the diner. His sister had a heart the size of Texas and had never been able to stand by when someone was in need. Casey, on the other hand, was a little more cynical, and his gaze was quietly assessing as he took in the woman talking to his sister in front of a faded black van.

She was standing side-on to him, but he could see she was boyishly slim, with short, white-blond hair. She was wearing a pair of black skinny jeans with a white T-shirt, and her black Chuck Taylor sneakers were splattered with paint. As he watched, she gestured with her right arm and he registered a brightly colored tattoo on her bicep.

City girl, was his first thought.

"Casey. Come meet Eva," Sierra called, gesturing for him to join them.

The blonde woman turned to face him fully as he approached, and he found himself looking into a pair of very blue eyes as she smiled at him.

"Casey. Great to meet you," she said, offering him her hand.

"You, too," Casey said, a little surprised by the wiry strength in her grip and how pretty she was, something he hadn't picked up from her profile.

"Please tell me you had a chance to check out the trailer before we got here," Sierra said.

"Gave it a once-over. Bar fridge is working, but the stove isn't."

"That's fine," Eva said quickly. "I can barely cook toast, so I don't need a stove, just somewhere to rest my weary head for a day or two."

"Unless you get the commission," Sierra said.

"Right. But let's cross that bridge when I come to it. If I come to it," Eva said, flashing his sister a smile.

She had a dimple in her cheek. Casey tried not to stare at it, or to notice the way her small breasts pressed against the fabric of her T-shirt when she slid both hands into the back pockets of her jeans.

"Eva is an artist," Sierra explained. "She's hoping to get a commission to paint a mural on the grain elevator out at the Clarke place."

Casey nodded. He'd never been great at small talk, especially with strangers. "Good luck with that."

"Thanks," Eva said, her gaze traveling down and then up his body, checking him out.

"Well, let's get this over with, put you out of your misery," Sierra said.

The two women moved off, and Casey's gaze gravitated to Eva King's butt. Small and shapely, it looked as though it would fit perfectly into a man's hands.

He frowned, a little thrown by the strength of his reaction. Eva King was not beautiful or built, but there was something in the way she walked and the way she'd met his eye that spoke to him.

She was *sexy*, and he found himself following her and his sister, drawn like an iron filing to a magnet.

"I love it. It's perfect," Eva said the moment she rounded the corner of the barn and saw the trailer.

Situated on a concrete apron, the shiny aluminum Airstream had been in place for more than thirty years and was framed by well-established trees and bushes, giving it a homey, cozy appearance.

"Wait until you see inside," Sierra warned.

"I'm pretty low maintenance," Eva said. "Unless there's a cesspit in the middle of the floor, I am about to be eternally grateful that I sat next to you at the diner this afternoon."

She stepped up into the trailer and glanced inside, then turned to address Sierra.

"No cesspit. I'm now officially your slave for life."

"Get out of here," Sierra scoffed, laughing.

Eva grinned, and Casey took a step backward, alarmed by the surge of animal interest that pulsed through him at the sight of her all lit up with pleasure.

Yep, she was definitely sexy. Maybe a little too sexy for his peace of mind.

Just as well she was only staying a night or two.

"If the offer is still open, I would love to rent this place for a couple of nights," Eva said.

"Of course. Done," Sierra said.

Eva's gaze shifted to Casey as though seeking his agreement, too, and he dipped his chin in a nod and offered her a quick smile.

"Fantastic. Phew. That is such a load off, I can't tell you," Eva said.

She glanced over her shoulder into the trailer, relief and satisfaction radiating off her. The action showcased her small breasts for the second time in as many minutes and Casey forced himself to look away.

"You need help with your bags?" he asked.

"Oh, thank you, but I'm fine."

"Don't mind helping out," he said.

"Thanks, but I'm good," she said. "I always make a point of traveling light."

Sierra hopped onto the bottom step. "I'll show you the trick to folding the bed down."

Both women disappeared inside the trailer, and Casey

hovered for a beat.

Then he realized what he was doing—angling for more face time with Eva King—and turned away.

He had stuff to finish in the barn, and it was his turn to start dinner.

Plus, there was no point investing any energy in a woman who was going to be gone in two days, no matter how hot she was.

Only a fool would do that.

Chapter Two

EVA SHADED HER eyes, tilting her head back so she could take in the full width and height of the old Clarke grain elevator. Her laser measure told her it was one hundred and twenty feet high by forty-two feet wide, but it seemed much larger. Its timber boards were silvered with age, some still boasting the faded, peeling remnants of barn-red paint.

She'd have to sandblast the whole south-facing wall before she could even think about painting, and prep it with a suitable sealer and primer to ensure the longevity of her work. Any rotten boards would have to be pulled out and replaced.

But what a canvas it would make, truly heroic in scale.

She could feel the thud-thud of her heart within her ribcage as she absorbed the potential of the site. So many possibilities, and no matter what the subject, the finished work would be imposing.

Maybe even inspiring.

The late afternoon sun beat down on her as she walked back to the van to grab her digital camera and tripod. The one advantage of having driven Big Bertha all the way from LA was that she hadn't been forced to be stingy with her gear, which would have been the case if she'd flown. Setting up the tripod, she took a series of shots of the elevator, trying to capture a sense of the structure in its environment. Later, she'd download the images and use them to finalize her pitch for tomorrow's meeting.

Her stomach did a nervous loop-the-loop as she thought about how important the next twenty-four hours would be for her career. Her whole life, really. If she could convince the Marietta Chamber of Commerce to take a chance on her, she was off and running. If she couldn't… She didn't want to think about the hard choices she'd have to make if she couldn't get someone to believe in her.

She needed to make this work. Needed to bring her A game and put her best foot forward.

And yet annoyingly—distractingly—an image kept insinuating itself into her thoughts as she worked: Casey Carmody stepping out of the shadow of the barn and walking toward her, his lean, hard body showcased to perfection by worn jeans and a plain black T-shirt.

It had been more than two hours since that moment in the Carmodys' yard, but every time she thought about it, Eva experienced an echo of the visceral jolt she'd felt when she'd looked into his eyes for the first time.

She lived in LA, surrounded by some of the most beautiful, manicured, sculpted people in the world, but she was pretty sure she'd never seen a man as beautiful as Casey Carmody. Not in the flesh.

And yes, beautiful was the right word, even though there was nothing remotely feminine about his features. He had the same true green eyes as his sister, the same dark hair, but his jaw was clean cut, his cheekbones chiseled.

And then there was his body—broad shoulders, flat belly, lean, muscular legs. Pretty much every woman's fantasy cowboy, really.

Eva had had trouble focusing on what Sierra was saying, she'd been so caught off guard. And now here she was, thinking about Casey Carmody when she should be concentrating on her work.

You don't have time for this kind of crap, King.

She so didn't. Not to mention she was still licking her wounds over her breakup with Dane. She honestly hadn't had a sexual thought or urge in months—until Sierra's brother had walked out of the shadows and she'd had a whole, messy bunch of them all at once.

Crazy, and stupid, and more than a little inappropriate. And it was going to stop *now*, because she needed to concentrate.

Shaking her head, she removed the camera from the tripod and took a number of atmospheric landscape shots, focusing particularly on including majestic Copper Mountain with its snow-capped peak. It was so much a part of the landscape, it would be criminal not to include it in her pitch document. Then she drove into town and tried to capture the essence of Marietta within the frame of her camera. She shot the stately courthouse, with its curved dome, along with the Main Street Diner, inside and outside. She shot the grand library, and the well-tended park, and the neat, charming storefronts on Main Street. She felt like she'd hit the mother lode when she stumbled on the deserted fairgrounds on the other side of the river, home to the town's annual rodeo, using up a large portion of her memory card on a bronze statue of a horse and rider she found there, and the empty concrete bleachers and shuttered concession stands.

She made a final stop at the supermarket to pick up some bits and pieces for dinner, then made her way back out to the Carmody ranch.

There was no sign of any of the Carmodys as she parked and gathered her things. Eva shot a glance toward the low, ranch-style house with its wraparound porch, noting the row of roses that grew along the front and the huge yellow pine that shadowed the rear corner of the yard. Sierra said she lived her with her two brothers. She hadn't mentioned any wives or partners. So did that mean Casey was single?

None of your freaking business, idiot.

Annoyed with herself, she hefted her shopping bags and started across the yard. She was here in Marietta for one purpose, and one purpose only. End of story.

"SORRY I'M LATE, got held up," Casey said as he swung through the door of his friend's garage.

He'd heard the rest of the guys jamming as he drove up, and they kept playing as he unpacked his Gretsch acoustic guitar, Danny throwing him a smile to let him know they got it.

All four members of The Whiskey Shots had full-time jobs they had to put ahead of their music, and they'd all been late to practice one time or another.

"All right, let's get this show on the road," Wyatt said,

his fingers stilling on his Yamaha keyboard as Casey settled his guitar strap over his shoulder. "You got any updates on 'Been Too Long,' Carmody?"

Casey pulled copies of his latest effort from his back pocket and handed them out to Danny, Wyatt, and Rory, watching their faces as they quickly scanned the pages.

"Hey, I like what you did with the bridge," Rory said.

"Yeah, cool chord progression. Why don't we play it out and see how it sounds?" Wyatt suggested, pushing his black-framed glasses back up his nose.

"Let's do it," Casey said with a shrug.

It might be his song, but he wasn't against making changes or trying new arrangements. None of the Shots ever let their egos get in the way of finessing a promising song. It was one of the reasons they worked so well together—they'd all agreed early on that egos and bullshit would be checked at the door. None of them wanted to get caught up in drama when they could be making music.

Danny counted them in, tapping his drumsticks together to find the beat, then they all jumped into the opening verse.

"It's been too long, baby, and there've been too many miles between us, too many nights I've spent drinking on my own…" Casey sang.

He felt the familiar tingle at the back of his neck when the song built momentum as they headed for the first chorus. Rory caught his eye, grinning and nodding, and Casey's chest seemed to expand as the music swelled and Wyatt added his backup vocals to Casey's.

"Something's gotta change, because I can't live with this pain, something's gotta change around here…"

The beat drove them all forward, everything coming together, and by the time he was singing the final verse Casey knew they'd found their next song. It wasn't perfect, but it was close, and they were all silent for a long moment when the song was finished. Then Danny hit the crash cymbal and gave the bass drum a mighty kick.

"That was fucking awesome," he said, grinning ear to ear, and Casey could only laugh in agreement.

"Did it again, Case," Rory said, patting him on the back.

Casey was already pulling out a pencil and making notes on his copy. "Still not completely happy with that bridge. Felt like we lost something there at the very start. What do you boys think?"

The rest of the session flew by as they noodled around with his song some more before finalizing the set list for their monthly gig on Thursday night at Grey's Saloon. They were still arguing over whether to end with a ballad or Casey's new song when Wyatt announced he had to go.

"My turn to do dinner, and you know Louanne will destroy me if I'm late home," he said.

"It pains me to see you scared of your own wife, man," Danny said, shaking his head in mock commiseration.

"It's true, I'm a pitiful creature," Wyatt said, beaming happily.

Everyone knew he didn't mean it, not for a second, and they were all smiling to themselves as they began packing away their instruments. Since it was Danny's garage, this meant simply tossing an old bed sheet over his kit before helping himself to a beer from the battered fridge in the corner.

As always after a session, Casey felt loose and light and just a little wired. Music had always had that effect on him, even from a young age. Which explained why he couldn't let it go, even though he knew his energies would probably be better directed elsewhere. The ranch could always absorb extra man-hours, and if he was less engaged with his music, it stood to reason he'd be putting in more back home.

The thing was, he couldn't imagine his life without this time with the boys, without songs in his head, and the itch to pick up his guitar to flesh out an idea. Didn't want to imagine it.

"You boys got anything exciting going on for the rest of the week?" Rory asked as he wound up the cord for his amp.

"Nothing exciting this end," Danny said with a shrug. "Case?"

For some reason the memory of a woman with deep cornflower blue eyes and slight yet provocative curves filled Casey's head.

"Same old same old," he said. "You know."

"You guys kill me," Wyatt said. "I'd be out every night if I was a free man, making the most of my youth."

"Dude, do you have any idea how old it makes you sound when you say crap like that?" Rory asked.

"Yeah, you're twenty-nine, only a year older than me and Casey. Get a grip on this Old Father Time routine," Danny said. "Next thing you know, you'll be wearing thermals and talking about getting enough fiber."

"Here's a deal—I'll stop acting old if you two start acting young," Wyatt said, indicating Casey and Danny, both of whom were single. "Next time we're at a gig and the girls come up afterward, take down a few numbers."

"Thanks for the dating advice, Grandpa," Danny said.

They all cracked up.

"Fine. Have it your way. I'm going home to my wife and children," Wyatt said.

"Whoa, before you go," Rory said, reaching out to grab Wyatt's arm to haul him back. "Did you guys hear they're running a competition for undiscovered bands out of Radio KUPR in Billings?"

Danny's eyebrows went up. "Yeah? What's the prize?"

"Time in a recording studio and ten thousand cash. Plus all finalists get air play, regardless of who wins," Rory reported.

Danny and Wyatt glanced at Casey, waiting for his reaction. Like it or not, as lead singer he tended to be the default leader of the band.

"Don't look at me. What do you guys think?" he said.

"We could always enter, just to see what happens," Wyatt said, feeling his way into the idea.

"Be kind of cool to hear one of our songs on the radio," Rory said. "And the studio time would come in handy if we want to start selling stuff online."

Again, they looked to him, and Casey shrugged, even though his heart was sinking. The Whiskey Shots were his escape, his happy place, an indulgence he allowed himself to feed the part of his soul that needed music. He'd never harbored dreams of the band hitting it big because he'd always known they'd need to go on the road to build a profile to get anywhere, and he wasn't in a position to walk away from his obligations on the ranch. He'd thought the other guys were in the same place—they'd explicitly talked about being a local band and having other commitments when they first formed two years ago.

And yet right now there was no doubt that all three of his bandmates were keen to take a shot at the big time if the opportunity presented itself.

"Hey, if you guys want to put a song in, let's do it," he said, but even he could hear the lack of enthusiasm in his own voice.

"You don't want to?" Danny asked.

Casey shrugged again. "I don't lie in bed at night dreaming about us selling out stadium concerts. That was never what the Shots were about for me."

"Sure, none of us jumped into this with stars in our eyes, but the Shots have been pulling bigger and bigger crowds. You honestly telling me you don't feel a bit of an itch to see how big this thing could get?" Danny asked.

Casey could see they didn't understand where he was coming from. He was loath to reveal too much about private family business, but he felt as though they deserved an explanation for his tepid response.

"We've got some money problems out at the ranch at the moment." He could feel heat rising up his neck as he spoke, but he owed the guys some background so they understood where he was coming from. "We're pretty much cutting everything to the bone. I can't afford to take time out to do anything more with the band than what we do now. I can't let Jed, Jesse and Sierra down like that."

"Sorry, man. I didn't realize," Danny said, looking about as uncomfortable as Casey felt.

"We're not exactly shouting it from the rooftops. And we'll come good. It's just tight right now, you know?" Casey said.

Wyatt was nodding as though he understood. "Louanne's father has been saying the same. Lost too much feed to game during the winter, and the market's been low for too long. It's a bad combination."

"And don't get me started on the tariffs," Rory said.

Danny held up his hands to stem the flow. "Don't ruin my post-jam buzz, boys."

Casey laughed along with the others, but he felt bad. He didn't want to be the handbrake holding everyone back.

"Fuck it, let's put a song in. Just to see how we do, like a benchmark," he said.

He didn't say it out loud, but there was bound to be plenty of competition. Worrying about winning was pretty much the definition of putting the cart before the horse.

"We've said for a while it would be cool to be able to make our stuff available online," Rory said. "I know we can record on Danny's setup here if we really have to, but some real studio time would be good. If we win, we can just blow off the huge recording contracts we'll be offered left, right and center and tell Garth Brooks we're not interested in touring with him."

The guys all laughed again.

"All right, I've gotta go, but we should all have a think about what song to put in," Wyatt said, shouldering the strap for his keyboard carrier.

"Everyone picks one song, and we'll vote. Deal?" Rory suggested.

"Cool," Casey said.

He walked out to his truck with the guys, waving them off before reversing out of Danny's driveway and heading back to the ranch. As always, he felt himself get tense as he approached the spot on the state highway where his parents had died thirteen years ago. It had been fast—a head-on collision—but Casey never drove this way without thinking about them and that night.

Ten minutes later, gravel crunched beneath the wheels as he turned into the driveway. Band practice had pushed their houseguest from his mind and the sight of her beaten-up black van in front of the barn made him blink with surprise.

Kind of funny, given how much he'd been thinking about her, on and off, ever since he'd met her this afternoon. Despite his best intentions.

He figured it was because she was so different from the women he knew locally. Her skin was city-pale, and her tattoo and short hair marked her out as a rebel. Then there was the frankness in her gaze, a quality he found undeniably hot.

He parked beside his brother's truck, then grabbed his guitar and headed inside. Jed was in the kitchen making himself a coffee when Casey entered and he raised his eyebrows and lifted the jug, silently asking if Casey wanted a cup.

"Thanks, I'm gonna grab a beer," Casey said, helping himself to a bottle from the fridge.

"How'd practice go?" his brother asked, stirring sugar into his coffee.

"Good. Same as usual. Fine-tuned the new song."

"The one you've been working on lately? It's a good one."

"Thanks, but it still needs work." He took a pull from his beer, then did his best to sound casual. "You met our houseguest yet?"

"You mean our tenant? Yeah, she came up to the house to talk to Sierra after you left."

"Kind of interesting," Casey said.

"In what way?"

Suddenly Casey felt incredibly transparent. He shrugged casually. "Apparently she's an artist, or something like that."

His brother gave him a long look before hiding a half-smile behind the rim of the coffee mug. "Yeah, I heard that."

"I'm going to go check on the horses," Casey said.

Before he exposed himself any more.

"I'm turning in after this," Jed said, raising his mug. "So I'll see you in the morning. Still set to go into town first thing?"

"Yep, all good."

Casey exited via the kitchen door, stepping onto the porch. His boots were loud on the wooden planks as he made his way to the steps at the front of the house.

Why on earth did he bring up Eva King with his brother? So he could talk about her? Fish for more information?

Dumb. Now Jed was going to give him hell. And God help him if Sierra ever got wind of him being interested in their temporary tenant.

He didn't bother switching on the light in the barn, not wanting to disturb the horses unnecessarily. He did a quick check on their two pregnant mares, making sure they had enough feed and water. He was rubbing the swollen side of a heavily pregnant mare when he registered the faint sound of music coming through the barn wall. He cocked his head, trying to discern what it was.

The syncopated beat clued him in before he discerned the lyric of Chet Faker's "Talk is Cheap."

Interesting choice.

He pictured Eva in the trailer, listening to Chet Faker while she did…whatever it was she did. Painting? Drawing?

He shook his head, turning toward the door. He seriously needed to stop thinking about Eva King. He was starting to come off as desperate, even in the privacy of his own mind.

He stepped out into the dark yard and was just in time to catch sight of something in his peripheral vision before their new tenant walked into him with a startled yelp.

"Oh my God. You scared the crap out of me," she said.

The only light source was the stars overhead but he could see she had one hand pressed to her chest, as though checking to make sure her heart was still in residence.

"Sorry. Didn't mean to startle you."

"No, it's my fault. Normally I would have used the light on my phone but the reason I'm out here is because I need the charger and I left it in the van," she said with a self-deprecating laugh.

She'd changed out of her jeans and T-shirt into a tank and what looked like a pair of men's boxer shorts. The laces on her Chuck Taylors were undone and he guessed she'd been ready for bed when her phone died.

"There's a switch in the trailer for the barn lights. And

SARAH MAYBERRY

another one just here. Sierra should have pointed them out to you."

He indicated the waterproof switch to the left of the main door to the barn.

"She probably did and I forgot. Sorry for the drama. I had no idea my voice could get that high."

"No drama. Grab your charger and I'll show you the switch in the trailer," he said.

She hesitated a fraction of a second before responding. "Sure. Great. Thanks."

She walked the final few feet to her van and unlocked the side door, pushing it wide on its sliders. An interior light came on, bathing her in a yellow glow. She leaned into the van, one foot propped on the floor, rummaging for the charger.

He allowed himself a single brief glance at her toned legs before looking away.

"Got it. Was starting to think I must have left it in Salt Lake City last night," she said, sliding the van door shut.

He watched as she carefully locked it again.

"Not a lot of grand theft auto around here," he said. "You probably don't need to stress about security."

"Old habits die hard. I grew up in Detroit."

"You still live there?"

"I've been based in LA for the last few years," she said.

She was standing a few feet away, but the darkness made their conversation feel oddly intimate. He was acutely aware of her bare arms and legs, as well as his own reaction to her presence.

Gut tight, senses heightened, pulse a little fast.

Get a grip, dude.

"I'll show you the switches, for next time," he said, gesturing toward the barn.

"Cool. Thanks."

She followed him as he walked to the waterproof switch mounted to the left of the barn door.

"This'll give you light here and down the pathway," he said, flicking it on.

She laughed as they were bathed in light from the gooseneck lamps mounted either side of the door.

"That was almost Biblical," she said.

"The miracle of electricity."

She shot him an appreciative look, her mouth curling at the corners.

"So there's another one of these in the trailer?" she asked.

"Next to the fuse box."

She fell in beside him as he walked past the barn and down the gravel path beside it.

"So what do you guys farm here? Or grow. Is that even the right term?" she asked.

"We're a cattle operation, mostly, but we also breed horses for ranch work. Crop-wise, we grow our own feed as much as we can, but that's about it."

"So next time I'm eating a steak, I should think of you guys?"

"If you like," he said, glancing across at her.

She looked at him at the same time and their gazes clashed and held for a long beat before she broke the contact. They'd reached the Airstream and he paused at the foot of the steps.

"Okay if I go in?" he asked.

"Hey, it's your trailer, not mine," she said.

"It's yours for the next two nights," he reminded her.

He opened the door and stepped inside.

"This box set into the wall is the fuse box. And this switch here turns the barn lights on and off," he explained.

Eva stopped just inside the doorway, her attention focused on the fuse box. "So it's a two-way switch, then?"

"That's right. You can turn it off here, I can turn it on at the barn, and vice versa," he said, demonstrating by flicking the light off.

With the loss of the barn lighting, the only illumination came from the reading lamp above the bed and Casey was suddenly acutely aware of how alone they were, and how close she was.

"Thank you. I promise I won't ambush you in the dark again," she said.

He turned the barn lights back on, and the shadows—and intimacy—receded.

"No harm done," he said, turning to go.

He expected her to step back, out of the doorway, but she didn't immediately move and for the second time that night they were standing too close. He could smell her perfume, something sweet and earthy, and couldn't seem to stop his gaze from sliding from her face to her body. Which was when he made the discovery she was braless beneath her tank top, her nipples clearly visible against the fabric.

He forced his gaze back to her face and knew she'd caught him looking. The world seemed to still as they stared at each other, the silence thrumming with a hundred unspoken thoughts, most of them dirty. He'd wondered if she was as aware of him as he was of her, and now he knew.

She'd thought about him in the hours since they'd met, in the same way he'd thought about her. He could see it in the way she swallowed, the slight flush to her cheeks, and the barely visible flutter of her pulse at the base of her neck.

He'd never felt so drawn to a woman before, so compelled and fascinated. Everything in him wanted to close the distance between them but at the same time the sheer intensity of his need made him hesitate. And then she stepped back down the steps, retreating outside, and the potential of the moment drained away like water from a bathtub. Taking his cue from her, he exited the trailer.

"Thanks for your help. I appreciate it," she said.

"You have a good night," he said.

Lifting a hand in farewell, he walked away from what could have been and didn't stop until he was in the privacy of his own room.

Sinking down onto his bed, he reviewed what had just happened and let out his breath on a frustrated sigh, annoyed with himself for not following his instincts.

She'd wanted him. He'd seen it in her eyes.

Then he ran a hand through his hair and sighed again, his shoulders dropping a notch. The truth was, he'd never been a fast mover with women like his rodeo star brother, Jesse. Not that he was lacking in experience or anything, he'd just never been the kind of guy who'd pursued a woman just to get her into bed. For him, it had always been a package deal.

But maybe he'd just never met a woman he really wanted

to fuck before. Because that was pretty much all he could think about when he was around Eva King.

Might as well own it, since it was true.

Anyway. He hadn't made his move, and she hadn't, either, so there was no point dwelling on it. Standing, he went to brush his teeth and prepare for bed.

Chapter Three

*W*HAT THE HELL *were you thinking?*
The question kept circling Eva's brain as she brushed her teeth at the small bathroom sink and crawled into bed. Here she was, on the eve of what could be the most important, momentous meeting of her life, and she'd almost leapt on a man she'd just met and torn his clothes off. It beggared belief, it really did. She should be focusing on her pitch, not getting all hot and bothered over a beautiful cowboy.

It was ridiculous. Self-destructive, even.

Lying in the dark, she went over the tense, breathless moments after she'd caught Casey Carmody checking out her breasts. There was no reason in the world why the knowledge he'd noticed she was a woman should have affected her so profoundly. She'd had men check her out before, plenty of times. Some of them had been pretty hot, too. None of them had emptied her brain of all thought except the need to get naked and sweaty, however.

Not a single one.

There was some serious, nuclear chemistry going on between her and Casey Carmody. It seemed pointless to deny it, since the evidence was still vibrating its way through her body ten minutes after he'd walked away. She wanted him, and he wanted her, in the most basic, carnal, instinctive way. Which was pretty much the best example of bad timing Eva had come across in her life. She did not have the headspace or energy to spare on a distraction right now. She needed to be laser-focused, at her absolute sharpest.

Just as well common sense had reasserted itself before she'd done or said anything she couldn't take back. Otherwise she'd be rolling around on this very bed right now, a hard, hot cowboy pounding into her.

"Oh, for Pete's sake," she said.

Rolling onto her side, she squeezed her eyes shut, ignoring the needy throb between her thighs and willing herself to sleep. It took some serious concentration, but she finally felt the worries of the day slip away from her, and the next thing she knew it was morning and she could hear a car engine starting outside in the yard.

Struggling out of the mess she'd made of the sheets and duvet, she blinked blearily. Then she remembered how much work she had to do today, and she kicked the covers off and scrambled to the edge of the bed to grab her laptop.

She spent two hours adding yesterday's photographs to her pitch document before hunger pangs drove her to stop. She stuffed her face with a couple of granola bars, then had a shower and went back to work, finessing copy, researching details online, tweaking the layout. By two o'clock she was satisfied she'd created an attractive, professional document. She'd brought her portable inkjet printer with her, and she printed a proof copy and checked it over. Only when she was satisfied she hadn't tripped herself up with a dumb typo did she print off several copies for her meeting at four.

By then it was three and she had to rush to get ready and leave enough time to drive into town. There was no full-length mirror in the trailer, so she had to hope that her slim black trousers, long white shirt and fitted black waistcoat looked presentable. She had a last-minute panic when she could only find one of her prized, handmade Italian brogues, but she finally thought to check in the van and found it wedged under the front seat. How it got there she had no idea, but searching for it had chewed up precious time and she was feeling distinctly panicky by the time she'd gathered her papers and computer and transferred it all to the car.

Being busy all day had kept the worst of her nerves at bay, but there was nothing to do but drive as she headed into town and she could feel adrenaline spike in her belly as she contemplated the meeting ahead.

She knew getting the commission was a long shot. She only had an interview because she'd called up and literally pleaded with them to give her an opportunity to pitch alongside Dane. She suspected they were only giving her a hearing because she'd been so insistent and persistent. They'd probably already made up their minds to go with the man whose name was on all the art Eva had helped create. And why not? Dane had a reputation—he'd bring interna-tional cachet to the project. He was a known quantity.

Her armpits were cold with nervous perspiration by the time she arrived at the library. Despite her concern about being late, she was actually ten minutes early and she sat in Big Bertha and tried to calm the hell down.

You've done this a dozen times. You know your shit. They'll see that. Just go in there and let them see how much this means to you.

That was the problem, though—this meant too much to her. She didn't want to come across as desperate or nervous.

But it was entirely possible that wasn't a factor she could control.

She took a deep breath, then let it out, visualizing all her nervous energy flowing out of her body. Then she collected her printouts and laptop and made her way into the library.

A tall, good-looking man and a slim, blond-haired woman were standing together in the foyer, talking quietly, when she entered. They were both wearing work clothes—Dickies pants, and some kind of uniform polo shirt. The woman's hair was up in a high ponytail, and her steel-capped boots were scuffed. Eva almost walked past them before noticing the logo on the breast pocket of the man's polo—McGregor Construction.

"Hi," she said, stopping in front of them. "Almost missed you. I'm Eva King. Thanks so much for seeing me."

She could feel more nervous words filling her throat but she managed to stem the flow somehow.

"Heath McGregor," the man said, offering her his hand. "And this is my wife, Andie."

"Good to meet you, Eva," Andie said, her gaze warm and direct.

"Good to meet you. Hope I didn't keep you waiting?" Eva asked. It would be too freaking ironic if she'd been sitting in her car killing time when they'd been waiting for her.

"We're early," Andie assured her. "And Jane's not here yet."

"Hate to contradict you there, Andie."

They all three swung around to face the blond, well-dressed woman who had just entered, a slightly harried air about her.

"Jane McCullough, good to meet you," she said, shoving a hand at Eva. Her focus was on Heath and Andie, however. "I'm slammed, so this needs to be quick for me."

"I can be quick," Eva said, smiling brightly even as her stomach got tight with anxiety. She was almost certain no one had told Dane he would have to be quick when he had his meeting. Which meant she'd been right when she guessed she was not really a genuine contender for the project.

Despair made her eyes burn with sudden emotion, but Eva had never given up on anything in her life without putting up a fight.

"All right, let's go through to the conference room," Jane said, juggling her coat, handbag, and papers as she bustled ahead of them.

Eva smiled at Andie and Heath, hoping they couldn't see how rattled she was, and fell in behind Jane. She edited her presentation mentally as she walked, making lightning-fast cuts in her mind to ensure she could hit the highlights in the time allotted.

Ahead of her, Jane flung open a heavy, ornate door to a wood-paneled room that boasted a huge table surrounded by at least a dozen chairs.

"There's power there if you need it," Jane said, indicating an outlet on the wall near the door.

"Thanks, but the battery is fully charged," Eva said, pulling out a chair near the head of the table and setting down her things. Aware she was on the clock, she opened her laptop and hit return a couple of times to bring it to life before passing a printout of her proposal to Heath, Andie and Jane.

"Since time is short, should I just jump in?" she asked.

"Yes, thanks. Sorry, I know it's not ideal, but we've got a bit of a crisis in the works and if I don't smooth some feathers tonight we might lose a major sponsor for this year's rodeo," Jane explained.

"Totally understand," Eva said. "So let me just get this out of the way first up—I know I'm the underdog in this process. I know you sought Dane out because you've seen his work. But that means you've also seen my work. For five years, we've worked side by side on every project. I'm familiar with every technique, every process, every logistical consideration required to complete a project like the Clarke grain elevator. I want you to know that I can deliver this project on time and on budget."

Heath and Andie both nodded, but Jane was busy taking notes on her phone. At least, Eva hoped that was what she was doing. Eva swallowed the lump in her throat and pressed her shaking knees together under the table.

Come on, Universe. Give me a break here.

"What I can't give you is Dane's name. I know that, and that's why I would be prepared to take on this project for half of what you'd pay him," Eva said.

Heath's eyebrows shot up, while Andie frowned.

"Is that viable for you? My understanding is that this

process can take several weeks, maybe months to complete," Andie said.

"I want the boost to my profile this project would give me," Eva said frankly. "I'm prepared to put something on the table to win the commission. It means a lot to me. Which is another reason why I'm a good choice for this project—I will give you everything I've got, and more. I'm hungry, I'm talented, and I'm passionate. This won't be just another job for me."

Andie glanced at her husband, and Jane looked up from her notes to consider Eva for a beat.

"Do you have any examples of your solo work we can look at?" Jane asked.

"Of course. If you turn to page ten of the printout, you can see some pieces I did in my home city of Detroit," Eva said.

Everyone dutifully turned to page ten, and Eva watched as they studied her work, flicking through the five pieces she'd included.

"These are on a much smaller scale than our project," Jane said.

"I know, but I can assure you, that won't be a problem for me," Eva said.

Jane glanced at her watch, and Eva decided to just go for it.

"Here's what I'm thinking for the site at the moment," she said, turning her computer around so she could show them the graphics she'd mocked up this morning. "The elevator is one hundred and twenty feet by forty-two feet. That's a huge and beautiful canvas. The timber boards are in good condition, and I think repair work would be minimal. I'd like to propose a triptych on this structure, three portraits that represent the community of Marietta. I'd stagger them to make full use of the height, and Copper Mountain would serve as the backdrop, uniting the three portraits."

Eva clicked through to the graphic depicting her proposed allocation of space. The images she'd used as placeholders were taken from studies she'd made before for previous projects with Dane, the style more her own than what the finished works had been.

"You don't think a more tourist-type idea would be more suitable? A landscape, or something referencing the local industry?" Jane asked.

"People connect with people. It's like when you look through shots from somebody's holiday—the ones with the people in them are always the most emotional and compelling. My job will be to tell the story of Marietta *through* the portraits," Eva explained.

Heath asked a question about the sort of equipment she'd require on site, and Eva spent the next ten minutes answering questions. She was heartened somewhat by the fact that Jane instigated many of them—surely, if giving the commission to Dane was a done deal, the other woman wouldn't bother making Eva jump through so many flaming hoops?

"I'm sorry, but I need to run," Jane said suddenly, wincing as she checked the time on her phone. "Eva, it was great to meet you. I love how passionate you are about this project, and thank you for your honesty."

"Thanks for the opportunity to pitch for the commission. I know I pretty much forced myself on you all," Eva said.

"Sometimes you've got to make your own opportunities," Heath said, and Eva hoped she wasn't fooling herself that there was a glint of approval in his eyes.

Jane gathered her things and threw goodbyes over her shoulder as she left, and Eva offered her best, most confident smile to the McGregors.

"Do you have any more questions?" she asked.

"You've been really thorough. I think we've got everything we need to make a decision," Andie said.

"Can I ask when you think that will be?" Eva asked.

"We want to get the ball rolling as soon as possible, so we'd be hoping to sign off on things tomorrow. If you got the commission, when would you be able to start?" Andie said.

"Straight away. My schedule is clear at the moment. Although that may change," Eva fibbed.

"Great. We've got your number, and we'll read through all of this properly," Heath said, indicating her proposal. "We'll let you know sometime tomorrow."

"Thank you. And thanks again for your time," Eva said, standing and leaning across the table to shake hands with them both. Her hands were shaking as she reached out to gather her papers, and she hoped they didn't notice.

She left the McGregors in the meeting room, exiting to the marble-floored corridor before heading for the exit. She didn't let herself relax until she was in her van and on the road. Then she let out a huge sigh and felt her shoulders drop.

Well, it was done. She'd done her level best in the time available. They'd listened, they'd asked questions. She sensed she'd caught their interest with her offer to halve her fee. And all three had appeared impressed with the mock-ups of her ideas.

But had she done enough to make herself a true contender?

She had no idea.

And now that she was done and there was nothing left to do but wait, she felt jittery with residual adrenaline. The time between now and tomorrow seemed to stretch ahead of her like a desert highway, endless and comfortless.

God, she hated waiting.

Almost without consciously willing it, she steered Bertha back to Main Street. She was pretty sure she'd seen a bar or a saloon along here somewhere yesterday, and the thought of a calming shot of something fiery and alcoholic sounded pretty good to her right now.

She found Grey's Saloon just a block down from the diner, but had to go a block further to find a parking spot for Bertha. Tucking her laptop under the seat, she locked up the van and headed for the bar.

She had to push her way past honest-to-God saloon doors to enter. The space she found herself in featured a battered bar on one side, booths on the other, with tarnished mirrors on the walls reflecting the late afternoon sun coming through the front window.

Eva headed straight for the bar where she slid onto an empty stool and waited for the bartender to notice her.

"Afternoon. What can I get you?" the man asked once

he'd finishing drawing beers for a group of cowboys down the far end of the bar.

"Vodka, straight up," Eva said. Then she thought about it and added, "Make that two."

"Sure thing."

Eva knocked the first drink back ten seconds after it was in her hand, wincing as the alcohol burned its way down to her belly.

The bartender raised his eyebrows. "Bad day?"

"Don't know yet," Eva said. "The jury is still out on that one."

The bartender went off to tend to another customer and Eva gave a small, heartfelt sigh as the warming alcohol worked its way through her bloodstream, throwing a warm, calming blanket over the adrenaline still pinballing around her body. Her phone beeped with a text as she sipped her second drink more slowly.

It was from her sister, Syd, back in LA:

Yo. Want to let me know you're alive and well? People who give a crap would like to have proof of life.

Eva smiled and tapped out an answer to her sister: **Sorry. Phone reception sucks out where I'm staying. But all good this end.**

Her sister immediately fired back: **So how did the big pitch go? It was today, right?**

Eva took another sip of vodka before typing out her response: **Just finished. Won't know until tomorrow. No idea how I went. Sacrifice chocolate to the god of good things for me.**

Dots filled the screen before Syd's response appeared: **Will do. Hang tough, babe. Gotta go now, but love you.**

Eva was just selecting the blowing kiss emoji when the sound of deep male laughter made her glance toward the group of cowboys at the end of the bar. Her gaze sharpened as she recognized one of the three men as Casey Carmody. He had a beer in hand and was talking with his friends, his expression relaxed and open.

He tilted his head back, swallowing beer, and she admired the way his biceps flexed and the muscle at his throat rippled.

Okay, that's enough of that.

But before she could look away, he glanced across and caught her eye. For a beat he simply looked at her, his expression arrested. Then he nodded, his mouth tilting up at the corners ever so slightly as though he was pleased to see her.

Eva lifted her vodka glass in his direction in silent acknowledgment before shifting her attention back to her phone.

If he comes over, do not encourage him, the voice in her head ordered. *Stay smart, stay focused.*

Eva kept fiddling with her phone, even though she was really waiting for him to make an approach, trying to decide what to say, how to handle it. When a minute passed, and then another, and he still didn't come over, she risked a second glance his way.

He was laughing with his friends again, apparently oblivious to her.

That's a good thing, in case you were wondering, the smartass in her head pointed out.

Eva rolled her eyes and swallowed more vodka, which

was when she registered that the glass was empty and the world was looking more than a little fuzzy around the edges. She frowned—she was no lightweight when it came to drinking—then it occurred to her that she hadn't had anything to eat since breakfast. No wonder the vodka had hit her so hard and fast.

"Excuse me, do you have a menu?" Eva asked the bartender.

"Absolutely. Give me a shout out when you know what you want, but these will keep you going in the meantime."

The bartender slid a basket of pretzels in front of Eva as well as a laminated menu offering the usual bar fare—buffalo wings, burgers, nachos, fries. Eva was trying to decide between nachos with the lot or a burger when she became aware of a large group arriving, their noise and laughter causing her to glance across her shoulder toward the door.

Her stomach did a drop and roll when she saw who it was—Dane, with his crew. Who used to be her crew, too.

Damn. Shit. Damn.

Eva whipped her head back around and closed her eyes, fervently, desperately hoping Dane wouldn't notice her.

Just go to a booth, be your usual self-centered asshole self, and give me a chance to get out of here.

Even though she hated the idea of scampering away because he'd arrived, she really, really didn't want to see him or talk to him.

"Eva."

Fuck.

How unlucky was she? In town less than twenty-four hours and she'd already run into her ex.

She opened her eyes and turned face the man she'd once thought was the love of her life.

"Dane."

His dirty blond hair was longer than when she'd last seen him, caught up on the back of his head in a man-bun, and his beard had been trimmed back to three-days'-growth length. His black linen shirt was wrinkled, his eight-hundred-dollar jeans folded at the cuff. A wallet chain hung against his thigh, the links made up of tiny black skulls.

She'd bought that chain for him for his birthday last year. She wondered if he remembered that.

He was looking her over, too, his expression verging on disdainful.

"You're wasting your time here," he said.

Great, they weren't even going to pretend to be polite.

"That's not your call to make."

"You know I could sue you for trying to steal this commission out from under me," he said.

"Knock yourself out. I look forward to discussing the way you denied me credit on every project we worked on in a court of law, for all the world to see."

He laughed, the sound nasty and hard and mocking. "You are so arrogant and deluded. You were my *assistant*, Eva. That's all you ever were. Every commission we did together was because of *me*, because of *my* vision, *my* talent, *my* reputation. You should be grateful I let you ride on my coattails as long as I did."

She could feel anger bubbling up inside her as he mouthed the same old lies. They both knew how hard she'd worked behind the scenes to help build his career. The calls she'd made, the website she'd built for him, the stories she'd shopped around to art magazines to burnish his reputation and grow his profile, the commissions she'd hustled for him. They had spent hours sketching ideas and talking about themes for projects, all of it based on the exhaustive, deep research she pulled together, and she had stood side by side with him on cherry pickers, cleaning rigs, and scaffolds around the world, helping to bring his vision to life.

But according to him, she'd just been his assistant.

"You wouldn't have completed a single work in the last five years without my help," she said. "In your heart you know that. If your ego wasn't so ridiculously fragile, you'd acknowledge me and give me the credit I'm due."

"Here's what I'll acknowledge—you were great at keeping the bills paid, and you made things run like clockwork. You always booked great hotels, and you are an awesome technician when it comes to painting. But you're not an artist, babe. You know how I know? Because you sat by for five years and never did a stroke of original work. It'd kill me to do that. Seriously, my fucking head would explode if I couldn't get my ideas out there into the world. So don't sit there and blame me because you don't have a career—that's on you, Eva. All of it."

He was so self-righteous, she wanted to punch him in the face. She sucked in air, ready to remind him the reason she'd done none of her own work during their relationship was because she'd poured all her energy into *his* projects, *his* career, because she'd wanted to help and support him, and because she'd always—stupidly—believed that once he was established and they could afford to hire someone to replace her, it would be her turn.

And then she remembered that they'd been over and over this ground, and that she had made a promise to herself not to let him undermine her like this again. Even engaging in the discussion gave him power and the opportunity to get into her head.

She didn't need to prove anything to him, or to hear him acknowledge the truth. She knew what she'd done, how much she'd contributed. That was enough.

"You know what? Let's not do this," she said.

His mouth curled at the corner in a derisive smile. "What's wrong? Can't handle the truth?"

"Go away, Dane. I've wasted enough time on you," she said, proud of the steady calm in her voice.

She gave him her shoulder, reaching for the glass of water the bartender had left in front of her earlier. By some miracle, her hand was steady, even though her gut was churning.

She could feel him hovering, hating being dismissed. He loved having the last word, always had.

"Wait, I forgot, there's something else you're good at," he said. "No one sucks dick like you, babe. Good to know you've got something to fall back on if things get tough."

She didn't think about it, just turned, the glass gripped tightly in her hand. She jerked her arm forward and water hit him square in the face. Fury riding her, she swapped the glass for the basket of pretzels and tossed that at him, too.

"You psycho bitch," Dane said, deflecting the basket with his arm.

She hadn't even realized she'd stood and moved toward

him until a strong arm came around her waist, holding her back.

"Easy now," Casey Carmody said near her ear.

"Let me go," she said, trying to wriggle free, determined to inflict pain on her ex.

Dane pushed his wet hair off his forehead, then pulled his damp shirt away from his chest. "You're lucky I don't charge you with assault."

"*Let me go*," Eva said, straining against Casey muscular arm for all she was worth.

"Take a deep breath," Casey said, which was when she registered that the hard, warm surface pressed against her back was his chest.

It threw her so much she stopped trying to get away.

"If I were you, I'd go while you can," Casey told Dane.

"I'm not afraid of her," Dane said.

"Wasn't talking about her," Casey said.

Eva saw the exact moment the threat registered. Dane's gaze assessed Casey's height and build. He frowned. Then he glanced across to where Zack, Tess, and Amy were watching from a booth. Eva could almost see him assessing his options—stand his ground and risk getting his ass handed to him by a real live cowboy, or back down in front of his team and lose face.

Dane lifted his chin. "Don't know who you are, buddy, but take it from me, she's more trouble than she's worth."

Rage exploded in Eva again and she gripped Casey's arm, using it as leverage as she kicked out at Dane with both feet. He dodged backward, out of reach.

"Okay, time for us to get some fresh air," Casey said.

Before she could do more than yelp in protest, Casey was frog-marching her toward the door.

"Stop. Let me go," Eva said, trying to dig her heels in and failing spectacularly.

He didn't stop until they were three storefronts away from the saloon, the cool night air a shock after the warmth of the bar.

"I'm going to let you go now. Try not to ruin my good looks," Casey said in her ear.

Then the warm band of his arm was gone and she was free.

Chapter Four

CASEY WATCHED AS Eva made a big deal out of straightening her waistcoat and shirt, clearly feeling very aggrieved that he'd interfered in her personal affairs.

"You didn't need to do that," she said.

"Yeah, I did. The sheriff was sitting in one of those booths. He was about to jump in before I did."

Eva frowned. Her face was flushed, her eyes a little glassy. He'd been watching her pretty much since she'd come into the saloon, and he'd seen her down two straight vodkas in rapid succession in the ten minutes before the asshole in black had arrived. She wasn't fall-over drunk, but she was definitely tipsy.

"I can handle myself," she said.

"Saw that. Nice shot with the water. Next time, you should just kick him in the nuts."

She stared at him. Then she let out a crack of laughter, her blue eyes bright with appreciation.

"Then I really would be in trouble with the law."

"Probably," he agreed.

He didn't blame her for losing it. He'd heard what the asshole had said to her—half the bar had—and he'd already been pushing to his feet when Eva threw her glass of water.

Not that she was Casey's to protect—not even close— but he wasn't about to stand by and watch a man insult a woman without doing something about it.

She pushed her hair off her forehead, leaving one side sticking up unevenly.

"I s'pose I should thank you for saving me from myself," she said grudgingly.

"You can sleep on it if you like, decide if you want to in the morning," he suggested.

She pointed a finger at him. "You're funny."

"You're pretty drunk, aren't you?" he asked.

"I just need something to eat. I forgot to have lunch."

"Right." Casey glanced up the street, assessing his options. There was no way he could let her drive home in the state she was in, and he couldn't just abandon her, either. "They do good burgers at the diner."

"Thanks for the hot tip." She gave him a mock salute.

He hid a smile. "All right, off we go," he said, laying a hand on the small of her back and propelling her into motion. "Let's get some food into you."

She made a small sound of protest, but when he took his hand away, she remained at his side as he crossed the road and headed up Main Street toward the diner.

"You're probably wondering who that guy was," she said after a small silence.

"None of my business," he said.

She threw him a look. "Come on. You're not even a little bit curious?"

"I know all I need to know about him already," he said.

She processed that for a beat, then shrugged. "He's my ex. Ex-boss, ex-collaborator, ex-everything."

Casey frowned. "Any reason you're both in Marietta at the same time?"

"Oh yeah," she said. "The Marietta Chamber of Commerce approached him four months ago to commission him to do a mural. We were in the middle of breaking up at the time. I offered my services as an alternative. They agreed to hear my pitch, and *voila*, here we are."

She punctuated her speech with a wide, dramatic sweep of her arm that inadvertently smacked into his chest.

"Sorry. Don't know my own strength," she said. Then she grinned at him, amused by her own silly joke.

The sooner he got a burger into her, the better.

"Here we are," he said, steering her up the steps and into the diner.

Flo was at the counter and she acknowledged him with a wave and pointed him toward an empty booth. He guided Eva into one side and took the seat opposite her, sliding a menu in front of her.

"The chicken burger is good, but the cheeseburger is better. And the fries are legendary," he said.

"What are you having? I'm buying you dinner," Eva announced.

"You don't need to do that."

"Yeah, I do. It's cheaper than bail, right?"

He laughed at her logic. "Yeah, I guess it is."

Flo approached the booth, offering them both a weary smile. "Evening. What can I do you for?"

"I will have the cheeseburger and some of your legendary

55

fries," Eva said, before looking at him with her eyebrows raised.

"Same for me, thanks Flo. And how about a couple of chocolate shakes?"

"Done and done. Won't be long," she said, giving him a friendly wink before bustling off.

"She's a nice lady." Eva pronounced it like a queen issuing a decree.

"She is."

"She was going to try to find me somewhere to stay before Sierra stepped in." She frowned as if something had just occurred to her. "Hey, that makes it two times now that I've been rescued by a Carmody."

"We're a helpful people," Casey said.

She narrowed her eyes, studying him from across the table. "Why did you come to my rescue? You don't even know me."

"Didn't seem like a very fair fight," he said.

"I could totally take him," Eva scoffed. "I grew up in Detroit. I fight dirty."

"Right. That's what I said."

She laughed. "Thanks for the vote of confidence."

Their shakes arrived and Eva immediately went to work on hers, lips pouting and cheeks hollowing as she sucked on her straw. Casey frowned and focused on his own drink, disturbed by how often and how quickly his thoughts turned to sex around this woman.

Plus she was tipsy-drunk, and it felt like he was taking advantage somehow by noticing how hot she was while she was under the influence.

"Okay, you were right, I needed that," she said when she finally came up for air.

Then she pulled her straw out of her drink and licked it, her tongue curling around the length of it with erotic dexterity.

Holy shit.

Casey shifted in his seat.

"So. When do you find out who won the commission?" he asked.

"Tomorrow." She pulled a face.

"You don't like your chances?"

"He's the one with the name. I might have helped build that name, but that doesn't mean anything in the big scheme of things."

"What's next for you, then?" he asked.

She poked her straw around in her drink, her mouth pressed into a straight, unhappy line. "Don't know. Back to LA. Might have to give up my studio, move in with my sister."

Casey frowned. "Sounds like a tough call."

"What can I say? You find me at a crossroads in my life, Casey Carmody. Anything could happen next."

He liked the way she said his name, almost as though she was daring him to do something.

What, he wasn't sure.

"Here we go. Let me know if you need anything else. We've got that coffee walnut cake you love on today, Casey," Flo said as she slid two loaded plates onto the table.

"I'll try to save a little room," he said with a smile.

Eva grabbed a fry from her plate and popped it into her

mouth as Flo sailed off again.

"You should use your powers wisely, you know. With great power comes great responsibility."

"Excuse me?"

"That smile of yours. You should use it wisely."

Casey frowned at her, genuinely bemused. She paused in the act of getting a grip on her burger.

"Are you seriously telling me you don't know what I'm talking about?" she asked.

Casey's frown deepened. "That's exactly what I'm telling you."

"Your smile—the one you just aimed at poor Flo without even considering the consequences—is a weapon of mass panty destruction. You must know that."

He shook his head. She eyed him for a moment as if trying to work out if he was bullshitting her.

"Huh. The last of a dying breed—the hottie who doesn't know he's hot," she said. "They ought to put you in a glass display case and charge admission."

Casey could feel his face starting to get warm. "Think we could talk about something else now?"

"Why? Is me objectifying you making you uncomfortable?" she asked, eyes dancing with mischief and challenge.

"A little."

"Okay. I will cease and desist. Just promise not to use that smile on me, okay? My defenses are down."

He gave her a look across the table. "Eat your burger."

The sooner she was sober, the better. For both of them.

Eva eyed the burger in her hand as though it was a challenge, then took a generous bite out of it. Casey watched, fascinated, as she closed her eyes, ketchup dripping down her chin.

"Oh my God. This is the best burger I've ever eaten. Either that, or I'm really hungry," she said.

"Probably a little of both."

She took another enthusiastic bite, then used a scrunched-up napkin to blot her chin. Which was when Casey realized he was staring, and forced himself to focus on his own burger.

He couldn't help wondering if she was as enthusiastic about other things in life. Her work, for example.

And sex.

And there you go again.

"So what do you do around here when you aren't cowboying?" she asked, one elbow propped on the table.

He gave her an amused look, guessing that "cowboying" in her mind probably consisted of woolly concepts she'd garnered from TV and movies.

"I sing in a band. Play a little ball in summer. Not much time for anything else with just the three of us on the ranch."

"What sort of band? What sort of music do you play?"

"We're a four piece—two guitars, keyboards, drums. And we play rock and country music. Crossover stuff, I guess."

"What's the band called?"

"The Whiskey Shots."

"Cool name. Do women throw their underwear at you when you're on stage?"

He reached for his shake to wash a mouthful of burger down. "No. What's this obsession with me and underwear?"

"What's this obsession with my obsession?" she asked, eyebrows raised in mock outrage.

He laughed again. She'd finished her burger, and she dusted salt off her fingers before undoing the buttons on her waistcoat and shrugging out of it. His gaze dropped to her breasts before he could stop himself. She was wearing a bra today, the texture of the lace discernible beneath her shirt. It made him think of the way he'd been able to see the outline of her nipples last night, the soft shape of her.

"You said no time for anything else. Does that mean no girlfriend?" she asked.

Her gaze was very direct across the table and he knew she'd caught him looking again.

"No girlfriend."

"No boyfriend?" Eva asked.

He smiled. "No."

Her gaze dropped to his mouth, then to his chest. He watched her checking him out and wondered what she'd taste like, how she'd feel beneath him.

"You want dessert?" she asked after a long moment.

"I'm good. But you have some if you want it."

"God no, I'm done. But thanks for suggesting this place. I didn't realize how hungry I was."

"Not a problem."

She eased to one side, pulling her wallet from her back pocket.

"You don't need to do that," he said, pulling out his own money.

"Shut up and take it like a man," she said, throwing money on the table.

She had a mouth on her—there was no denying that. He liked it, a lot. Liked that she gave as good as she got, that she didn't hold back or back down.

They stood simultaneously, and Casey was a little surprised to discover all over again how slight she was—she had such a big personality, while they were sitting down he'd forgotten he was almost a foot taller than her. They headed for the door, and Eva stopped at the counter to thank Flo personally for their meal. Then they were outside, in the quiet darkness of the street.

"Where are you parked?" she asked.

"Just past the saloon," he said, indicating the direction they'd come from.

"Same," she said, pivoting on her heel.

He matched his stride to hers, shooting her a quick, assessing glance. The glassy-eyed look from earlier was gone, and her gait was steady. But she'd seemed pretty tanked when she launched herself at her ex and he wondered if she was safe to drive now.

"I'm fine," she said, looking at him.

"If you say so. I can drive you home and bring you back to pick up your van tomorrow, if you want to be sure."

She was silent for a moment, and he liked that she seemed to be genuinely considering his offer, not just rejecting it out of hand.

"Thanks, but I'm okay. I just needed some food to soak up the vodka and adrenaline."

They were about to pass the saloon and he watched as she glanced at the front window, a quick, furtive check to see if her ex was still there.

There was no guessing what she was thinking as they continued past the bar. He wondered if she was still hung up on the guy. In his experience, the kind of anger he'd witnessed earlier indicated there might be unfinished business on both sides.

Eva stopped and he saw they'd arrived at her van. She pulled her keys from her pocket.

"Thanks again for riding to my rescue," she said.

"Actually, this is your first thanks. You were gonna sleep on whether you were actually grateful or not, remember, and get back to me with an answer."

Her mouth turned up in a rueful smile. "What a pain in the ass I am, huh? An ungrateful, rude, pain in the ass. Let me do this properly—Casey Carmody, thank you for saving me from an assault charge. Your gallantry is noted and appreciated."

"Don't mention it," he said, and she cracked up laughing.

"All right, I'm going to quit while I'm ahead. I'll see you out at the ranch." She turned to unlock the van.

"Keep an eye out for deer on the highway. They tend to move around a lot after dark," he said.

She looked over her shoulder at him, a worried frown pleating her forehead. "What should I do if I see one?"

"Not drive into it."

She blinked, then gave him a wry smile. "Right. Thanks for the insider intel, cowboy."

"Pleasure, ma'am," he said.

He walked across the road to where his pickup was parked and got in. She was just pulling away from the curb as he did a U-turn, and he wound up following her out of town. He put the window down and rested his forearm along the top of the door as he drove, keeping a safe distance as he trailed her out to the ranch. The night was still warm, and the radio was playing an old Dire Straits song, "Brothers in Arms." Watching Eva's taillights, Casey let himself think about the moment in the diner when she'd asked if he had a girlfriend.

There was something between them, something they both felt. An attraction, a magnetism.

She was unlike any other woman he'd ever known—a bit wild, fun, maybe even a little dangerous. If he hadn't been there to hold her back tonight, he could only guess at what she'd planned on throwing at her ex next. A barstool? A fist?

He admired her fighting spirit and her refusal to concede, and he was becoming increasingly obsessed with the need to find out if her mouth was as soft and sweet as it looked.

And he really, really wanted to fill his hands with her perky little breasts.

He could feel himself growing hard and he eased off the gas a little. He was getting way ahead of himself. Reading too much into some heavy-duty flirtation and the heat in her eyes. They'd had fun over dinner, but it didn't mean anything. It definitely didn't mean that anything was going to happen between them tonight.

And she was leaving tomorrow.

Ahead of him, Eva's left turn signal came on and he followed her up the bumpy gravel drive to the house. He parked beside her and made himself take his time getting out of the car, refusing to rush like a horny teenager just for the pleasure of scoring a few more minutes' conversation with her in the dark.

He took his time gathering his jacket and phone, then got out of the car. She was waiting in front of her van, her face cast in shadows, hands tucked into the pockets of her pants. She looked as though she was supremely at ease, but as he drew closer he could feel the tension in her.

The edginess.

He pretended to inspect the front of her van.

"Didn't bring any deer home. Good work," he said.

"Had my heart in my mouth the whole drive."

He wished he could see her face properly, wished he was the kind of guy who acted first and thought second. She was so damned pretty and sexy.

"Think you'll drive back through Salt Lake City on the way home tomorrow?" he asked, because it was safer than saying the things he really wanted to say.

She laughed, the sound low and husky. "You don't really want to stand here talking travel routes with me, do you, Casey?"

He was still trying to work out what to say in response when she turned and headed for the path beside the barn.

Damn. Real smooth with the frickin' Google maps routine, Carmody.

"You coming or not?" she called over her shoulder.

For a moment he was so thrown he didn't know what to do. And then he did, and he was moving, following her through the dark like a heat-seeking missile.

EVA'S HEART WAS pounding so hard it was a wonder it didn't hammer its way out of her chest. She could hear Casey following her and she got a little breathless thinking about what was about to happen.

Him, her, no clothes, a bed.

She'd been thinking about it—about him—all the way home.

The feel of his strong arm banded across her body. His voice in her ear, deep and low. The way he'd watched her across the diner table, his green eyes dark with hunger.

Last night, she'd told herself not to be distracted by him, but the chances of her winning the commission were almost zero, and she was going home tomorrow.

And she wanted to fuck Casey Carmody, big time.

She'd wanted it from the moment she'd first laid eyes on him, and she didn't see any good reason to deny herself the pleasure of riding his big, hard body. Getting the chance to lie skin to skin with him might be the only good thing that came out of her trip to Montana.

She stepped up into the trailer and leaned across to flick on the reading light over the bed. Then she started on the buttons on her shirt. She had half of them undone by the time Casey filled the doorway and stepped inside. Once again he seemed to suck up all the available space, but tonight that was exactly the way she wanted it.

His gaze went to where she was working on her buttons.

"If you don't mind, I like to unwrap my own presents," he said.

He stepped closer, gently easing her hands away. Then he undid the remaining three buttons, his fingers warm against her ribcage and belly, his gaze intent on the task. When he was done, he pushed her shirt open and took a good, long look at her breasts. She was wearing a white lace balconet bra, and the way his gaze went from one breast to the other told her she'd made a good choice.

"Gorgeous," he said, the single word thick and low with desire. He traced the frivolous, lacy edge of one bra cup and she felt herself get even hotter and wetter with need.

"Fair's fair," she said, reaching out to grab the hem of his T-shirt. She pulled it up, exposing the astonishing topography of his belly, chest, and shoulders.

"Holy fuck," she whispered. "How can you be real?"

His shoulders were broad and bound with smooth muscle, his pecs covered with dark hair that narrowed to a silky, enticing trail that bisected his cut abs before disappearing beneath the waistband of his jeans.

He laughed. "I was going to say the same thing about you."

And then he closed the remaining distance between them, pulling her close and ducking his head to find her mouth. His lips were soft but firm on hers, and she gave a little moan as she realized how much she needed this. He took it as encouragement, his tongue tracing the seam of her lips, and when she opened to him, his groan echoed hers as his tongue swept into her mouth.

He tasted like chocolate and warm nights and hot man, and she gave back as good as she got, clinging to his shoulders as they kissed as though their lives depended on it. He was the first to break the contact, muttering something under his breath as he trailed kisses to her ear and then down her neck. Need rocketed through her as he licked and nipped at her sensitive skin, his hands sliding up her ribcage to cup her breasts.

"Yes," she encouraged. "Please."

He pushed her bra up, and she almost forgot how to stand on her own two legs as his calloused fingers brushed over her nipples. The achy, needful throb between her thighs became a demand as he teased her, plucking and squeezing and soothing her with his clever hands.

Pushing him away, she ignored his muffled protest and concentrated on unbuckling his belt before tackling his fly. He was wearing gray boxer briefs, his cock pressing against the soft fabric. Impatient to see him, she pushed his underwear down with shaking, urgent hands. He was everything she'd hoped for and more—thick, long, and incredibly hard.

The thought of having all of that wonderful, hot hardness inside her made her even more frantic, and she pushed his jeans down his hips.

"We in a rush?" he asked, amusement in his voice as he obligingly kicked off his boots and stepped out of his jeans and underwear.

"Yes. Get on the bed," she said, already working on her own pants.

He looked as though he might be about to object to her bossiness—then she pushed her pants and panties down, revealing the neat patch of her pubic hair. His face got very intent then, his features hardening, his cock twitching against his belly.

Half naked, she placed a hand in the middle of his chest and pushed him toward the bed. He went willingly, sitting on the edge of the mattress to watch her shrug out of her bra and shirt. She liked the way he looked at her, as though everything he saw pleased him.

As though he wanted to be inside her as much as she wanted him to be there.

She kicked her clothes to one side and took the two steps necessary to join him on the bed. Eyes holding his, she straddled him, snugging the hot, wet heart of her right against his hard cock as her breasts pressed against his chest. It felt good—amazing—to be skin to skin with him, and she angled her head and kissed him. His hands slid onto her breasts as their tongues danced together, his work-hardened hands once again driving her crazy as he played with her nipples.

So much had happened in the last few days. She was stressed out, worried, angry, scared about her future—and right now, none of it mattered because Casey Carmody's mouth was on hers, his body hard and ready.

She made a small, regretful sound as he broke their kiss, only to shudder with pleasure when he immediately lowered his head to her breasts. The pull of his mouth on her nipple was nothing short of electric, the sensation shooting straight to her pussy. Need rippled through her as he split his attention between both breasts, sucking and teasing her with his hands and mouth.

"You like that?" he asked, the words blurred by her flesh.

"What do you think?" she asked, barely able to think, let alone speak.

"What about this?" he asked, one big hand sliding over her hip and belly to where she was spread wide for him.

Two fingers delved there, sliding over her slick flesh before plunging inside her.

She bit her lip, pressing down on him, loving the feeling of being invaded, of being full.

"You are so fucking hot," he said, lifting his head to gaze at her in wonder. His eyelids were heavy, his cheeks flushed, his mouth slightly wet from her kisses.

Maybe it was what he'd said, or the look in his eyes—either way, she was done. Leaning across, she grabbed her makeup bag from the counter and extracted one of the three condoms nestled inside. Her eyes locked with Casey's, she tore the foil pack open with her teeth, then shifted back just enough to get her hands on his cock. He felt smooth as silk and incredibly hard as she rolled the condom onto him.

The moment the contraceptive was safely deployed, she took him in hand and rose up onto her knees, guiding him to her entrance. His hands found her hips as she slid down onto him, his thickness filling and stretching her.

"Oh, God, *yes*," she sighed.

Hands gripping the hard muscles of his shoulders, she closed her eyes and started to move, savoring the slide, the pressure, the pounding of her own heart. It was perfect, exactly what she'd needed, what she'd craved.

Then she felt the heat of his mouth on her breasts again, and it stole the last of her sanity.

Chapter Five

PANTING, DESPERATE, SHE rode him as though her life depended on it, as though the fate of the universe hinged on the tension ratcheting tighter and tighter within her body. His own urgency growing, Casey slid his hands onto her ass and used the leverage to thrust up into her, rocking her hips back and forth to increase the contact between them.

It was too much, too perfect, and suddenly she was gone. The world fell away, and for precious seconds there was nothing but pleasure as her body throbbed around his. He groaned, his cheek pressed to her breast, his breath hot on her skin as he found his own release mere seconds later.

She could barely keep her head up afterward, sliding off his lap and onto the bed in one boneless movement. Her body felt warm and loose and damp as she lay with her eyes closed, her breathing still labored.

She couldn't remember the last time she'd been so turned on and so desperate for satisfaction. And he'd been perfect. The way he'd kissed her, the way he'd tortured her breasts, his lovely cock…

The mattress dipped as Casey moved around beside her

and she cracked an eye, only to realize he was taking care of the condom, wrapping it in a tissue before lobbing it toward the small trash can at the other end of the trailer.

"He shoots, he scores," she said when it landed dead center.

He glanced across at her and treated her to one of his devastating smiles. "Hell, yeah."

She smiled in return and closed her eyes again, unable to keep them open.

"I think you just ruined me, cowboy. Thanks for being so freaking hot."

"Feeling's mutual, trust me."

The mattress dipped again and she opened her eyes to find him lying on his side beside her, head propped on his hand, his gaze roving lazily over her body.

"Tell me about this," he said, tracing the curving edge of the tattoo on her arm.

She glanced down at her own arm. The tattoo was so much a part of her now she often forgot she had it. An abstract design, it zigzagged jaggedly down her upper arm in a black stroke that looked as though it could have been painted with a brush. Behind it were bright sprays of color— purple, yellow, green, blue, red.

"A friend started tattooing in LA, and I wanted to support her," she explained. "It's a sort of homage to my early days in street art. That ridiculous squiggle used to be my tag."

He angled his head, trying to "read" it, and she laughed.

"Don't bother trying to see my name in it. We deliberately kept things vague so we didn't get caught."

"I'm getting the sense you were trouble," he said.

"Depends on how you define trouble," she said, wiggling her eyebrows.

His gaze dropped to her breasts, lingering on her nipples, before skimming over her belly to focus on the damp triangle of hair between her legs. There was no mistaking the hunger in his eyes, or the way his cock was already hardening once again.

"It's barely been five minutes," she said laughingly, not sure she was up for round two just yet.

"Your fault," he said. "These drive me crazy." He leaned his head forward and lapped at her right breast, the rough, wet velvet of his tongue bringing her nipple to instant attention.

She felt the stir of renewed desire between her thighs, and the fog of satisfaction clouding her mind slipped away.

Apparently round two was not out of the question, after all.

His hand cupped her left breast, his rough thumb teasing her to hardness even as his mouth did the same on her other breast. She lifted her hips restlessly, needing more already. As if he could read her mind, Casey slid a hand down her belly and between her legs.

She spread wide for him, unashamed of how much she wanted him, of how good he made her feel. He stroked her with strong, confident fingers, before zeroing in on the spot that made her moan. Then he really went to work, stroking her pussy and kissing and sucking on her breasts until she was gripping the sheets in both hands and trembling with the building tension.

"Tell me what you want and it's yours," he said, his voice a gravelly promise.

Images flitted across her mind's eye, each more decadent and dirty than the last. Then she felt the press of his erection against her thigh and knew that no matter what, she had to have him again.

"You, inside me," she panted.

He left her briefly to grab another condom, and she watched impatiently as he slid it on. Then he rolled on top of her, his hairy legs rough against hers, his weight bearing down on her, and there was nothing in the world except the two of them.

She lifted her hips, welcoming him, and he thrust inside her, so hard and hot she whimpered with how good it felt.

This time around he was in charge, and he set a punishing pace, driving into her hard and fast. It was exactly what she wanted, what she needed, and it wasn't long before she was arching off the bed, a second climax rippling through her. Then and only then did he slow the pace, his thrusts becoming almost leisurely as he stroked into her again and again. She watched his face, watched the pleasure taking him over, saw the hitch in his breathing, the way his neck muscles got tense and his mouth opened as he finally came.

His weight came onto her fully for a long moment afterward, his face pressing into her neck. Then he caught himself, stirring lazily.

"Sorry."

Withdrawing, he rolled off her, and she was surprised by the odd sense of loss she felt. Thrown, she reached out to snag the quilt and pulled it over both of them.

"Now I really am ruined," she said.

"Never say never," he said. His eyes were closed, and a small, slightly smug smile curved his mouth.

She figured he'd earned that smile, because it had been a long time since she'd felt this good. And to think, she'd almost denied herself this pleasure.

She pushed her pillow into a more acceptable shape and studied his profile, her brain still moving at half speed thanks to all the post-great-sex endorphins.

His nose was straight, and his cheeks were just starting to darken as his beard grew in. She had a sudden urge to reach out and test the texture of his stubble with her fingers, but instead she curled her hand into a fist.

There would be no tender after-play with this man. She wasn't stupid enough to walk into that bear trap.

"Tell me something I don't know, Casey Carmody," she said instead.

"What about? Quantum mechanics? Comparative religion? World championship chess?"

She laughed. "Do you know anything about any of those things?"

"Enough to sound stupid, but that's about it." He opened his eyes and turned his head to look at her. "Maybe you should narrow the field a little."

"Tell me about the ranch. Is it Jed's place, and you and Sierra are just helping him out, or do you all own it or what?" she asked, figuring it was a pretty safe topic.

"All four of us own it—me, Jed, Jesse, and Sierra. You haven't met Jesse. He's a pro saddle bronc rider and he and his girlfriend CJ usually only come home when the circuit brings them back to this part of the state."

"It's pretty cool that you like your family enough to invest with them. I love my sister, Syd, but no way would I go into business with her."

Casey hesitated a moment. "We actually inherited the place after our parents died in a car accident."

"Shit." Eva closed her eyes. So much for the ranch being a safe topic. "I'm so sorry."

"It was thirteen years ago," he said with a shrug.

Eva did the math in her head. She figured Casey was around her age—twenty-seven—which meant he couldn't have been more than fourteen or fifteen when his parents died.

"So you were just a kid? It must have turned your world upside down."

"Pretty much. Jed had to leave agricultural college, come home and hold us all together. And Jesse kind of went off the rails for a while."

"What did you do?"

He frowned, his gaze on the ceiling. "Kept to myself, mostly. Couldn't play my guitar, 'coz Dad gave it to me." He glanced at her. "Not my favorite year."

"Hell, no. I can't even imagine." The words felt utterly inadequate.

"In the end, having to keep this place going saved us," Casey said. "At first we just needed to pay the mortgage, put food on the table. Then it became more about preserving their legacy. They bought this land, built the house, developed the herd. They lived in this trailer for over a year when they first started out, if you can believe it."

"For real?" Eva looked around the small space, trying to imagine sharing it with another person day in, day out. "They were either very happily married, or incredibly tolerant."

"Bit of both, I think," he said with a smile, his eyelids drifting shut.

Eva watched his face soften as he drifted into a light sleep. She closed her own eyes, enjoying the lassitude in her body. But instead of falling asleep, her mind started sifting through the events of the evening, anxiously parsing the meeting with the McGregors and the woman from the Chamber of Commerce, trying to assure herself she'd done everything humanly possible to advocate for herself. Inevitably her thoughts moved on to the fight with Dane at the saloon, and she felt a prickle of embarrassment, along with a wash of anger and hurt as she remembered what he'd said to her, the coldness and disdain in his eyes.

It was hard to believe that things had gotten so ugly between them. She'd spent five years with him. They'd had amazing adventures together—but it had all been on his terms. She could see that clearly now, and as soon as she'd started to advocate for herself, to ask for something that might progress her career and ambitions, he had become angry, resentful, and finally, openly selfish.

And now she could add nasty to the list.

She had to take a deep, steadying breath as she remembered the way he'd essentially called her a whore in front of the whole bar. She might have made a spectacle of herself, throwing water in his face and following it up with the basket of pretzels, but she was glad it was rage she'd felt, and not hurt.

Not then, anyway.

Now… Now she felt weary and sad and stupid that she'd wasted five years on a man whose first move when he felt threatened was to try to humiliate her using the oldest, most obvious weapon at hand—her virtue, or lack thereof.

Do you really want to do this now?

No, she did not. Tonight might have started badly, but it had ended with a big, happy bang, and she was going to hang on to the memory of Casey Carmody worshiping her body when she hit the road tomorrow. It was going to be the highlight of her trip, the silver lining, and she wasn't going to taint or dilute the experience by lying in bed next to him brooding over her ex. It was wasted energy.

She deliberately refocused her thoughts, thinking instead about what Casey had told her about the ranch and his siblings, about the ranch helping save his family after his parents had died. There had been gravel in his voice when he talked about preserving their legacy.

It was a noble calling, and she tried to imagine what it must be like to have such a strong sense of connection to the land and a way of life.

Life. Love. Legacy.

The words drifted across her mind as sleep rose up to take her.

Then suddenly the idea was there, clear and crisp and undeniable.

"That's it," she said, sitting up with sudden urgency. "Oh my God, *that's it.*"

"What?" Casey murmured.

"The grain elevator. I just worked out what the theme should be," Eva said, scrambling out of bed to find her sketchpad and pencils.

She pulled it out of her backpack with urgent hands and climbed back onto the bed. Legs crossed, she dragged the corner of the quilt around her shoulders and flipped to a fresh page in the pad.

Then, her brain racing, she started to sketch.

CASEY LAY WITH his arms cradling his head, still pleasantly drowsy after some of the best sex of his life. He could hear the scritch-scratch of a pencil on paper and guessed Eva was busily sketching something, trying to capture an idea before it evaporated. He'd done the same with song lyrics, and he waited for her to finish and rejoin him under the covers. He knew for a fact that there was one condom left in her toiletries kit and once he recovered enough he had definite plans to use it.

In the meantime, he closed his eyes and listened to Eva draw or take notes or whatever it was she was doing. After a few minutes, she still wasn't done and he opened his eyes and saw how engrossed she was.

Huh.

He shifted in the bed, making a big deal out of adjusting the quilt. Eva didn't so much as glance up.

Okay.

Clearly, she was very absorbed in her work. Lucky he wasn't the sort of guy who was insulted easily.

He glanced toward her toiletry bag, but his hopes for

round three were rapidly dwindling. He gave it another ten minutes, then Eva flipped to a fresh page in her sketchbook and started on a new sketch.

"I can go, if you prefer," he offered. Better to ask what she wanted rather than assume anything.

Eva barely looked up. "Oh. Um, sure. If you want. Up to you."

And then her head was back down, her pencil moving over the page.

Casey raised his eyebrows. His reaction was wasted on her, however, because she was utterly focused on her work. He sat up and threw back the covers. Shifting to the edge of the mattress, he stood and reached for his jeans. Eva continued to sketch, and he glanced across at what she was drawing.

It was a woman's face, weary and careworn, her gaze focused on something in the distance. Eva had used powerful pencil strokes and delicate cross-hatching to create shadow, and even though it was only a bare-bones portrait, quickly rendered, he was struck by the emotion in the woman's eyes. He didn't know much about art, but even he could tell Eva was good at what she did.

She muttered something under her breath and flipped the page, immediately starting to sketch in the outline of a new portrait.

He realized he was standing there, naked, jeans in hand, and gave himself a mental shake. He stepped into his jeans, yanking them up, then found his T-shirt on the counter, on top of her computer. He shoved one boot on, then the other. He paused after he'd pocketed his keys and phone, wondering if it was even worth interrupting her. She must have sensed his diffidence because she looked up, her expression distracted.

"Thanks for tonight. I had a good time."

"Me, too," he said.

She smiled, but he could see her mind was still in her work.

"What time you heading off tomorrow?" he asked.

"Not sure yet," she said.

"Well…okay," he said, unsure if he should say goodbye or if he'd maybe catch her tomorrow.

"Sleep tight," she said, and then her gaze dropped to her sketchpad and she was drawing again, sucked into some world only she could see.

Bemused and maybe a little offended, Casey let himself out of the trailer. The warmth of the day was well and truly gone now and his stride was long as he made his way up to the house, entering via the kitchen door.

Sierra looked up from where she was making herself a hot chocolate, her expression surprised.

"Hey. Didn't hear your truck come in," she said.

Casey hesitated, unsure what to say in response to his sister's casual comment. Sierra's eyebrows rose in silent query as she registered his weirdness.

"I was, um, talking to Eva," he said. "We ran into each other in town. Got talking."

"Okay," Sierra said, her tone telling him she suspected there was more to the story than he was offering.

"Got those plant stakes you wanted from the hardware store," he said. "They're in the back of my truck, I'll grab them for you in the morning."

He headed for the door, eager for the privacy of his bedroom.

"Wait. Hang on. You can't just walk out. We were having a conversation," Sierra called after him.

Interrogation, more like. He'd seen the look in his sister's eye, and he knew he'd been dumb enough to give her ammunition when he hesitated before responding to what was, in hindsight, a perfectly innocent comment.

Realistically, bailing on Sierra now only meant a delay—his sister would be sure to pursue him tomorrow because she was nosy as hell when it came to her brothers' romantic lives—but right now that seemed like a good trade-off.

He took care of his teeth, then shut his bedroom door and stripped for bed. Stretched out under the covers, he tried to analyze his own feelings.

He felt…dismissed. There was no other word for it.

Kind of dumb, when he considered what he and Eva were to each other. She was going home to LA tomorrow. Neither of them had any claim on the other. And it wasn't as though she'd kicked him out—he'd volunteered to leave, mostly out of stupid pride because she'd moved on so quickly from what had been a pretty damn notable event for him.

But maybe she had great sex like that all the time. Maybe the sense of affinity he'd felt with her was entirely one-sided.

Jesus, can you hear yourself?

He could, and it was pissing him off. As he'd already established, she was going home tomorrow. Him lying in his bed brooding over how he felt and what she'd said or not said was bullshit.

They'd had their one night. It was over, before it had even started. And there was nothing he could do or say that was going to change that.

EVA SKETCHED UNTIL her hand cramped and her neck ached. Taking a break, she registered three things all at once: she was cold, her bladder was full, and it was very late. Unfolding her cramped legs, she stood and stretched, then quickly leafed through the sketches she'd made. Some of them were good, a lot were so-so, but a couple were great.

Were they enough to swing the decision in her direction? She had no idea—but she had to try.

She'd been so close to giving up, just getting in Bertha and driving away. But she knew now that she couldn't leave Marietta without sharing her new ideas with the committee somehow. She couldn't leave anything on the table, other-wise she would always wonder what might have happened if she'd only pushed a little harder.

But right now, she really needed to go to the bathroom. Hustling to the other end of the trailer, she took care of business, then stood in the tiny bathroom staring absently at her reflection as she brushed her teeth.

She felt simultaneously wired and tired, her body ex-hausted by her epic session with Casey, her mind busy with ideas and plans.

The way she saw it, she had two options tomorrow—she could try to get an audience with Jane, who was apparently in the middle of some kind of work crisis, or she could hunt the McGregors down and pitch to them.

It was a fairly easy decision to make—it may have only been an illusion, but she'd felt as though Heath and Andie McGregor had been more sympathetic to her cause. Probably she was misreading pity and politeness for something else, but what the hell.

Conveniently, she happened to know where she had a good chance of finding the McGregors tomorrow morning, since their housing development was adjacent to the grain elevator. She would get up early, take the best of her sketches, and go make her Hail Mary pitch. And if that didn't move the needle, then she'd get in her van and start the long drive home.

Which meant she really needed to go to bed now, because despite the hope fizzing through her veins, the odds were good she'd be on the road tomorrow.

Turning off the light in the bathroom, she walked the short distance to the bed and clambered onto the mattress. The pillow still held the impression of Casey's head, and when she lay down she detected the faint scent of his deodorant.

Now that the urge to give life to her ideas had faded a little, she remembered the way he'd left and winced. If the shoe were on the other foot, and he'd left the bed to go deal with business while she was still enjoying the afterglow, she was pretty sure she'd be a little ticked off, to say the least.

Damn it. She'd been an asshole, and he'd been so sweet and lovely tonight, intervening in the bar, escorting her to dinner, and then helping her enjoy two world-class orgasms.

She'd apologize to him tomorrow, explain her urgency to

him. Hopefully he'd understand. It would be sucky indeed if he was left with the impression she was an ungrateful, selfish sex maniac. She didn't want him to think badly of her, not when she would be taking home such awesome memories of him.

BETWEEN ANXIETY OVER ambushing the McGregors and guilt over Casey, it took her a while to fall asleep, but she finally dropped off, waking with a start when the alarm she'd set on her phone sounded. The first thing she did was scramble to the edge of the bed to review the sketches she'd made last night.

She hadn't been in the grip of a post-sex fever dream— they were good. She closed her eyes and sent a little prayer out into the universe before tearing out the three sketches that best captured her vision. Then she hit the shower. Twenty minutes later, she was out the door, sketchbook under her arm. It was still dark out, dawn only just turning the horizon peachy-pink. There was condensation on her windshield, and the steering wheel was cool beneath her hands as she started the van and did a three-point turn to head down the driveway.

Mindful of Casey's warning about deer, she went a little slower than she might have usually. Dawn arrived just as she was pulling off the highway onto the side road that led past the grain elevator, and she was relieved to see several pickups and SUVs parked near the portable site office when she turned into the first street of the development.

She took a moment to steady her nerves, flipping down

the visor to make sure she wasn't sporting eye booger. She looked fine, which meant she had no more excuses. She pushed the door open, grabbed her sketchpad, and strode toward the site office.

The metal stair treads clanged beneath her Chuck Taylors as she climbed, and she knocked briskly on the closed door. She couldn't hear anyone inside, and she was starting to think she'd beaten the McGregors to work when the door opened to reveal Andie.

"Eva," she said, surprised. Then she laughed. "That's so weird—we were just talking about you."

"I won't take up too much of your time, I promise, but I had what I guess you could call an epiphany last night, and even though I know the committee might have already made a decision, I didn't want to leave without telling you about it," she said, her words coming out a little too fast and loud.

"Okay. Sure. Come in," Andie said, standing back and gesturing for Eva to enter.

The small space featured a desk at the far end, a bookshelf, and a bar fridge, which doubled as a table for a coffee maker. Heath was filling a mug as Eva entered, and he turned and offered it to her with a small smile.

"Figured you might not have had one of these yet," he said.

"I haven't, thanks," Eva said, wrapping her clammy fingers around the warm mug.

"Sit, please," Andie said, indicating a battered guest chair.

Eva sank into the seat, then leaned forward and set her coffee on the desk.

"I know you're busy. I just wanted to show you these. Last night, I was talking to Casey Carmody, and he said something that got me thinking about families, community, and legacy. And I realized that the triptych shouldn't just be about Marietta *now*, it should be about Marietta *before*, and Marietta *after*, too."

Andie and Heath were frowning, and Eva could tell she was making a hash of conveying her vision. She pulled out the three images she'd chosen from last night's work and set them side by side on the desk, hoping they'd speak for themselves.

The first sketch was a woman, her hair pulled back in a no-nonsense bun, her stern face weathered by the elements. She wore a simple, old fashioned dress, and one hand shaded her eyes as she kept watch over her land. Next was a depiction of a modern-day cowboy on horseback, his gaze aimed straight down the barrel as he stood ready to take on the world. And the last sketch featured two children, a boy and girl, each in jeans and plaid shirts and miniature cowboy hats, their faces turned up toward the sun, laughter and hope in their faces.

"Past, present, future," Eva said simply.

It had felt so right, so fitting last night, and she held her breath, waiting for Andie and Heath's reaction.

"I love it," Andie said. Then she shot Heath a slightly sheepish look. "I know I probably shouldn't say that, given the situation, but it's a great idea, and I love these sketches."

Heath was studying the pictures, and he glanced at Eva assessingly.

"The reason Andie and I were just talking about you is

because we were going to call you first thing," he said.

Eva had been so focused on what she needed to say and do, Andie's words had barely registered when she first arrived. Now Heath had brought them to her attention, however, they seemed loaded with portent.

"Right." She reached forward to grab her coffee, needing something solid to wrap her hands around.

"We talked with Jane last night, and we were all on the same page—we can't decide."

"Oh," Eva said. Then it hit her what he meant—that she was still in with a chance—and she sat up straighter.

"So what we decided was that we'd like to see a more detailed proposal from both contenders," Andie said.

"More detail. Sure, I can do that," Eva said, trying to stop herself from grinning like a demented person.

Contrary to what she'd thought, they'd taken her proposal seriously. She still had a chance of winning the commission.

This could actually happen.

"We're not sure how these things normally work," Heath said. "We've got a limited budget for the project, but we can kick in some money to cover your accommodation costs for the week, if you think that would be enough time for you to pull something more detailed together."

"So, a full week, or a working week?" Eva asked, even though she was prepared to work around the clock if it was the latter.

"A full week. We'd like to see sketches, an artist's statement, and any other details you can provide," Heath said.

"Of course. Absolutely," Eva said, nodding to let him

know she was on board with everything he was saying.

Andie smiled then, her pretty face lighting up. "You probably guessed, we weren't expecting to be this torn. We thought we knew which direction we wanted to go in, but your presentation was really impressive. Scratch that—*you* were really impressive."

The praise was so unexpected it brought the burn of tears to the back of Eva's eyes. Embarrassed, she blinked rapidly and focused on her lap.

"Sorry," she said, aware of hot color flooding into her face.

Andie's hand landed on her shoulder, warm and reassuring. "It's *fine*."

Eva shook her head, only looking up when she was confident she wouldn't cry. "You snuck up on me with the niceness. I wasn't expecting it," she said. "And it's been kind of a tense few months."

Andie smile sympathetically. "I get it. We've had our fair share of those lately, getting this development off the ground."

Heath parked his butt on the edge of the desk and took a mouthful of his own coffee, apparently unfazed by shows of female emotion.

"Let us know if you need help finding somewhere to stay. I know there's an agricultural show happening in Livingston and most places around here are booked up," he said.

Eva frowned. She hadn't thought about accommodations. She was reasonably confident Sierra would be happy for her to stay on in the trailer, but she couldn't help wondering what Casey would make of her extending her stay. Neither of them had fallen into bed last night anticipating Eva would be sticking around.

Worry about it later, on your own time.

Right. She was chewing up Heath and Andie's work day.

"I think I'll probably be fine, but if I hit a snag I'll let you know," Eva said. Then she stood, slipping her sketches back inside the pages of the pad for protection. "Thanks for hearing me out, and for giving me a chance to flesh out my proposal. I'm really excited by the opportunity."

"We're happy to be in a position to have two amazing artists to choose from," Heath said.

"Jane will be in touch to talk about contributing to your accommodation expenses, okay?" Andie said.

"All right. Great, thank you."

Andie walked her out, and Eva waved goodbye to the other woman before walking across to the van. Aware of Andie and Heath standing talking in the doorway to the site office, she started the engine and drove out of the development. Only when she was safely parked in front of the grain elevator, well away from any witnesses, did she let out a whoop of triumph. Grabbing her phone, she rang her sister in LA, only remembering it was still very early there when Syd's sleep-muffled voice answered the phone.

"Ev. What's wrong? Is everything okay?"

"Sorry. I forgot the time difference. Do you want me to call back?" Eva asked, ready to button off.

"I'm awake now. What's up? I assume this is not a life or death situation?"

Eva winced. Syd was not a morning person at the best of

times.

"I really am sorry. I was ringing to let you know I'm in the running for the commission. The committee couldn't make a decision, so they're giving Dane and me a week to flesh out our proposals with more detail."

"What? That's freaking *fantastic*," Syd said, her voice high-pitched with excitement. "I'm so proud of you for going in to bat for yourself, babe. I knew it would pay off."

"It hasn't paid off yet, don't get too excited. But it's a good start. They admitted they really only spoke to me out of politeness, but I convinced them with the thoroughness of my proposal."

"Of course you did, because you're awesome."

Eva laughed and let her head drop back against the seat. Her sister had always been her biggest cheerleader.

"I'm so relieved," she admitted.

"I know. This is going to happen for you, Ev. I feel it in my waters."

"Your bladder is predicting the future now? That's impressive," Eva said.

"I mean it. I have a good feeling about this project. I think this is going to be your launching pad."

Eva squeezed her eyes shut tight. She wanted to believe her sister, because she needed and wanted this so badly, but she knew that she was still the underdog in this competition.

"Talk to me, Ev," Syd said when the silence stretched too long.

"I saw Dane last night, at a bar in town. He told me I wasn't really an artist. That the reason I didn't have a profile was because I'd been content to ride on his coattails and didn't have the urge to create my own art." She hadn't meant to tell her sister what Dane had said. Hadn't ever wanted to think about it again, because she was terrified there was some truth in his words.

"What a piece of excrement," Syd said hotly. "He wouldn't have a career if it wasn't for you, and he *dares* to try and tear you down? I swear to you, if I ever see him again, he's going to be wearing his testicles as earrings."

The quivering, fervent outrage in her sister's voice went a long way toward making Eva feel better.

"I may have thrown a glass of water in his face, along with a basket full of pretzels," Eva confessed.

"That's my girl. Imagine how furious he must be that you're in serious contention for this commission. Imagine how afraid he must be, deep inside, where he knows you were the secret to his success."

Eva pulled a face. "Yeah, I'm not sure there's any part of Dane that's ready to admit I'm a threat to him. His ego is pretty much titanium-plated."

"I'm so glad you're not with him anymore, Ev. So glad."

Eva sighed. "Me, too. Even though it sucks having to start from scratch, at least I know I'm working for a good cause this time—me."

She talked for a few more minutes, then let her sister go so she could prepare for her day. The van seemed very quiet as she ended the call. She took a moment to simply breathe and get her thoughts in order.

She needed to refine her ideas, work up some art that she could mock up into a digital model for the committee. And she needed to start seriously considering what she'd need, and how long it would take if she actually won this thing.

But first she needed to check with Sierra to see if she and the rest of the Carmodys would be okay with Eva staying in the trailer for the week. She was pretty sure she knew what the answer was, but it never paid to take anything or anyone for granted.

Her thoughts flashed to Casey, to the way he'd made her feel last night, the things she'd said to him, the things he'd done to her.

If she'd known she was going to be sticking around, there was no way she would have complicated her living situation by jumping him the way she had.

And yet the truth was, she didn't have it in her to regret what had happened between them. He'd made her mindless with intense, breath-stealing pleasure, and she'd needed the release he'd provided last night. It had been very good between them. Insanely good.

Don't even think about it.

Because only a crazy woman would even consider going back for more when she had so much on her plate.

And Eva wasn't crazy, no matter what her ex had told the patrons of Grey's Saloon last night. No way was she going to let herself get derailed and distracted by a beautiful cowboy.

No way.

She punctuated the mental declaration by throwing the van door open and approaching the grain elevator. When she was close enough, she reached out and laid a hand on the roughened wood, tilting her head back to contemplate the structure's epic scale.

For a few seconds, she let herself imagine that her sister's prediction was true, that this really was going to be the springboard she needed to launch her career.

It could happen. It really could. She could feel how close she was.

All she'd ever asked for was a chance. Now she just had to make it count.

Chapter Six

CASEY SPENT ALL day thinking about Eva King. He'd hoped to have an opportunity to say goodbye this morning, but when he'd stepped outside after breakfast, her battered black van was already gone.

Obviously she'd decided to get a head start on the long drive back to LA.

To say he was disappointed was an understatement. He'd felt…gutted. Which was dumb, because saying goodbye wouldn't have changed anything between them. It wasn't like they were suddenly going to start a hot and heavy long-distance relationship. Despite how much fun they'd had last night, how good it had been between them, they barely knew each other, and she was clearly very focused on her work. He had only to remember her preoccupation last night to understand that.

None of that stopped him from thinking about her and the way she'd made him feel. The truth was, she'd blown his mind with her boldness and honesty and hotness—and he was never going to see her again.

He had to make a run into town for parts for one of the automatic waterers late in the afternoon, and it was nearly six by the time he was pulling into the yard. A familiar black van was parked in front of the barn and he tapped the brake in surprise, sending up a spurt of gravel.

So she hadn't gone back to LA. She was still here.

The surge of triumph that rocketed through him was more than a little disturbing.

Chill, dude. She probably got held up or something and decided to start out tomorrow instead. This is not about you.

He knew it wasn't, and to prove it, he made a point of carrying the parts for the waterer into the barn before heading inside to see if Sierra knew what was going on with their guest.

The sound of feminine laughter from the kitchen alerted him to the fact that his sister wasn't alone as he entered the house, and he took a moment to take off his hat and check his hair in the mirror next to the coat rack at the front door.

Sure enough, he had hat hair, and he finger-combed it a few times before deciding he looked presentable. There was dirt and dust on his jeans and boots, and he needed a shower, but the need to see Eva again was stronger.

Doing his best to seem casual, he strode toward the kitchen. Both women looked up when he entered. They were standing at the counter, a pile of sliced and diced vegetables in front of them, along with an open bottle of wine and two half-full glasses. Eva was wearing a black tank top and a pair of jeans cut off at the knee, and she looked hotter than any person had a right to in such androgynous clothing.

"Perfect timing," Sierra said. "I was just about to fire up the grill but now you can do it."

Casey was too busy locking eyes with Eva to pay much

attention to what his sister had said. A hundred sense memories from last night bombarded him as he met her blue gaze. Suddenly she was in his lap again, her mouth on his, her small breasts pressed to his chest.

Then he blinked, and she looked away, and he realized his sister was at the fridge, pulling out steaks for him to grill.

"…might as well get them started while I make the potato salad," she said.

He accepted the plate, then glanced at Eva again. She was dusting off the counter with her hand, collecting stray bits of bell pepper and carrot.

"Thought you'd be halfway to LA by now," he said.

"Eva's staying with us for another week," Sierra said, and Casey shot his sister a frustrated look.

Eva was the one he wanted to hear from.

"Does that mean you got the commission?" he asked, his gaze on Eva again.

"It means they want more information before they make a decision. But I'm in with a chance," Eva said, her mouth quirking up in a brief smile that disappeared as quickly as it had appeared.

Maybe it was his imagination, but she seemed uncomfortable—and it wasn't a huge stretch to think it was because of him. Because of what had happened between them last night.

Which knocked him off his stride. He'd been thinking about her all day, and here she was, struggling to make eye contact with him.

As though she was embarrassed about what had happened between them. As though she regretted it.

It was a bucket of cold water, and he took a physical step backward.

"Congratulations," he said.

Then he headed for the back door, escaping to the porch. He set the plate of steaks on the bench seat beside the barbecue and took a moment to sort through his thoughts and feelings.

He'd had a great time last night. But apparently the feeling was far from mutual. Apparently Eva had been done with him the moment her skin had cooled.

He busied himself pulling the vinyl cover off the barbecue, annoyed with himself for giving a shit. He'd had a good time—that was all he should be worried about. And no promises had been made—he'd stepped into the trailer last night believing she was going the next day, which was pretty much the definition of a one-night stand. He had no right to feel wounded or rejected. It made no sense. Any other guy would be high-fiving himself for scoring big time with no strings attached.

It was too good to be a one-off. We fit too well together.

Casey shook his head as he lit the grill, wishing he could shake the thought loose. The problem was, he hadn't liked a woman as much as he liked Eva for a long time. She was bold, unpredictable, a bit dangerous. She was also smart, and driven, and she knew how to laugh at the world and herself.

And being inside her had been insanely good.

He fired up the burners, then automatically went through the process of scraping down the cast-iron grill before throwing the steaks on. He very deliberately didn't let himself think about anything except the task at hand, and after a few minutes he felt his shoulders relax.

He knew where he stood now. That was the takeaway from the little scene that had just played out in the kitchen. They'd both had a good time, but it had meant nothing, and even though she was staying another week, it wasn't going to happen again.

He was a grown-up; he could deal with that.

The sound of the kitchen door opening made him look over his shoulder. It was Jed, two beer bottles dangling from the fingers of one hand and a plate in the other.

"For the meat when it's done," Jed said, handing the plate over before offering Casey one of the beers.

Casey took it gratefully, taking a long pull from the bottle and welcoming the cold as it hit the back of his throat.

"All good out here? Anything I can help with?" Jed asked.

"Nope. These'll probably only need a few more minutes," Casey said.

"Did you hear we're going to have a tenant for another week?"

Casey was conscious of his brother shooting him an assessing look but Casey kept his expression neutral. At least, he hoped he did.

"Yeah. Good timing—the extra rent money will just about cover the parts for the automatic waterer," he said.

Jed seemed to be waiting for him to say more but Casey kept his focus on the grill, lifting one of the steaks to see if it was done yet.

"That all you've got to say?" Jed asked.

"What did you want to hear?"

"Ask her out for dinner or something. Not every day you meet someone who does it for you."

Casey was momentarily speechless. Apart from a single, incredibly awkward five-minute conversation to confirm Casey understood the ins and outs of procreation and contraception before his senior prom, he and Jed had never had a conversation about their private lives. Not that there had ever been much to talk about—his brother pretty much lived like a monk, as far as Casey could tell, devoting all his energy to the ranch, and Casey hadn't had a girlfriend for a couple of years now.

"Not much point when she's going to leave in a week's time," Casey said.

"Don't miss out on something good just because it might be complicated," Jed said, and there was a weight—a heaviness—behind the words that made Casey turn to study his brother's face.

"You all right?" he asked.

"Sure. How much longer on those steaks?" Jed asked.

"Not long."

"I'll tell Sierra."

Jed let himself back into the house and Casey resumed his station in front of the barbecue.

Not for a second did he believe his brother when he said nothing was up, but the man was like Fort Knox when it came to talking about his feelings.

The steaks were done, and he loaded them onto the clean plate before turning the gas off and heading inside.

Sierra was just placing the salads in the middle of the table as he entered, and both Jed and Eva were already seated.

Casey handed the meat over to his sister before washing his hands at the kitchen sink.

His shoulders were tight again, and he rolled them before reaching for the dish towel to dry his hands. He wasn't looking forward to sitting down to eat with Eva and pretending nothing had happened between them.

The irony wasn't lost on him—he'd spent most of the day regretting the fact he'd never see her again, and now he'd gotten his wish and didn't want it.

"Steaks look great, Case," Sierra said, taking the seat next to Eva.

Which left Casey sitting opposite her.

Awesome.

He flicked her a quick look as he sat and was just in time to catch her glancing at him, too, before focusing on the plate in front of her. So he wasn't the only one feeling uncomfortable. He wasn't sure if that made him feel better or worse.

"Help yourself, Eva," Sierra said, offering their guest first pass at the salads and steaks.

"Everything looks amazing," Eva said as she forked a steak onto her plate and reached for the salad servers.

"Especially compared to the feast of instant noodles you had planned instead, right?" Sierra said with a laugh.

"Knew I was going to regret telling you that," Eva said, flashing his sister a bright smile.

He couldn't help remembering the way Eva had laughed last night as she flirted with him over burgers at the diner, which naturally led to the memory of her on top of him, her head thrown back as she gave herself over to pleasure.

Get a grip, dude.

Determined to distract himself, Casey reached for the water jug and filled everyone's glasses, focusing on the small task with everything he had.

"So, Eva, I take it you're going to be painting a mural on the old Clarke grain elevator?" Jed said, dusting off his best company manners to make their guest feel welcome.

"Oh, no. At least, not yet," Eva said with a small laugh. "I'm in the running to create the mural, that's all. They want to see and hear more, so they've given both of us a week to prepare a more detailed pitch."

"So it's like a competitive tender, but for art?" Jed asked.

"Exactly like that, except her competition is her ex," Sierra said.

Jed took a pull from his beer before responding. "So I guess you're fixing to slam dunk this thing, then?"

Eva smiled. "That's the plan."

"Well, good luck to you. Hope you get what you came here for," Jed said.

"Thanks. And thanks for letting me stay for the week."

Casey kept his eyes on his plate, grateful for possibly the first time in his life for his reputation for quietness. He'd always been reserved around people he didn't know, and neither Jed nor Sierra would think it was strange he wasn't rolling out the welcome mat for their visitor.

It was a small blessing, but he'd take it.

"You should hear her ideas," Sierra said. "Tell them about your pitch, Eva. It's so cool."

Eva shifted in her chair, and Casey could tell she was uncomfortable with his sister's suggestion. "They don't want to be bored by my mural ideas."

"They're not boring, they're amazing," Sierra said. "That idea about representing the past, present, and future of Marietta is pure genius."

"Well, thanks, but it's still just an idea at the moment. I need to flesh out the concept, put together some proper studies."

Casey frowned down at his plate. Was that what she'd been doing last night before he left? Sketching studies?

"You're as bad as Casey, refusing to toot your own horn," Sierra said. "Being modest is practically un-American, you know that, right?"

"I'll try to be better," Eva said meekly.

Sierra laughed. "I knew I liked you. If you don't want to brag about your amazing concept, tell me what Australia is like. You said you did a commission down there a couple of years ago, right? I've always wanted to go there."

"Hot. And dry. And scary," Eva said. "But also beautiful and wild. And the coffee…some of the best coffee I've ever had in my life."

Casey listened as they talked about Eva's travels in Australia for the next fifteen minutes, allowing himself an occasional glance in her direction. She was a good storyteller, and not afraid to tell a joke against herself. When she laughed her whole face lit up, transforming her from attractive to stunning.

She had charm to spare, and he was uncomfortably aware of the tug of continuing attraction. Apparently it didn't matter that she was done with him, he still wanted her.

The realization made him claim he didn't want any of his

sister's truly excellent apple pie, and he made an excuse to leave the table early.

Only when he stepped outside did his shoulders climb down from around his ears. He made a point of checking on the mares, just in case Jed followed up on his manufactured excuse, lingering over the chore as long as he could. Then he collected his guitar from his room and made his way round to the very back of the house where the porch was protected by the branches of the big pine tree and he could look out across the darkened fields for miles. He kept an old chair out there for nights like this, and he sat and stared into the darkness, his fingers sliding restlessly over the guitar strings. A rhythm came to him, a collection of notes that swiftly arranged themselves in his mind. He gave himself willingly over to the music, channeling his disappointment and confusion into the work.

After a while, his noodling resolved into a grinding, dirty rhythm and ideas started to spark. After ten minutes, he stopped and pulled out the battered notebook he always carried in his back pocket and scribbled down the lyrics floating in his brain. Then he went back to playing, refining his ideas, searching for a bridge, finding a chorus.

It was a boozy, sexy song, meant for late nights and dark bars, different from the stuff he'd been writing lately, but it captured the essence of last night perfectly. The promise, the flirtation, the lust, the gratification. The earthy, consuming realness of being with a woman who'd grabbed his attention and held it from the moment he first laid eyes on her.

He was going over the bridge again when he caught the scuff of shoes on wood. He knew straight away that it was

Eva, even though it was too dark to see anything that wasn't up close and personal—there was a sudden vibration in the air, and within himself, and his hands stilled on the guitar.

"I didn't meant to interrupt," she said.

"It's okay," he replied.

"Cool song. Is it one of yours?"

"Maybe, if I get it right."

"Sounded pretty amazing to me."

She moved closer, and he could see the gleam of her eyes and the outline of her body.

"Am I invading your special place? Is this your songwriting corner?" she asked.

"No, and yes. But it's not a tree fort. Girls are allowed."

Her teeth showed briefly as she smiled.

"I wanted to talk to you about last night," she said, and his stomach was suddenly as tight as a drum.

"Okay," he said, and he could hear the wariness in his own voice.

"I can get caught up in my own head sometimes, and it wasn't until you left that it occurred to me I'd just done the equivalent of wham, bam, thank you ma'am. And that was not cool, at all, and I've been feeling like crap about it all day. So I wanted to say I'm sorry for being rude."

It was so not what Casey had been expecting and it took a moment for her words to sink in.

"You don't need to apologize," he said, even though her words had taken a weight off his mind.

"Yeah, I do. You gave me such a good time, but then I was so inspired by what you said about your folks and this place, I had to get my ideas down on paper before they disappeared. And you tried to remind me you were still there, but my head was somewhere else entirely and I didn't realize until after you'd gone."

He tried to remember what he'd said last night that might have been inspiring, but he'd been so wiped after climaxing twice in quick succession that all he had was a vague memory of talking about the accident.

"You don't remember what you said, do you?" She moved closer, parking her butt on the porch railing so she was directly in front of him.

Almost within reach.

"You told me that keeping this place going was about preserving and honoring your parents' legacy, and I couldn't stop thinking about how special that was, which led to me thinking about Marietta's legacy, and then I needed my sketchpad. And then I disappeared down a rabbit hole and didn't come back up until after you'd gone."

"I'm glad it helped," he said. "It's great you've got a real chance at the commission now."

She sighed. "Okay. I guess I deserve all that politeness. I'll let you get back to your song. And don't worry, I'll be working twenty-four seven on this proposal, so you'll hardly ever see me."

He blinked, taken aback by her words. She pushed away from the porch rail and he shot out a hand to catch her forearm before she slipped past him and disappeared into the darkness.

"You think I regret last night?" he asked, barely able to believe it.

"I could understand why you might. If a guy was that

dismissive of me, I'd probably want to key his car."

Her arm was warm in his hand, and he could feel the sinewy strength beneath her soft skin. Even though he wanted to keep touching her, he forced himself to let her go.

"I'll admit, my ego took a hit, but I get it. Sometimes when I'm writing a song, I tune out so much, Sierra claims she has to jump up and down in front of me to get my attention."

"Except we'd just had earth-moving sex and you were naked in my bed. Slightly different situation."

He felt a stab of gratification at her words. "Define earth-moving for me."

There was a small pause before she responded. "Fishing for compliments, Carmody? I didn't scream loud enough to tip you off last night?"

"Maybe I just want to hear you say it."

"I'm not sure that's a good idea. You're a little distracting, and I need to stay focused."

"I thought about you today, too," he said, and she laughed outright.

"You're not going to make this easy, are you?"

"Funny, I thought I was bending over backward to be easy."

She laughed again, then she took a step closer, almost as though she couldn't help herself. "Funny, and hot. How am I supposed to resist that?"

"Don't know why you'd even try," he said, shamelessly offering her his best lazy smile.

She shook her head. "I thought we talked about you using that smile for good instead of evil."

"I promise my intentions are nothing but good."

Reaching out, he hooked his finger into the belt loop on her jeans and pulled her closer, only stopping when she was standing between his legs. She watched as he slipped his finger free of the belt loop before tracing her skin along the top of her waistband. She shivered subtly when he stopped at the stud on her jeans.

"You're probably wondering how good I can be, right?" he asked.

She closed her eyes in a long blink. "The thought did cross my mind."

He slid the stud free.

"When I do something, I like to do it properly."

She swallowed audibly as he gripped the tab on her zipper and slowly slid it down.

"That sounds very…thorough."

"Thorough. That's a good word for it," he said, then he shifted forward in the chair.

He pulled her jeans open and leaned forward to press his lips to the soft, warm skin of her belly. Her hips rocked forward a little and he opened his mouth and tasted her skin.

As he already knew, she tasted *good*, and he wanted more.

She made a small, low sound as he gripped her hips and pulled her closer still, peppering kisses across her smooth belly to the lacy top of her panties. Her hands found his shoulders, her fingers digging into the muscles there as he continued his journey south, kissing the gentle rise of her mons through the delicate lace.

Her jeans impeded further progress so he kissed his way back up, opening his mouth hungrily when he reached her bare flesh again.

"Oh, God, that feels so amazing," she whispered brokenly.

She sounded so lost in pleasure, it went to his head. All he could think about was getting her clothes off so he could make her lose her mind entirely. Gripping the waistband of her jeans, he started peeling them down, past her hips—just as he heard the unmistakable sound of the kitchen door opening around the corner. The distinct sound of footsteps made Eva jerk with alarm, then she brushed his hands aside and yanked her jeans back up in a lightning-fast move. By the time Sierra rounded the corner, Eva was leaning against the porch railing again, arms crossed over her chest.

"Case, I know you said you didn't want pie, but I saved you a piece anyway because I'm a good and kind sister," Sierra said.

Her steps slowed when she realized he wasn't alone and Casey could practically hear the wheels turning in her mind as her gaze went from him to Eva and back again.

"Thanks, appreciate it," he said.

"Sorry, I didn't mean to interrupt," Sierra said.

"You didn't. I just heard Casey playing out here and stopped by for a free performance before I headed back to the trailer," Eva said. "Speaking of which. I've got a ton of work to do."

She stepped away from the railing, clearly keen to be gone.

"Don't go on my account," Sierra said. She took a step backward, signaling her intention to return inside. "Make sure he plays 'Montana Dreaming' for you while you've got him cornered. It's one of his best."

Then she pivoted on her heel and disappeared back around the corner of the house.

Casey waited until he heard the door close behind her before catching Eva's eye.

"Come here."

"No way."

"Didn't take you for a chicken."

Her chin came up. "I'm not, but you can't be trusted. And apparently neither can I when I'm around you."

Casey smiled and reached down to collect his guitar. Then he stood and closed the small distance between them. She had to tilt her head back to continue looking him in the eye as he lowered his head to capture her mouth in a short, hot kiss, just because he could and because he was that freaking desperate to be close to her.

She could pretend all she liked, but they both knew where this was headed.

"Here's what's going to happen—I'm going to go inside, put my guitar away, and grab a shower. Then I'm going to come out to the trailer, and you're going to be naked on the bed, ready for me. Got it?"

Her eyebrows rose and she gave him a look. "Bossy, aren't you?"

He answered her with another kiss, pressing his body against hers this time so she could feel exactly how much he wanted her. They were both breathing hard when he came up for air.

"Not a stitch on. Got it?"

Then he left her standing in the darkness.

Chapter Seven

*B*OOM. *B*OOM. *B*OOM.

Eva lay in the dark, the sound of her own heartbeat loud as a tom-tom in her head as she waited for Casey to come to her. In line with his orders, she was naked and the warm night air caressed her bare skin as she counted down the minutes.

She'd thought about defying him, just to see what he'd do, how he'd handle it. She'd thought about meeting him at the door fully dressed and telling him she'd changed her mind, that this was a distraction she didn't want or need.

But that would have been a lie, and she was done with denying her own wants and needs. She'd pushed down her ambition for five years to support someone who was never going to reciprocate. She wasn't about to deny herself the intense pleasure she knew she'd find in Casey Carmody's arms. Maybe that was stupid, given everything that was at stake, but that didn't change her decision.

She wanted more of him. It was that simple.

And so she waited, on the alert for the sound of his approach, her breathing ragged as she anticipated what he was going to do to her, what they were going to do together.

Last night, he'd teased her breasts until she was aching with need. He'd sucked and kissed and licked her until she'd seriously thought she could come from breast play alone.

She wanted him to touch her like that again. She wanted it to last for hours.

She also wanted him pounding into her again, his body hard and hot with urgency. Her inner muscles clenched as she remembered what it had been like to be filled with his beautiful cock. He'd been tireless, driving her higher and higher with every thrust of his hips.

She shifted on the bed, squeezing her thighs together. She didn't need to check that she'd fulfilled the second part of his command: she was so aroused it almost hurt.

The scuff of a shoe on cement made her tense, and she held her breath as she heard the door open. She was so ready for this, so hungry for it, she was trembling, her mouth dry, every nerve straining.

"No lights? Don't tell me you're shy." Casey's voice was low and deep in the darkness.

"Didn't want to intimidate you," she said.

"Baby, I love a good challenge. I'm going to turn the light on, okay?"

"Knock yourself out," she said, drawing her bent knees up and rolling them to one side in a classic pinup pose a second before the light came on.

As she'd hoped, he laughed when he saw her.

"See anything you like?" she asked in her most sultry voice.

He'd kept her waiting, now it was her turn to tease.

Holding his gaze, she slowly peeled one thigh away from

the other, opening herself up to him. The smile dropped from his mouth, hunger flaring in his eyes.

Casey pulled his T-shirt over his head and let it fall to the floor.

"Lucky the Airstream is tucked in behind the barn the way it is," he said, his hands making short work of his belt buckle. "Because I'm going to make you scream so loud."

He pushed his jeans down and she saw he was already hard, his cock jutting proudly. Suddenly the trembling was back and she was almost scared of how much she wanted him, how much she wanted this.

Almost.

He walked toward the bed, six feet of prime male, then the mattress shifted beneath his weight as he climbed on board. His gaze was fixed on the heart of her, taking in everything she had to offer with an avid, appreciative intensity. A shiver ran through her as his hands landed on her knees, his work-roughened hands smoothing up her thighs but stopping just short of touching her where she was aching for him.

"You ready for this?" he asked.

"Are you?" she countered.

"I've been ready for this since I rolled off you last night. I've been thinking about it all day. Wondering how you taste, how much you can take."

"I can take anything you're offering," she said boldly.

His fingertips pressed into the soft skin of her thighs as his grip tightened briefly. "Let's see."

Then he lowered his head and licked along the seam of her intimate flesh, his tongue firm and hot and wet. Sensation rocketed through her and she moaned shamelessly because it felt *so good*.

"Fuck. Knew you'd taste amazing," he murmured, coming back for more.

His shoulders pressed her thighs wider as he scooped his hands under her butt to control her hips. Then his mouth was on her, and the world fell away. There was nothing but the delicious pressure of his tongue as he licked and sucked her most sensitive, delicate flesh. He consumed her—there was no other word for it—his mouth open and eager, leaving her no place to hide, stripping her of any illusion of control or dignity.

She was lost, ruined, devastated, hands clenched in his hair, back arched, breathing ragged. Pleasure wrapped itself around her and squeezed until she was pleading with him for release, unable to take any more.

And then he gave her what she needed and she was sobbing through one of the most intense climaxes she'd ever experienced, her whole body shuddering with the force of her release.

He didn't let up until he'd wrung the final moan from her, and she didn't need to see his face to know he was feeling pretty damn pleased with himself.

Sure enough, he was smiling like a marauding conqueror when he lifted his head, shifting so his weight was supported on his elbows.

"How are we doing? Still with me?" he said.

She eyed him through heavy, half-closed eyes, her body limp with satisfaction. "Barely took the edge off," she lied.

"Better step up my game, then."

She watched as he sat back on his heels and collected a condom from the pocket of his jeans. His gaze moved from her wide-spread thighs to her flushed face as he tore the foil packet open and rolled the condom slowly down over himself. Watching him handle himself was nothing short of mesmerizing, his fist stroking down the length of his shaft one of the hottest things she'd ever seen.

"Roll over," he said.

She hesitated a moment, tempted yet again to defy him just to see what he'd do. Then she thought about how hard he was and how ready she was and she rolled over and pushed herself up onto her knees, presenting him with her backside.

"Very nice," he said. Then he surprised her with a single, firm slap on the butt.

"*Hey.*"

She was about to tell him she was not into pain with her pleasure, but then she felt the hot, hard press of his cock at her entrance, and a moment later it was all she could do to keep breathing as he seated himself deep inside her.

"You feel so good," he said, his voice barely more than a growl.

He started to move, withdrawing from her in a smooth slide before returning to fill her once again. It felt so right, so perfect, she rested her head on her clenched fists and closed her eyes and gave herself over to him.

He pumped into her over and over, smoothing a hand along her spine and up to the nape of her neck, then back down again. She pushed back against his thrusts, finding his rhythm, urging him on. Tension spiraled through her, pleasure building with each firm, hard stroke inside her.

She was already close when he slid a hand between her legs, finding her with his clever fingers. She made an approving sound and spread her thighs wider, tilting her hips to provide him with even greater access. He took her encouragement and ran with it, increasing the pace until the only sound in the small space was the slap of his skin on hers and their mutual panting.

And then she lost track of everything as her body was racked with intense, throbbing pleasure. She was aware of Casey shuddering into his own release, his grip tightening on her hips as he held himself deep inside her, his body hard as steel as he bowed over her for long, drawn-out seconds.

When it was over, she flopped onto her belly, ruined yet again by a cowboy with clever hands and, it turned out, an even more clever mouth. She was conscious of him hitting the mattress beside her, and she cracked her eyes open to see if he was as destroyed as she was. He lay on his back, one arm thrown over his head, eyes closed, cheeks flushed. His chest rose and fell as he fought to catch his breath.

She allowed herself a small, slightly smug smile—she'd done that to him.

His eyes flickered open, his focus quickly sharpening when he realized she was watching him.

"See anything you like?" he asked, echoing her earlier words.

"A few things spring to mind."

He smiled lazily. "Give me a minute and I'll be right with you."

She shivered, her body cooler now that the first flush of

desire had faded, and he reached down and pulled the covers over both of them.

"Better?"

"Thanks."

He closed his eyes again, arms crossed behind his head now, and she allowed herself the small pleasure of admiring his handsome features. He'd be a pleasure to draw, his body full of intriguing dips and curves, his face beautifully masculine.

And yes, that was totally a thing.

"I can feel you staring at me," he said without opening his eyes.

"I'm thinking about how pretty you are."

"It's my skin regimen. I exfoliate religiously."

He was so deadpan she cracked up laughing, and suddenly she couldn't hold back the question that was at the forefront of her mind.

"Why are you single?" she asked.

His eyes opened and he looked at her. "Is that some kind of trick question?"

"No trick. Just curious. You're pretty. You play the guitar. You're funny. Your body is...well, you know. And you're passably proficient at sex," she said. "So why hasn't one of the good women of Marietta pinned you down yet?"

"Passably proficient? You're gonna pay for that, you know that, right?" he said with a lazy smile.

She reached out to poke him in the ribs. "Answer the question."

"There is no answer. I had a girlfriend a few years ago. There wasn't enough between us to keep us together, so we broke up and there hasn't been anyone else serious since. That's about it."

He shrugged. She studied his face.

"That's it, really?"

"Sure. Plus there's my perverse sexual tastes. It takes a very particular type of depraved woman to satisfy me, and once word got around town, it was slim pickings. Until you showed up." Again, he was so matter-of-fact she couldn't help but smile.

"Lucky me."

"Funny, I've been feeling pretty lucky myself."

A quick glance down his body told her he'd had enough recovery time. Determined to make the most of this night of self-indulgence, she shifted closer and threw her leg over his hips. Using her knees for leverage, she shifted so her body was lying on top of his, breast to chest, hip to hip.

His eyebrows rose in surprise, but his hands landed warmly on her backside, holding her in place.

"So the interrogation is over?" he asked, lifting his hips to increase the pressure between them.

"Yes."

Then she kissed him and stopped thinking about anything except how good he made her feel.

CASEY WOKE WITH his arms full of warm woman.

The last thing he remembered was slipping into darkness, his body heavy with satisfaction after he and Eva had made each other crazy a third time. She'd collapsed beside him on the bed, one arm thrown over her eyes, and he'd gone to the bathroom to dispose of the condom, turning the light out on his way back to the bed. Then he'd stretched out beside her and closed his eyes for what he'd thought would be a few minutes.

That had been a mistake, obviously, because his internal clock told him it was now early in the morning, maybe four or five.

He hadn't intended to stay the night. After the way things had ended last time, that had seemed like the smart way to play it. And yet here he was, with Eva plastered to the side of his body, her head on his chest, her arm around his waist, one slim leg tangled with his.

He hadn't figured her for a snuggler. She clearly didn't mind getting up close and personal when pleasure was on the agenda, but she was so fiercely independent, so determined, he'd figured she was more of a sprawled-starfish-don't-touch-me-I'm-sleeping type person than a spooner. But apparently not, because there was nothing standoffish about the way she was welded to his side.

It had been a while since he'd shared a bed with another warm body for anything other than sex. Not through active choice, it had just worked out that way. He'd broken up with his last girlfriend, Annie, two years ago, and even though there had been a few women he'd dated briefly in that time, none of them had clicked for him.

He didn't know what he was looking for, he just knew he hadn't found it yet.

Not that he'd been looking too hard. Truthfully, Eva was the first woman in a long time to really grab his attention. He didn't know what it was about her that got him going, but she did, and he knew himself well enough to understand he was on the precipice of doing something stupid if he allowed himself to savor this quiet, intimate moment too much. He might not talk much, but he was a songwriter and a musician, and he'd done a fair amount of navel-gazing in his time. He knew he wasn't built for casual sex, that he preferred to really connect with the person sharing his bed.

He also knew that while Eva might have unconsciously sought closeness from him in her sleep, she was not seeking it in her waking life. She was in town for one reason only, and even if she won the commission, she'd only be here for a handful of weeks, max.

Plus she was fresh out of what sounded like a pretty shitty relationship.

Two strikes. If he wanted another one, he could throw in the fact that her life was located in the LA art scene, too.

In short, there was zero chance of anything serious happening between them. Zero, nada, zilch.

So the smart thing to do right now would be to carefully disengage from her embrace and ease his way from her bed. Doing so would ensure that they both understood exactly what this was—and, equally, what it wasn't.

Beside him, Eva stirred, her grip tightening across his torso. He listened to her breathing for a moment as he tried to decide what to do. He could smell her shampoo, something beach-y and coconut-y. He could feel the warmth of her exhalations against his chest. His arm was wrapped around her back, his hand resting on the roundness of her shoulder.

One of the things he loved about her body was its inherent contradictions. She was slight, but strong, her arms and legs toned and subtly muscled, and while she was slim-hipped and small-breasted, her nipples were exquisitely sensitive, and he loved the way she squirmed and moaned when he teased them.

He could feel himself getting hard again, which wasn't going to help anything. He needed to go, not find a way to draw this encounter out any further.

Carefully he lifted the shoulder supporting her head, hoping she might pick up on the subtle signal. She stirred, but didn't shift, and he was forced to use his free hand to lift hers from where it was clamped across his belly and return it to her side. Next he slipped his leg from beneath hers. Then—finally—he gently eased away from her, sliding his shoulder from beneath her head in slow increments. She murmured a protest but didn't wake, and he scooted to the edge of the bed and reached for his clothes.

There was enough moonlight leaking through the curtains to find his jeans, and he pulled them on, then pushed his feet into his boots. His T-shirt was harder to find, and he finally gave in and pulled out his phone, switching the flashlight function on for long enough to see it crumpled on the floor, halfway to the door.

He scooped it up, then tugged it on and turned to consider Eva. She was still deeply asleep, her arm flung out across the empty bed now. He was reluctant to leave her, which was exactly why he needed to. Forcing himself to turn away, he moved as quietly as he could to the door and let himself out of the trailer. He walked briskly up to the house, slipping in via the kitchen door. Even though it made him feel like a teenager, he paused long enough to ease off his boots, then made his way to his bedroom in his socks. Such was the price of privacy when you lived with two siblings, one of whom would be more than happy to make dissecting his private life her entertainment should he be stupid enough to hand her the opportunity.

He stripped and climbed into bed, but after five minutes of lying in the dark, he realized his brain was too busy to let him sleep. It was too early to consider getting a head start on the day, so he settled for flicking on the beside lamp and pulling out his song journal.

He ran an eye over the song he'd jotted down after dinner, half expecting it to suck, but was pleasantly surprised to realize it was okay. Good, even. Propped up on one elbow, he read over the few lyrics he'd written down and instantly knew what came next. His hand sped over the page as he channeled his half-formed thoughts and feelings. It was light outside when the distant flush of a toilet roused him from his journal.

He was itching to pick up his guitar and see if he'd nailed the song, and he figured that if one of his siblings was up already, the other wouldn't be far behind. He grabbed his guitar and sat naked on the edge of his bed to pick out the new chorus he'd written. He tweaked a note or two, then played the whole thing from beginning to end. As he'd hoped, it was good, but there was something missing still. He tried a couple of ideas before setting his guitar down.

He couldn't keep his brother and sister waiting while he indulged himself.

His head felt clearer, despite the lack of sleep, and he was feeling at peace with the world in general as he dressed and headed out to the kitchen. Sierra and Jed were at the table eating waffles, and Sierra wordlessly pointed him in the direction of the jug of batter on the counter so he could make his own.

"What time do the Shots start tomorrow night?" she asked as he poured batter into the waffle maker.

"Eight, same as usual," Casey said.

"I was thinking of bringing Eva along, if she's interested," Sierra said.

Casey shot her a look, checking to see if she was fishing, but she was busy dabbing at some spilled syrup on her jeans. Most likely she was just being friendly, worrying that Eva would be lonely because she didn't know anyone locally.

He checked on the progress of his breakfast and used a fork to flip two golden brown waffles onto a plate. Then he loaded them up with syrup and joined his brother and sister at the table.

He wasn't sure how he felt about Eva coming to watch the Shots play. A little nervous, but also kind of excited.

Maybe even a little proud that she'd get to see the Shots doing their thing.

You don't need to impress her. And even if you do, it's not going to change anything. She's still going to leave.

Casey stared at his plate, troubled by the fact that he had to keep reminding himself of that fact.

"I'll go saddle the horses," Jed said, pushing back his chair and draining the last of his coffee. They were checking the fences today, a time-consuming task that had to be done regularly to ensure they didn't lose stock.

"Two minutes and I'll be with you," Casey said, shoveling waffle into his mouth.

Sure enough, a minute later he was rinsing his plate in the sink before sliding it into the dishwasher. Then he went to brush his teeth, very deliberately pushing all thoughts of Eva King out of his mind, where they belonged.

EVA WOKE FROM deep sleep to the sound of a horse whinnying. For a wild moment she forgot where she was, and then memory came flooding back—Marietta, Dane, the grain elevator, Casey.

She lifted her head, suddenly very awake, but the bed was empty beside her.

Huh. She hadn't heard Casey leave last night, she'd been so deeply asleep. And obviously he'd decided against waking her to say goodbye.

Thoughtful of him. But Casey *was* thoughtful, as well as generous, sexy and very, very thorough.

She grinned suddenly, remembering the way he'd teased her with that word last night. He hadn't simply been bragging, either—she'd had no idea another human being could make her feel so good. It wasn't as though she was a shrinking violet when it came to sexual matters, either. She'd had her fair share of lovers—but none of them had ever made her lose her mind the way Casey had.

She didn't know what it was about him that got her so wound up. The intuitive way he touched her, maybe? He just seemed to know what she needed, giving it to her exactly the way she wanted it.

And the way he'd gone down on her last night… Holy hell, he had destroyed her.

She made an impatient noise and threw back the covers. She didn't have time to wallow in sensual memories, she had a kick-ass proposal to pull together.

She showered and ate a granola bar for breakfast, then grabbed her laptop, camera, and phone and jumped in Big Bertha. Ten minutes later she was approaching the turnoff from the highway, but the sight of a shiny black SUV and a bright yellow cherry picker parked in front of the grain elevator made her hesitate.

Dane.

Ugh.

She put her foot on the gas, speeding past the exit, her stomach churning with a sudden injection of acid.

Damn it. She should have guessed Dane would be doing the same sort of groundwork as her, checking out the site more thoroughly, trying to get a firmer grip on the parameters of the job. The difference was that he had the resources to do it properly. She'd give a lot to be able to inspect the grain elevator's weathered timbers up close to confirm her best guesses regarding the kind of preparation work she'd need to do, but there was no way she could afford to hire a cherry picker for the day.

She told herself it didn't matter. She'd come back later, when he was gone, and do what she could from the ground. And she'd make sure that every other aspect of her proposal was spot on. She'd always been the one to do the background research and leg work on his projects, and she was as sure as she could be that Dane wouldn't be taking on the task personally himself now. He was too big for that, too important. He'd probably send Zack along to make some token enquiries and pull a few books from the library.

She'd planned on hitting the library herself this afternoon, but it wouldn't hurt to reverse her schedule if it meant avoiding him.

She tensed as she registered her own thought. Then she sighed and signaled before executing a sweeping U-turn.

She wasn't afraid of Dane, and she wasn't going to let him change her schedule for the day.

She could see Dane and his entourage clustered at the foot of the elevator as she approached the turnoff, and she put her best game face on before pulling off the highway. Heads turned to note her arrival, Dane's mouth thinning into an ungenerous line as he glared at her through the windshield.

Good. She hoped it stuck in his craw that she was here. She hoped he was so distracted he could barely concentrate.

Ignoring him completely, she gathered her things and slid a pair of sunglasses on. Then she approached the elevator and did a long, slow lap of the entire structure. Her path led her past the cherry picker where Dane and entourage were now huddled, but they didn't so much as look her way or acknowledge her existence as she walked past. She stopped at the opposite corner to make notes, glancing across as the cherry picker rumbled to life. Slowly Dane and Zack rose into the sky, Zack holding what looked like a new X-Pro with a wide-angle lens. Eva glanced down at her own ten-year-old DSLR and felt a stab of envy.

It's just stuff. They'll be making the decision based on ideas and execution, not because he's got the coolest and latest gear.

She knew it was true, but she also knew that all the technology and equipment he had at his fingertips gave him a distinct advantage. And he was already the front-runner, because he was the name, and she was a nobody.

The cherry picker was still high in the air when she left an hour later. She stopped to pick up a sandwich from a coffee shop near the library, eating it quickly in the van before heading inside. She spent the afternoon trawling through books on the town's history and peering at old newspaper editions stored on microfiche. She had pages of notes and sketches and a fistful of photocopies to take home with her when she was done, and she headed back to the ranch feeling as though she'd put in a good day.

But it wasn't over yet. Once she got home, she made herself some instant noodles, then spent several hours doing more studies. Her eyes were bleary with tiredness by the time she peeled off her clothes and slipped under the covers.

She flicked the light off, and then and only then did she let herself think about Casey again. She hadn't seen any of the Carmodys all day, but she'd heard a truck start up at some point in the evening. Had that been Casey, heading off somewhere?

None of your business.

It wasn't, but that didn't mean she didn't want to know. She imagined him going into town, hanging out at the bar again the way he had the other night when he'd saved her from herself, and she'd given him a hard time.

The memory made her smile as sleep rose up to take her. It had been a lot of fun, giving Casey Carmody a hard time.

It was her final thought for the day.

Chapter Eight

THE FOLLOWING DAY was just as consuming. Eva got an early start, hitting the library for more research, followed by a visit to the Marietta Historical Society. She returned to the trailer loaded down with yet more photocopies, as well as a number of books she'd bought on the history of the region.

She was absorbed in a gripping recounting of the town's short-lived mining boom when a knock on the door drew her out of the 1800s and back to reality.

Her heart kicked out a couple of extra beats: Casey.

"It's just me," Sierra called, immediately killing Eva's little fantasy.

Just as well. You've got enough on your plate, remember?

She unfolded her legs and groaned when her circulation came back to life as she hobbled to the door.

"Hey. Sorry I was so slow—I don't think I've moved for a couple of hours and my legs have forgotten how to work."

"Just doing a welfare check, since we haven't seen or heard from you for a couple of days now," Sierra said, her gaze assessing as she took in Eva's rumpled appearance.

"I've been working. A week isn't a lot of time to come up

with all the stuff they want." Eva stretched, then circled her shoulders. "But thanks for checking on me."

"I think you should take a break. Come into town with me. The Whiskey Shots are playing, and we can be amused by all the women throwing themselves at Casey without a chance in hell. It'll do you good to get out of this little tin can."

Eva frowned at the mention of Casey beating off hordes of women. "I happen to be very fond of this tin can," she said. "And even though it sounds fun, I think I should stick with this."

Plus it would be easier to stick to her all-work, no-play promise to herself if she didn't have to actually be in the same room as Casey. Much easier.

"There are reams of scientific studies that show productivity tapers off when exhaustion sets in. Give yourself some time out, let your hair down, and come back to it fresh tomorrow," Sierra said.

She was very persuasive, her smile bright and beguiling, and Eva couldn't help thinking about how good it would be to stop thinking for a few hours and get out among other people.

"You Carmodys need to rein in the charisma a little when you're dealing with us mere mortals. We're defenseless when you pull out the big guns," Eva said.

"I have no idea what you're talking about," Sierra said. Then she batted her eyelashes and widened her smile a fraction so it shifted from charming to dazzling.

"All right, all right. I'm on the mat already, no need to pummel me into mush," Eva said.

"Great. You've got ten minutes to get ready before we leave."

Eva looked down at her aged tank and floppy pajama shorts.

"I'm going to need at least fifteen."

"Band starts at eight, and we want to grab a booth if we can," Sierra said in a warning tone.

"Fine. But if people point and laugh, it's on you," Eva said.

Sierra laughed. "My money is on every eligible bachelor in town doing their best to get your attention."

"They can do backflips for all I care—I am officially not on the market."

"Because you're not interested or because you're with someone?" Sierra asked, and even though she threw the question out as casually as can be, Eva sensed intent behind her words.

"After Dane, I am officially once burned and twice shy," Eva said.

"Well, be warned—there are going to be some cowboys there tonight who are going to do their damnedest to change your mind," Sierra said as she disappeared out the door. "See you at the truck in ten."

Eva wasted no time shedding her clothes and jumping beneath the trailer's compact shower. She rinsed off the sweat and stress of a day spent inside her own head, then hastily toweled herself dry and contemplated her meager wardrobe. She needed to do some laundry, so there wasn't a lot of choice—her black skinny jeans and a dressy tank, or her black slip dress. It was a warm enough night that the dress seemed like the smart option, so she pulled on a pair of lacy boy shorts and matching bra, then threw the dress on. Five minutes later she was clattering down the steps in a pair of colorful wedge-heeled sandals, makeup on, hair styled.

Sierra was waiting by her truck as Eva rounded the corner of the barn.

"I knew you could do it in ten minutes," she said, opening the driver's door and sliding in behind the wheel.

Eva helped herself to the passenger seat as Sierra started the pickup. "I felt the pressure of living up to your high expectations," she said.

Sierra shot her an amused look as she headed down the driveway. "Sure you did, LA girl."

Eva waited until they were on the highway driving toward town to give voice to her curiosity.

"So, what am I going to see tonight?" she asked.

"Are you asking if the Shots are any good? Because I'm a little biased, in case you hadn't guessed."

"I guess I'm trying to imagine Casey center stage, enjoying the limelight. He seems so self-contained."

"He is, one on one. But he comes to life on stage. You'll see."

"You said something about women throwing themselves at Casey and not having a chance in hell. Why not?"

"Casey doesn't do casual. Never has," Sierra said with a shrug of one shoulder.

Eva glanced across at her, thrown. "Really? Never?"

"I'm not saying that. It's not like my brothers give me a weekly rundown on their private lives. But Casey's had a lot of opportunities to enjoy the Shots' success, if you know what I mean, and I've never seen him take advantage. Not once."

Eva frowned as she stared out the window at the dark fields rushing past outside. It was a little worrying that she'd felt a decided thud of triumph at hearing Casey didn't make a habit of sleeping around. Whether he was a player or not shouldn't matter to her one iota—they'd used condoms, and neither of them had made promises to each other. Sleeping with him had been about pleasure and distraction, nothing more, nothing less.

And yet there was no denying she was glad he didn't do this all the time. That she was the exception, rather than the rule.

How messed up and confusing was that?

It's called having your cake and eating it, too. Or being a dog in a manger. One of those things.

Even her inner smartass was confused by what she wanted when it came to Casey.

A car passed them, its headlights briefly illuminating the truck's interior, and Eva's attention was caught by the laminated ID hanging from the rearview mirror.

"What's this?" she asked, catching the tag in her hand and reading the small print. She looked at Sierra, surprised. "You can fly a helicopter?"

"I can," Sierra said.

"How come I didn't know this about you?"

"I was thinking of having a T-shirt made, but I thought it might be a bit ostentatious," Sierra joked. "It doesn't come up much, especially because I haven't had a chance to go up since you arrived."

"Well. You're officially a dark horse," Eva said. "Is this a hobby or something you want to do for a living or what?"

"Long term, I'd love to get my commercial license. That's what I'm working toward at the moment but you need a lot of flight hours and they're expensive. One of our neighbors, Gideon Tate, lets me use his chopper sometimes if he's in town, but he hasn't been around much lately. So it's probably going to take a while to get where I need to be."

Eva frowned. "Why do I know that name?"

Sierra's hands shifted on the steering wheel. "Casey might have mentioned him. He was driving the other car in the accident that killed our parents."

"Oh. Sorry."

"Don't apologize. It's a fact of life." Sierra was quiet for a beat. "The boys don't like me flying his chopper. They don't like feeling like we owe him anything."

"Was the accident his fault?" Eva asked.

"Nope. The accident report says Dad's truck hit some ice on a turn, and he lost control and drifted across the line. Gideon barely had a chance to brake before they hit."

Eva's gut clenched as her imagination threw up vivid images of what must have happened next.

"I guess it must be hard, knowing he's alive and they're dead," Eva said, thinking it through.

"Sure. And Gideon got Jed's back up in the early days, offering money to help out. At one stage, he even offered to buy the ranch outright."

Eva winced. "A little misguided."

She'd only just met the Carmodys, but it was obvious to her that they were deeply committed to the ranch their parents had built out of nothing.

"Just a little," Sierra said. "But I figure his intentions were mostly good. And the truth is, it will take me years to get where I need to be without his generosity, and the sooner I can get my license, the sooner I can start paying back all the money Jed has spent on lessons over the years. I want to contribute more, and if that means taking Gideon Tate's guilty charity, I will."

There was steel and determination in her voice and Eva figured the Carmody brothers were going to have a fight on their hands if they ever tried to clip Sierra's wings.

"You go, girl," Eva said approvingly.

Because it was her personal philosophy that everyone was entitled to their dreams, no matter how big or small they were.

They were rolling down Main Street by then and Sierra made an approving noise when she spotted a parking space opposite the saloon. She swung into it deftly and threw the truck into park.

"Time to brace yourself. It's going to be busy in there, so stay close, okay?" Sierra said as they exited the truck.

Eva glanced toward the saloon, and sure enough, there was a line of people waiting to enter. On a Thursday night.

"Are The Whiskey Shots the only band on the bill?" she asked.

"Oh yeah. They don't need anyone else," Sierra said. There was more than a hint of pride in her voice.

She led the way across the street, her long legs eating up the ground, and Eva had to almost run to keep up with her. Sierra called out greetings to a few people in the queue before joining the line and taking out her phone to text someone.

"Just checking to see if Cara has grabbed a booth yet," Sierra said. "Otherwise we might be standing."

Evidently she got good news from her friend because she punched the air a few seconds later.

"Awesome, we're in, and she's already ordered a pitcher of margaritas," Sierra said.

"I like her already," Eva said.

The line shuffled forward and a few minutes later Sierra was exchanging greetings with the burly security guy on the door. And then they were inside and it was *insane*.

It was like walking into someone else's surprise party, it was so crowded and noisy. Eva blinked, a little overwhelmed, and almost lost Sierra as she immediately plowed into the crowd, heading for the booths that lined the left wall. Lunging forward, Eva chased the other woman, ducking elbows and excuse me-ing her way past what had to be half the population of Marietta.

This was not what she'd envisaged when she'd imagined Casey playing a gig at the local bar. She'd pictured a few well-intentioned locals supporting live music played by people they knew, tapping their feet and singing along whenever they recognized a song.

Not in a million years had she anticipated this heaving mass of expectant, boisterous people, and Eva glanced toward the stage, beginning to suspect she'd seriously underestimated Casey and his band.

"There you are. I thought I'd lost you," Sierra said, reaching out to pull Eva onto the bench seat on one side of a booth already crowded with three other women, all of whom looked to be around the same age as Sierra.

"Eva, this is Cara, Ashley, and Jessica. Ladies, this is Eva—she's staying in the trailer out at the ranch while she's in town on business," Sierra said.

"Oh my God. When did you start renting out the trailer and when can I move in?" Ashley asked. A small brunette, she had an open, sunny face and a cute button nose.

The others laughed, and Sierra gave Eva a wry look. "Ashley is my brother's number one fan."

"And my good friend here refuses to set me up on a date with him," Ashley said, reaching across the table to give Sierra's arm an admonishing shake.

"I am not my brother's social secretary," Sierra said firmly.

"I'll make you maid of honor at our wedding," Ashley said, her tone light.

"What brings you to town, Eva?" Cara asked pointedly, very deliberately changing the subject. Slim, blond and angular, she had direct blue eyes and a no-nonsense demeanor.

"I'm in contention for a commission to do an art mural on the old Clarke grain elevator," Eva explained.

"I heard about that project," Jessica said, tucking blond curls behind her ears. "My mom does admin work for the Chamber of Commerce. I think she said it's going to be more than a hundred feet tall…? It sounds like it's going to be pretty epic when it's done."

"It will be if Eva wins the commission," Sierra said loyally, reaching for the jug in the middle of the table to pour a drink for herself and Eva.

The sound of applause prevented Eva from having to say more, and she looked across to see The Whiskey Shots had come on stage. Her gaze gravitated to Casey as he slid his guitar strap over his head and settled the instrument against his body. He was wearing a plain white T-shirt and well-worn jeans with boots, his overgrown hair pushed back from his forehead, but somehow he looked *more* now that he was up on stage.

Gilded. Special.

Such was the power of fame, even modest fame.

She half expected him to appear nervous, or intimidated by the capacity crowd, but he scanned the audience with a small, confident smile, said something over his shoulder to the drummer, then stepped closer to the mic.

"Evening, Marietta. Hope you're ready to raise the roof," Casey said, his deep voice filling the room and silencing the chatter.

Eva heard the drummer counting them in, then the room filled with sound as the Shots launched into their first song. It was fast-paced and high-spirited, with a rhythm that quickly had her wanting to tap her fingers on the table. A few people whistled their approval, clearly recognizing the song—and then Casey started singing and Eva was glad she was sitting down because otherwise she was sure she'd have fallen over.

Deep and resonant, with just a hint of emotional rasp, Casey's voice was so good, so delicious, so compelling she felt all the little hairs on her arms stand up.

"*Jesus,*" she said, unable to take her eyes off him as he commanded center stage.

"Told you," Sierra said in her ear. "He's amazing."

He was. Assured and playful, utterly committed and confident, he had the crowd in the palm of his hand as he sang about love and laughter and having it all. By then people were stomping their feet in time with the beat and singing along, and Eva couldn't keep the smile off her face.

Well, how about that. Apparently she'd been sleeping with a freaking superstar for the past two nights. No wonder poor Ashley had a crush on him—Eva suspected half the women in the room harbored X-rated fantasies about the hot, talented man singing his heart out on stage.

She watched, bemused, as the Shots powered straight into a second song, barely giving the audience a chance to signal their appreciation.

Glancing across, Sierra laughed when she saw Eva's face.

"It's a little shocking at first, I know," Sierra said, obviously enjoying Eva's bafflement. "He's the last person to draw attention to himself in everyday life, but up there, he owns it because it's about the music for him. That's all he cares about, making it as good as it can be, and people just respond to that passion."

It was an astute observation. Genuine passion combined with great skill was very attractive all on its own, but combined with Casey's hard body and pretty face, his appeal was undeniable.

"How have they not been discovered yet?" Eva asked, because she'd seen enough bands in her time to know that the kind of alchemy she was witnessing right now was rare and precious.

Sierra shrugged. "Beats me. But it will happen one day,

and I can't wait for him to be able to do what he loves instead of feeling torn in two all the time."

Eva wanted to ask what Sierra meant by that, but now was not the time or place to pump the other woman for information about her brother.

Or you could just let it go, because you're being smart and concentrating on what you came here for. Remember?

The crowd went wild at the end of the song, screaming and clapping so loudly Eva had to cover her ears. Casey smiled, lifting a hand in acknowledgment, then took off his guitar. Returning to center stage, he wrapped both hands around the mic as the opening bars of a ballad filled the space. Casey lowered his head, his hair falling forward to mask his face. Then the music opened up, and he lifted his head and started singing with a raw emotional intensity that gave Eva gooseflesh all over again.

Which was when she understood she was not going to be smart or sensible when it came to Casey Carmody. Far from it.

That ship had sailed the moment Casey walked on stage.

She was going to be reckless. She was going to indulge herself. She was going to let this beautiful, talented man do incredible things to her body, and worry about the consequences afterward.

The realization should have made her anxious, but Casey was on stage, and she couldn't look away.

She'd worry about tomorrow when it came. And tonight…tonight she would simply enjoy.

CASEY PUSHED HIS hair off his forehead and looked out over the crowd. A sea of faces looked back at him, the air vibrating with the force of the applause as the final notes of the final song reverberated around the bar.

"Marietta, you brought it tonight. Thanks for partying with us and giving us all the love. We love you guys," he said into the mic.

His words set the crowd off again, and when he glanced over his shoulder to see how the band was taking it, he could see they were getting off on it as much as he was, mouths stretched wide in crazy grins.

Nothing in the world matched this feeling. *Nothing.*

The crowd wouldn't let up, so he looked to Wyatt, eyebrows raised in question. Wyatt nodded and Casey faced front again and leaned into the mic.

"All right, you sweet-talking fools. One more, but it's gotta be the last or we'll be in trouble with the management. If you haven't kicked up your heels yet, now's the time."

He launched into "Blue Sky Dreamer," feeling the bass and the beat in his bones, loving the expansive feeling in his chest as he gave the lyrics everything he had.

Too quickly the song was over, and even though the applause was just as crazy and sustained, he didn't cave and sing another encore. The show had to end sometime.

Giving the audience one last wave, he slipped his guitar strap over his head and carried it offstage with him. Later, when the bar was empty, he and the boys would come back out and pack up their gear, but for now all he could think about was getting his hands on a cold beer.

"Oh, man," Wyatt said, collapsing into a chair in the

windowless room set aside for the entertainment backstage. "That was *epic*."

Casey smiled and reached for one of the beers waiting on ice for them. "Yeah, it wasn't too bad."

"Did you see them turning people away at the door?" Danny said.

"No shit?" Rory said, eyebrows raised. A slow grin stretched his mouth. "Well, how about that. A full house."

"We did good, boys," Wyatt said, lifting his beer in a toast.

They all leaned forward to clink bottles.

A knock sounded on the door before it cracked and Sierra peeked into the room. "Just me, plus one," she said.

Casey had already spotted Eva in the corridor, his gaze running over her scrap of a dress and bare legs and arms, her tattoo a bright, bold splash on her upper arm. He'd lost count of the amount of times he'd stopped himself from asking his sister if Eva had agreed to come see him play over the past two days. The thought that she might be in the audience tonight had added an extra buzz to the adrenaline coursing through him when he stepped on stage, but he hadn't known until this moment if she'd actually come or not.

Her gaze met his and she smiled, and he could tell by the look in her eyes that she'd enjoyed his music. It was a little pathetic how relieved he was that that was the case.

"You guys were so good tonight," Sierra said. "So. Good. I thought the roof was going to lift right off there at the end."

"This is why you are always welcome in the band room,

Sierra," Rory said.

"You had a good time?" Casey asked, his gaze still on Eva.

"I did, I had a great time. I'm officially a country convert," she said.

"She even stood on her seat at the end," Sierra said.

Eva shrugged a shoulder and laughed. "I got carried away, what can I say?"

There was something about the way she lifted her chin and shifted her shoulders that reminded him of the way she'd held herself when she straddled him that first night, and all of a sudden all he could think about was getting her alone and naked.

Okay, take a deep breath. You're high on adrenaline and endorphins right now.

It was true, he was, but that didn't diminish his need for her. He'd been thinking about her for two days, living off the occasional glimpse of her as she disappeared around the corner of the barn or headed off in her van, telling himself she had to make the next move because he wasn't going to be That Guy.

"All right, we'll leave you to it," Sierra said.

"Okay, good to see you, gorgeous," Danny said.

"You know you're still Plan B for me if Louanne gives me the heave-ho, right?" Wyatt said.

"Be still my heart, you old romantic," Sierra said, blowing him a kiss before switching her attention to Casey. "See you at home."

Casey nodded, doing his best to not stare at Eva like a hungry dog.

"Great show. Really amazing," Eva said, flashing him a smile before following Sierra out the door.

It took every bit of self-discipline Casey had not to go after her and stop her from leaving.

"Holy guacamole. Who is the smoking-hot blonde?" Danny asked, giving a long, suggestive whistle, the moment they were gone.

"Her name's Eva King. She's in town for the week, renting the trailer out at our place," Casey explained.

"You lucky bastard," Danny said.

Casey took a pull from his beer and lifted a shoulder, hoping it would be enough to change the subject.

"So, is she single?" Danny asked. "Because I know a guy who likes hot blondes." He gestured toward himself and the other guys cracked up.

"She's here for work," Casey said, and he could hear the tightness in his own voice.

Danny's eyebrows rose toward his hairline. "Uh-oh. Did I just step on your toes, Carmody?"

"She our guest, that's all. She doesn't need a bunch of horn-dog cowboys sniffing around like desperados," Casey said.

"Definitely stepped on some toes there," Rory said. "Good luck, buddy—I think you've got your work cut out for you there. She's got big-city girl written all over her."

Casey tossed his empty beer bottle into the nearby trash can. "I wasn't happy with the mix at the start of the gig. Anyone else notice the bass was out?"

Wyatt took the bait, and instead of taking apart his private life, they did an autopsy on the gig for the next fifteen minutes. By then the bar was closed and they filtered back to the stage to pack up their gear. He'd just returned from taking his guitar and amp out to his truck when Wyatt caught him in the corridor.

"Hey, Case—don't listen to what Danny said earlier. So what if she's a city girl? Louanne is from New York City. Doesn't get more big-city than that."

Casey bit back a sigh, aware his friend was coming from a good place. "She's in town for a week. Don't go picking out a tuxedo just yet," he said, trying to keep it light.

"Plans change, man. Feelings happen. Never say never, right?" Wyatt said before clapping him on the shoulder and heading outside.

Casey shook the moment off, but his friend's words came back to him as he took the road out of town fifteen minutes later.

Plans change. Feelings happen. Never say never.

It was ridiculous how much he wanted to take heart from Wyatt's wisdom, but he knew he'd be setting himself up for a fall if he pushed things with Eva. He already liked her more than he should, and she'd made it clear in lots of ways that what had happened between them was about sex and only sex for her.

He didn't hold that against her, but seeing her again had driven home to him that he was playing with fire.

If he let her, Eva King could break his heart.

He caught the glint of animal eyes on the side of the road and slowed, just to be safe, wishing he was built differently. More like his brother, Jesse, who never seemed to have trouble moving on or enjoying temporary dalliances. He'd never bragged about it, but Casey had a fair idea what the lifestyle of a pro rodeo cowboy was like.

Of course, Jesse was head over heels for CJ now, and that was unlikely to change anytime soon from what Casey had seen. His brother was about as lovestruck and besotted as it was possible for a man to be.

But Eva was not CJ. Not even close. No way was Casey going to talk himself into believing that, regardless of Wyatt's wildly optimistic advice.

It shouldn't be too hard to avoid her for the rest of her stay. She'd kept to herself the last two days. There was no reason to think she wouldn't keep doing so, given how immersed she was in her work. And if Sierra invited her to dinner again, he could handle that.

He just had to stay out of her bed. Definitely achievable, he figured.

Then he pulled into the yard and his headlights caught a slight, blond figure sitting on the porch steps and all his good intentions went up in flames.

Chapter Nine

H IS BODY GOT hot with instant lust and he took a deep, steadying breath as he got out of the car. She stood as he approached the steps, dusting her backside off with her hands.

"Hi—"

He kissed her, hauling her body against his, cutting off whatever else she'd been about to say. She came willingly, her arms wrapping around his shoulders as she strained closer. She tasted so fucking good, so addictively, insanely hot, he couldn't stop himself from moaning into her mouth. She responded by wrapping a leg around his hips and rubbing herself against him, her body shaking with need.

He needed to be inside her like he needed air, and he pushed her dress up and pushed his hand roughly inside her panties. His cock got even harder when he discovered how hot and wet she was. He pressed her against the porch railing as he slid a finger inside her. She started to shake, her breath coming in anguished sobs.

"Please… God… Feels so good."

He reached for his belt, ready to give her what she needed and wanted—and then an owl hooted and sanity made a hard, unwelcome return.

They were on the front steps to the house, in plain view of anyone who cared to look out the window. No way could he do what he wanted to do to her out here.

"Damn," he said, sliding his hand free from her panties.

"What?" she asked, blinking, her eyes heavy-lidded, her cheeks flushed.

She'd been so close, and he'd just pulled the rug out from under her.

"Take your shoes off," he said.

She blinked up at him for a moment, then leaned down to tug off her high-heel sandals. Taking her by the hand, he led her up the steps. As he'd hoped, the house was dark when he opened the front door.

His tread steady, he led Eva across the living room and into the hallway toward his bedroom. A light showed under Sierra's bedroom door, but Jed's was dark. His hand on the small of Eva's back, he steered her through the doorway to his bedroom and pushed the door shut behind him.

Flicking on the light, he took a moment to savor the way she looked right now—utterly wanton, her mouth swollen from his kisses, her nipples hard beneath the soft fabric of her dress.

"Where were we?" he asked.

"I'm pretty sure I was about to come," she said.

"Right. Let's see what we can do about that."

He reached for the hem of her dress, whipping it over her head to reveal a truly decadent bra and pantie set.

"Nice," he said, then he flicked open the front clasp and closed his mouth over one of her already-puckered nipples.

She arched her back, her hips pressing forward into his, hands clutching at his shoulders as he sucked hard on her straining flesh.

"Oh, God," she whispered, and she sounded so broken he felt like beating his chest and baying at the moon.

Instead, he abandoned her breasts to sink to his knees, taking in the glorious sight of her soft little mound covered with black lace.

"Did you think of me when you put these on?" he asked, reaching out to press a finger against the damp fabric of her panties.

"Yes," she said. "I thought about you doing this. Exactly like this."

He rewarded her honesty by leaning forward and pressing an open-mouthed kiss on her mons through her panties. Then he hooked his fingers into the waistband and pulled them down her legs so he could get more of what they both wanted.

Her legs were trembling as he urged her back onto the bed and down onto her back, her feet remaining on the floor. Then she spread wide for him, offering him a truly heart-stopping sight and he lost track of time for a while.

His world shrank to a few inches of delicate flesh, to the scent of her arousal, the spasmodic grip-release of her hands in his hair, the uncontrollable trembling of her thighs as he licked and sucked and teased her until her hips lifted off the bed and she shuddered into a silent, convulsive climax.

His cock was so hard it hurt, and he didn't bother fully undressing, just yanked his T-shirt over his head and pulled his belt free. His cock jutted out of his jeans as he opened them, quickly smoothing a condom over himself. He considered Eva's flushed, spread-eagled body for a moment, then grabbed the pillow from the head of the bed.

"Lift your hips," he instructed, keeping his voice down.

She tilted her pelvis and he slid the pillow under it, the added padding lifting her to the perfect height. He slipped a hand beneath each of her knees and lifted them toward her chest, opening her even further.

"Hold your knees," he told her.

"Wow, you are really bossy tonight," she said.

"You love it. Now, hold your knees."

Her eyes flared, but she did as instructed, closing her hands over her knees. His gaze locked to hers, he took himself in hand and positioned himself at her entrance. She sucked in an anticipatory breath, her breasts rising, and he pushed inside her in one long, firm stroke. Still holding her eyes, he slipped his hand between them, delving through her damp curls until he found the hard little pearl of her clitoris.

She didn't look away as he circled her with his thumb, but he could feel her tighten around him. He began stroking into her, long, strong, steady strokes, his thumb circling and circling. She started to pant, but she still refused to look away, and he watched as desire spiraled inside her, bringing out the cords in her neck, making her body tremble as she rose toward climax yet again.

Then she was gone, her head tilting back, and his self-control slipped the leash. Planting a knee on the bed, he came down over her, kissing her breasts, biting a nipple, and finally finding her mouth as he drove into her again and again. Her legs wrapped around his hips and her hands clutched at his shoulders, his back, his butt. And then he was coming, pleasure gripping him as he held himself deep inside her, his face pressed into her neck.

He allowed himself a few seconds to recover before lifting his weight off her, conscious of how much bigger he was. Her eyes were closed when he withdrew from her, her head turned away from him, her hands flung out to either side in utter abandonment.

"Say something," he said.

"Something," she said.

He smiled. Even after two orgasms, she still had attitude to spare. A tissue took care of the condom in the short term, and he joined her on the bed, lying beside her.

A moment of silence passed, then she opened her eyes.

"So, this is your bedroom, huh?" she said.

"Figured it was marginally more comfortable than the front porch."

She sat up, supporting her weight on her elbows as she surveyed his room. "Can I snoop?"

"Sure. You won't find much, but have at it," he said, crossing his arms behind his head and preparing to be amused.

"We'll see."

She sat up and slid off the bed, then crossed to open his closet doors.

"Wow. You have a lot of boots," she said.

"Some of them need to be thrown out," he admitted.

He'd never really had a chance to appreciate her body at leisure before—he'd either been crazy with need every time they were naked, or on the verge of slipping into a coma

from satisfaction—and he surveyed her slim form, admiring
her small but firm little backside and the neat proportions of
her body, as she considered his clothes. Her hips were on the
boyish side, and her breasts on the small side of average, but
she was hands down the sexiest woman he'd ever met and
parts of him were already becoming interested in round two
just from looking at her.

"Your clothes smell like sunshine," she said. "And I wish
my jeans were this soft. Ha. I knew there would be something good in here."

She pulled out his old letter jacket from when he was on
the high school football team, holding it at arm's length to
study it.

"I always wanted to wear a guy's letter jacket in high
school," she asked. "What's the statute of limitations on high
school fantasies?"

"There isn't one. Put it on, if you like."

"Thought you'd never ask."

He watched as she slipped her arms into his jacket. It was
predictably huge on her, her hands hidden by the too-long
sleeves, the hem hitting her mid-thigh. She struck a pose,
hand on one hip, the opposite knee bent.

"Why, sure, Bobby Lee, I would, like, totally love to go
to the prom with you," she said.

"Uncanny," he said. "It feels like 2009 all over again."

She laughed, then covered her mouth. "Sorry. I forgot
we're on the down low."

"More for you than me."

"You protecting my reputation, Carmody?" she asked.

"I'm protecting you from my nosy sister."

"That's very gallant, but I have a foolproof method for deterring nosy siblings—graphic and detailed descriptions of sexual positions. Works every time."

Casey laughed. "I bet."

She wandered over to his bedside table and lifted the aftershave bottle there, sniffing it. "So this is why you always smell like sandalwood and spice. Nice."

She put the aftershave down.

"Now, the million-dollar question—where does he keep his porn?" she asked, tapping her fingertips together as though she was pondering something of great importance.

"Haven't you ever heard of the internet? No one buys porn mags anymore."

"So if I check under the mattress, there won't be a well-worn copy of *Playboy* or *Penthouse* circa 2005? No nostalgic pinups of Pamela Anderson hidden away?"

"You sound disappointed."

"Porn is very revealing. I want to know what you're into. What you like."

His jacket gaped open as she talked, allowing a rosy pink nipple to peek out and offering him the briefest of glimpses of the silky thatch between her thighs.

"That's easy—I like you," he said. "I like your tight little pussy and your firm tits. And I love the noises you make when you come. Come back to bed."

She went still, as though he'd taken her by surprise. Then she stepped toward the bed, arms reaching up to push his jacket off.

"No, leave it on," he said. "I'm getting into this high school fantasy thing."

"In that case…" She climbed onto the bed and into his lap, the rough wool of his jacket scratchy against his bare skin. "Onto your back, Carmody. It's my turn to be bossy."

"Yes, ma'am," he said.

There wasn't a doubt in his mind that she planned to make him pay for his earlier high-handedness, but he didn't have a problem in the world with handing over the reins. Not with this woman.

Lying back, he gave himself over to whatever was going to happen next.

EVA LAY IN a pleasant haze, trying to muster the energy to get out of bed and sneak back to the trailer. It was hard to even think about moving when every part of her body felt so languid and satisfied. Plus Casey's bed smelled nice—the faintest hint of lemony laundry soap with a side note of his aftershave.

Also, she liked the feel of his warm, strong body against her side. Not because she wanted to have sex with him again—although that was also part of it—but because she'd missed the simple companionship of lying next to someone like this. Such a strange, animal thing, taking comfort from the press of another human body against her own.

It was one of the few things about Dane that she actually missed.

Casey stirred beside her, his hand coming to rest on her hip. She turned her head to find him watching her, his green eyes warm as they scanned her face.

"I'm glad you came tonight," he said.

"Me, too," she said, wiggling her eyebrows.

He smiled. "I meant to the bar."

"I know. Same answer. I had a great time."

"Good to hear."

She could tell it pleased him that she'd enjoyed his music, and it made her think about the way he lit up when he was on stage.

"What's it like, being on stage with all that attention on you?" she asked.

"It's pretty intense, in a good way. To be honest, I'm still kind of getting my head around it. When we first started gigging a year or so ago, we were playing to a handful of bored locals who really didn't want to listen to our music. But things have been slowly building, and for the past few months, it's been standing room only when we play at Grey's."

"That's because you guys are really good. I can't believe you haven't been signed to a label yet. Don't they have talent scouts in Montana?"

He shook his head, a small frown between his eyebrows.

"What does that mean?" she said, imitating the movement.

"I'm not interested in signing to a label," he said.

She blinked, a little taken aback. "Why not?"

"Because the Shots are about making music, not chasing fame and all that other bullshit."

Eva gave him her best side-eye. "For real? You don't want to hear them call your name out at the Grammys? You don't want a row of golden records hanging in your luxuriously fitted-out mega mansion?"

SARAH MAYBERRY

"Not really."

She rolled over to face him fully. "You don't want hordes of beautiful women throwing their underwear at you? You don't want to be a household name?"

He shrugged. "None of that stuff motivates me. I like playing to a room full of people who are into my music. That's the limit of my ambition."

Eva studied him, not sure if she believed him or not. She'd seen the joy he took in performing tonight, she'd felt the way the audience responded to him. How could he not want more of that?

"What about you? Do you want to be famous? Is that what your art is about?" he asked, turning the tables.

"I would never want to be famous just for the sake of it, like a Kardashian or Paris Hilton. I can't think of anything worse, actually. And it's definitely not what motivates me to create. But it's a sad fact of life that it's much easier to pay the bills when you have a big name. So, I guess that's my way of saying yes, I want to be famous. But more because it would mean I could stop worrying all the time about keeping a roof over my head than because I want people kissing my ass all the time."

"Come on, you'd love a little ass kissing thrown in. Be honest," he teased.

"A little bit," she admitted. "But not to excess. Enough to get me a good table at a restaurant, or tickets to a Broadway show."

"So what's the trajectory after you land the commission this week? What happens next on your journey toward fame and fortune?"

"You're very confident on my behalf."

"Why not assume the best outcome?"

It was a novel concept. She rolled onto her back and folded her arms behind her head, letting herself explore the idea a little.

"First I'd make sure all the major art publications knew what was happening. Then I'd make sure to document the process with lots of photographs so I could provide them with a good story if I can convince one of them to profile the finished project. Maybe I'd even film some video of me working, put it on my website so people could see it all coming together, share it on Instagram blah, blah. Then I guess I'd have to sit back and wait, see what crops up next."

He looked thoughtful. "So you'd just be waiting for someone to reach out to you with another commission?"

"Until I get some runs on the board, yes. I need to build my name, do all the things I did to grow Dane's profile, but for myself this time. This stuff doesn't happen overnight."

The challenge would be advocating for herself as confidently as she'd advocated for him. It was always harder to be your own cheerleader than to be pushy on someone else's behalf.

"You know, there are hundreds of old grain elevators dotted around Montana. Hell, they're probably dotted across the country," Casey said slowly.

"I stopped counting them on the way here," she said. "Every town used to have one, but a lot of them are being demolished now that they're defunct. Which I think is a huge shame—they're a part of the history of rural America."

"Speaking hypothetically, what if you could convince a

few towns nearby to follow Marietta's lead?"

"You mean, create a sort of art trail?" she said. "Dane and I worked on something like that in outback Australia. There's a whole region there with something like six or seven murals over one hundred and fifty miles. It's a huge tourist attraction."

"I bet there are plenty of small communities around here that would love a boost in tourist numbers, especially if the risk was low and the reward high," Casey pointed out.

Eva stared at him, struck by the simple genius of what he was suggesting: rather than wait for commissions to come to her, she would initiate them and become the driver of the project.

"If I could get a handful of towns to come to the party so I could create an art trail, I'd supercharge my portfolio," she said. "It would be huge. I'd get lots of coverage, make lots of noise. And I could approach them with the same idea I'm pitching to the Marietta Chamber of Commerce—a mural capturing the past, present, and future of the local community. I could celebrate local stories, local people. It would be amazing."

She could feel herself starting to get excited. She'd need to do a lot of research to get the idea off the ground, and she'd have to be shameless in her approach to local communities with viable grain elevators. But it was doable. Very doable.

She sat up, her earlier lassitude long gone, her brain ticking over with ideas and strategies.

"And you know what?" she said, thinking out loud. "Pitching the Marietta elevator as the first of many adds more value to the project, too. Suddenly it becomes a regional initiative, a bigger draw card, rather than just a solution to a local problem for a housing developer. This is my point of difference for my proposal. Oh my God."

She pushed her hands through her hair, overwhelmed by all the thought bombs going off in her mind.

"There's an old elevator in Reed Point. And there's one not far from Billings in Rapelje. Probably a bunch more that I haven't even noticed locally," Casey said.

"I need to make a list. I need a map. I need my computer," Eva said. Then she launched herself at him, throwing her arms around his shoulders and pressing a kiss to his lips. "Thank you. I'm embarrassed I didn't think of this myself. You're amazing."

His arms were warm as they came around her back. "Guess this means I'm going to lose you now, huh?"

His hands settled on her backside, squeezing lightly. As always, her body lit up in response to his touch.

"You can't drop a brilliant, potentially career-transforming idea into a girl's lap and then expect her to ignore it," she said.

"Not when that girl is Eva King."

Her heart gave a strange little squeeze at the way he said her name. As though it was special to him. As though it meant something.

His body was firm against hers, his arms strong around her, and she felt a swell of emotion as she looked into his eyes. She'd slept with him that first night because he was hot and sexy and she'd needed something good and uncompli-cated in her life, but she'd gotten so much more than she bargained for. He was kind and funny, clever and talented, and, it turned out, a lateral thinker who may have just changed her life.

"If I go, can I come back again another night?" she asked before she could stop herself.

"Sure. Why not?"

She dug her elbow into his ribs to pay him back for his casualness. He laughed and kissed her.

"On what planet do you think I am ever going to say no to you?" he asked.

There was so much warmth in his voice and the way he was looking at her. It should have alarmed her. This was supposed to be a hot and sexy fling. Pointless, light, and ultimately meaningless. There was no place in that equation for the way she'd felt tonight, watching him on stage, and the way he was looking at her right now.

And yet here she was, and here he was.

"What's wrong?" he asked.

"Nothing," she lied.

She kissed him, then forced herself to get out of the bed. He immediately threw back the covers and reached for his jeans, starting to dress alongside her.

"What are you doing?" she asked.

"Walking you home."

"All the way out to the trailer?"

"That's right," hc said, pulling up his fly and reaching for his T-shirt.

She stared at him, amused and touched and challenged by his gallantry.

How on earth was she supposed to keep her head when

he was so sweet and hot and lovely?

He shot her a quizzical look, and she made herself smile and reach for her dress.

A minute later they padded quietly through the house, pausing on the porch to pull on their shoes.

"I feel like a sixteen-year-old," she said.

"Welcome to my world."

They started down the steps together, and somewhere between the top and bottom step his hand found hers. She figured he was simply trying to steady and guide her but it was scary how right it felt to twine her fingers with his.

They walked in silence to the trailer, where he opened the door and reached in to turn the light on for her.

"Don't stay up too late," he said.

"I won't."

His hand found her shoulder, sliding around to palm the nape of her neck. And then he kissed her good night, a thorough, firm, demanding kiss that promised more next time they met.

She pressed her fingers to her lips as he walked away, the crunch of gravel loud in the quiet night. She wasn't stupid, she knew this was probably going to end badly. But as she'd already admitted to herself, she didn't appear to have a lot of self-control where he was concerned. She'd tried being smart and keeping her distance, but her puny stock of willpower was no match for his hotness and her own desire.

It seemed to her that the only choice she had left was to hang on, enjoy the ride, and hope they both landed on their feet at the end of this thing—whenever that turned out to be.

It wasn't much of a plan, but so be it.

In the meantime, she had some serious strategizing to do, thanks to the man who'd just disappeared into the darkness.

Letting her hand fall from her lips, she climbed the steps and got to work.

Chapter Ten

CASEY TOOK HIS shoes off again when he reached the house and let himself in through the kitchen door.

He'd barely registered the silhouette of someone standing at the open fridge door when Sierra's high-pitched shriek of alarm almost gave him a heart attack.

"Jesus, Casey. Are freaking kidding me?" she gasped, one hand to her chest. "What the hell are you doing, sneaking in the back door like a freaking cat burglar?"

The sound of urgent feet coming their way announced Jed's arrival and he skidded to a halt in the doorway, naked except for a pair of boxer briefs, a baseball bat in hand. The overhead light came on with a snap and all three of them stared at each other under the too-bright light.

"It's okay, Sierra just had a scare," Casey explained to his brother.

The tension instantly drained out of Jed's face. "Okay. Good."

Sierra gave Casey a look. "Hang on a minute—I did not 'have a scare.' You *gave* me a scare, sneaking in in your socks in the dead of night."

Jed's gaze went to the boots in Casey's hand.

"I was trying not to wake anyone up," Casey said. Annoyingly, he could feel his face growing warm.

"Since when have you ever given a crap about that?" Sierra demanded.

Casey sighed. Why did his sister always have to make things harder than they needed to be?

"I was walking Eva out to the Airstream," he said.

Sierra blinked. Then she frowned. "Oh."

Not exactly the reaction Casey had expected. Given the way Sierra had been previously fishing for intel regarding his feelings for Eva and how much Sierra seemed to like their tenant, he'd figured his sister would be happy to learn her suspicions had been correct.

But apparently not.

"That's my cue to go back to bed. Night," Jed said, turning on his heel and exiting.

Casey eyed his sister, but Sierra was uncharacteristically quiet.

"Just say whatever it is you want to say," he said. Might as well get it over with.

"Why would I have anything to say? It's your life, not mine."

Casey shook his head. It was late and he had a full day tomorrow.

"Cool. I'll see you tomorrow, then."

He headed for the door.

"Case."

He sighed and turned to face his sister.

"Just…don't get hurt, okay?" she said.

"That's not going to happen."

She rolled her eyes. "Okay, fine. I look forward to having this conversation when Eva's gone and you're moping around the ranch like a sad sack because she broke your heart."

"Wow, Sierra, tell me how you really feel," he said.

"Casey, she told me tonight she's officially burned once and twice shy, or something like that. She also said she's not in the market to meet someone."

"I know that."

"And yet here you are in your socks with your boots in your hand."

"You really want me to explain casual sex to you?"

Sierra shook her head. "Nope. You don't do casual."

He frowned. "What would you know about that?"

"I'm your sister. I know you better than almost anyone. You write poetry, for Pete's sake. I get that Eva is sexy as all get-out and pretty much the coolest person either of us has ever met, but she is going to chew you up and spit you out."

He'd heard more than enough.

"Okay, thanks. Glad we had this chat," Casey said, turning toward the door.

"I'm saying this because I don't want you to get hurt. That's all."

"How about you concentrate on your own shit for a change," he said, his back well and truly up now. He was not a country yokel, bumbling his way through his first romance and he resented the implication he was. "Maybe if you had more going on in your own life you wouldn't be so busy sticking your nose into mine."

Sierra flinched but he didn't have it in him to regret his

words. Not yet, anyway.

"And I write songs," he said on his way out the door. "Not poetry."

"Same difference, dickhead," Sierra called after him. "And don't expect sympathy from me when she rips your heart out and feeds it to you for breakfast."

Casey rolled his eyes as he strode toward his room. This was exactly why he'd kept his nights with Eva on the down low in the first place. There weren't many times he resented sharing a house with his siblings, but this was definitely one of them.

He threw his boots into the corner when he got to his room, not caring about the clatter. Almost immediately he felt like a five-year-old for letting his temper get the better of him. Sitting on the edge of his bed, he scrubbed his face with his hands.

She is going to chew you up and spit you out.

He made an impatient noise in the back of his throat. He did not need his sister's ominous predictions to tell him he was in over his head with Eva—he'd known that from the moment he met her. It hadn't stopped him from wanting to be with her, and Sierra's warning wasn't going to change his mind either. He wasn't going to miss out on being with the most exciting, sexy, challenging woman he'd ever met because he was scared. Fuck that noise.

And if he was left gutted when she left, he'd make sure the only person who knew about it was him and his music journal, because he was twenty-eight years old, not a little kid.

EVA WORKED TILL her eyes were gritty and her back ached from hunching over the computer keyboard. By the time she turned off the light, she'd created a regional map for herself with as many abandoned grain elevators marked on it as she could discover through cross-referencing local history sites, Instagram feeds, and other social media. She suspected she'd missed a few, and that some she had listed might have been demolished for safety reasons since they'd been documented, but she still had a list of more than twenty elevators to work with when she was done. Surely out of all of those she could find a handful of communities who'd like to work with her to turn an eyesore into a feature.

Surely.

She went to bed with hope in her heart and woke feeling lighter than she had in months. She worked all day on finessing her proposal document, tweaking the wording and layout until she was satisfied she'd conveyed her vision in the best way possible. She had several studies in her sketchbook by then, and spread them all out on the bed and spent an hour considering the merits of various ideas before settling on her final three.

By then she was so sick of her self-imposed solitary confinement, she decided to take a break to clear her head before breaking out her good cartridge paper and her airbrush to start on her final studies. Pushing her feet into her Chuck Taylors without bothering with socks, she emerged into the day and stood blinking in the bright afternoon sunlight.

"Hello, world," she said, feeling like a bear who had been hibernating for winter.

Rolling her head on her neck, she walked toward the

house, then changed her mind at the last moment and veered right into the corral, climbing through the post and rail fence. Several horses at the far end lifted their heads to consider her and she stopped in her tracks, wondering if they were going to object to her presence. What she knew about horses could fill the back of a postage stamp. Were they like bulls, territorial and inclined to defend that territory? Should she be worried right now?

For a long moment, she and the horses considered each other, then the animals lowered their heads and went back to cropping grass, their tails swishing lazily.

Feeling like an idiot, she crossed the corral, slipping through the fence again and out into open land.

The Gallatin Mountains formed a hazy blue-green ridge to her right, and Copper Mountain rose on her left, its sides blue and purple in the afternoon light. She walked for a few minutes, long enough to get her blood flowing and clear her head. Then she stopped and simply looked around herself, taking a moment to absorb the natural beauty of her surroundings—the tall trees in the distance, the endless blue sky, the vast swathe of open land that spread before her. A warm breeze lifted her hair and made her T-shirt billow, and she tilted her head back, closed her eyes, and let the sun warm her face.

What an amazing place. And Casey had grown up here, breathing in this air, working this land. It was so different from the concrete and congestion she'd grown up with, it blew her mind.

After a few minutes, her thoughts drifted back to work. She was happy with her progress today. If she could nail the final studies by tomorrow, she'd have a whole day left to rehearse her presentation and iron out any bugs.

Her hands flexed by her sides, itching to get back to work, and she opened her eyes and took a deep breath. Okay, back to it. Hands tucked into the pockets of her jeans, she turned back.

The horses gave her another disinterested once-over as she traversed their corral, and she glanced at the main house before turning toward the barn and returning to the Airstream. There was no sign of Casey, which was probably just as well, because she had trouble concentrating when he was around.

She got lost in her work after that, and the day quickly turned to night. She was rummaging among her groceries, trying to decide between more instant noodles or egg on toast when she heard footsteps outside. Sure enough, a knock soon sounded and she opened the door to find Casey standing there, a pizza box in hand.

"Thought you might need dinner," he said.

"You're a mind reader. Come in."

Casey stepped up into the trailer, and as always, the space seemed to contract. He glanced at the bed, which was strewn with her art supplies.

"Maybe we should eat outside?"

"Another excellent idea," she agreed.

He took the pizza outside, and she stopped to grab two beers from the fridge and a couple of paper napkins. There was only her one camping chair, and Casey gestured for her to take it.

"I'll sit on the steps," he explained.

"You take the seat, I'll take the steps. You're the guest. And you already brought the food," she said.

Casey looked as though he wanted to argue, but he shrugged a shoulder and sat, flipping the lid on the box and offering the first slice to her.

"Oh my God, please tell me that's hot salami," she said, her mouth watering like crazy.

"Mild. Wasn't sure if you could handle hot, but next time I'll know better," he said.

She took a bite of pizza and made happy noises. "I didn't realize how hungry I was until I saw that box in your hands," she admitted.

He was silent for a moment, chowing down on his own slice. Then he cleared his throat and looked at her.

"So you know, Sierra was in the kitchen when I came back to the house last night."

She wiped her mouth with a napkin. "Well, that was probably bound to happen, considering."

"Yeah. How did your work go today?" he asked, clearly done with the subject.

For the next twenty minutes they discussed their respective days and ate pizza. She learned he'd spent the day inspecting the various automatic waterers situated around the ranch, checking if the problem he'd found with one unit recently was an isolated incident, and she told him about the map she'd made last night, and the new details she'd added to her proposal after his suggestion.

"Sounds like you're on track to kick ass," Casey said, wiping his hands on a napkin and washing the last of his pizza down with a mouthful of beer. "You want the last piece?"

Eva eyed the remaining slice, seriously tempted, then shook her head.

"I think I'm done. I'll only regret it later if eat it."

"Then get over here," Casey said, patting his lap.

"Please," she prompted him.

"You don't have to beg, baby," he said, giving her one of his devastating smiles, and she couldn't help laughing at his cockiness.

"That's not funny. Just so you know," she told him.

"Made you laugh," he said.

There wasn't much she could say to that, so she went and did as instructed, perching on his knees. His arm came around her, drawing her closer so that her shoulder was leaning against his chest. Then he tilted her chin up and kissed her, and it was so exactly what she'd been waiting for that she simply clung to him and kissed him back.

He tasted of beer, fresh and malty, and when his hand slid beneath her T-shirt to cup her breast she made an approving noise and marveled at how he always seemed to know exactly what to do to make her feel good. Between his kisses and what he was doing to her breast, it wasn't long before she was a panting, needy mess, desperate for more.

"Come inside," she said.

"You all done with your work? I don't want to set you back. I know how much you've got riding on this thing."

There was no doubting his sincerity, despite the fact that she was sitting on the hot, hard evidence of his arousal. She forced herself to think beyond her own desire and genuinely consider his question.

"I probably need another hour or two," she admitted grudgingly.

"Then why don't I come back at ten?"

"Sounds good to me." She squirmed a little, almost too embarrassed to ask the question in her mind. "Any, um, instructions for me?"

He went still for a moment, and she saw the flare of desire in his eyes.

"You like that, do you?" he asked. "Me telling you what to do?"

"Turns out I do," she said.

He laughed. "All right, then. No clothes, blindfolded, legs spread. Got it?"

"A blindfold? What is this, the red trailer of pain?" she scoffed, even though the idea secretly excited her.

"Do it," he said. Then he lifted her off him and stood. "Or else."

She snorted out a laugh, but there was no denying the anticipation thrumming through her body.

"We'll see," she said.

He gave her a knowing smile before kissing her briefly. Then he collected the pizza box and disappeared around the corner.

It took her nearly twenty minutes to calm down enough to concentrate on completing the first of the three studies she planned to present to the committee. By then it was nearly ten, and she had time for a quick shower before she made her way to the bed.

She rummaged in her duffel bag, finally settling on the sash from her bathrobe as a suitable blindfold. Climbing onto the bed, she tied it over her eyes, then lay down and spread her legs for Casey as instructed, leaving the light on this time because she knew he liked it that way.

She imagined what he'd see when he arrived—her body stretched out on the bed, her nipples already hard, her pussy exposed, her eyes blindfolded.

A willing sacrifice, desperate for his touch.

She drew in a shuddering breath, trying to keep a grip on her own need. Never in her life had she imagined she could be so turned on by just the idea of a man and what he might do to her, the pleasures he might bring to her.

She almost sobbed with gratitude when she heard his boots on the gravel path outside. He didn't bother knocking, just opened the door and stepped inside. She knew the exact moment he saw her displayed for him, his sharp intake of breath loud in the small space.

"Do you have any idea how good you look right now?" he asked, and she heard the clink of his belt opening, followed by the almost imperceptible hiss of his fly.

"Tell me what you see," she said.

There was a small pause then something hit the floor. His jeans, she hoped. He moved closer to the bed and she imagined him surveying her, taking in everything that was on offer.

"I see smooth legs, and soft, creamy thighs. I see two perfect tits, with sweet, pink little nipples that are nice and hard for me. And I see this."

Her hips jerked instinctively as he stroked between her legs, his touch sure and firm as he glided through the slick folds of her sex.

"I see how ready you are for me. Do you want me to fuck you, Eva?" he asked.

"Yes."

"Do you want my mouth or my cock?"

"Your cock. *Now.*"

"Are you sure?" He stroked his fingers through her folds again, pausing to slide a finger inside her this time. "You don't want me to kiss you down here again?"

"Oh, God," she moaned, lifting her hips, practically on the edge of coming just from a few brief touches. "*Please.*"

"Since you asked so nicely…"

She felt him come over her then, felt the strength of his thighs as they came between hers, then the heat of his belly and chest against her torso. She held her breath, expecting him to enter her then, but instead his mouth closed over one of her nipples. Pleasure pierced her, tightening her sex, and she arched her back, her hands gripping his shoulders.

"Stop teasing, you bastard," she panted, even though she was loving every moment.

He responded by swapping to her other nipple, sucking and licking until she was sure she was about to come. She was trembling on the edge of release when he finally stroked into her, filling her with welcome, brutal hardness, stretching her and pushing her into a gasping, breathless climax.

Casey kept stroking into her as she fell apart around him, his thrusts almost frenzied, and she realized he was wildly turned on by her arousal, that her pleasure, her getting off, was the ultimate aphrodisiac for him.

He came quickly, his body shuddering into hers, his breath hot on her neck. For a few seconds, his full weight bore down on her, then he started to lift himself. Instinctively, she wrapped her arms and legs around him, halting his retreat.

"Don't," she said. "Not yet."

He let his weight come onto her again, and she listened to him breathe and felt the percussion of his heart as it banged against his chest wall. She felt the heated dampness of his skin, and smelled his aftershave and her own deodorant and the musky, earthy scent of sex, and she consciously savored the closeness, the intimacy of the moment.

It was one thing to have sex with someone, to allow a man inside her body, but it was another thing entirely to feel this sense of connection with another human being.

The way she felt when she was with Casey—the way he made her feel—was both rare and precious, and she wanted the moment to last forever.

But life didn't work like that, and after a moment or two he stirred again.

"I'm too heavy."

This time she let him go, reaching up to pull her blindfold off so she could see him. He rolled onto his back on the bed beside her, his legs sprawled, and closed his eyes. One hand rested on his chest, his fingers slightly curled in relaxation.

His eyes flicked open while she was studying him and he smiled slowly. Reaching out, he ruffled her hair, his touch gentle.

"I like it better when I can see your face properly, but that was fucking hot," he said.

She laughed, her introspection evaporating in the face of

his simple honesty.

"I want you to know that before I met you, I liked to be on top most of the time," she said.

"I like it when you're on top, too. I like it all ways with you," he said. His gaze shifted to the counter, where she'd stacked her art supplies in order to free up the bed. "Did you get your work finished?"

"I did. For today, anyway."

"Can I see?"

Surprise made her hesitate for a moment. "Sure."

She rolled onto her knees and crawled to the end of the bed to collect her sketchpad, not sure if he was simply being polite or if he was genuinely interested.

"This is the first of the three images I'm proposing for the site," she said as she flipped to the current page, revealing the study she'd finished this evening.

The portrait was a refined version of her original concept—a pioneer woman, her face etched with experience and hardship. She wore a homespun dress with an apron over the top, and there was both worry and hope in her eyes as she stood at a water pump, bucket in hand, her gaze fixed on an unseen horizon.

"Amazing," Casey said, adjusting the pad minutely on the bed so he had a better view. "I can't believe you're going to paint a one-hundred-foot-high version of this."

"If I gct a chancc," shc said.

She studied the piece, her gaze critical. She was happy with the technical aspects—the proportions were good, and she'd captured the emotion she'd wanted in the woman's face. She wasn't quite as confident about her color palette.

One of Dane's signatures had always been his monochrome color schemes, and for five years she'd worked with shades of gray, blue, black and white.

Marietta didn't feel like a monochrome community to her, though. It was vibrant and strong, rich with connection to the land. She wanted to capture that, and she'd used bright, bold colors in her mural—the sky was a piercing blue, a perfect match for the woman's eyes. Her gown was an earthy red-brown, the landscape around her green and verdant.

Casey was still studying the drawing, his eyes narrowed. "That's Copper Mountain in the background, right? Part of it, anyway."

"That's right. I want the mountain to link the three images, so the middle one will feature the peak, the final one the eastern slope."

"Really clever," he said, and there was admiration in his eyes as he looked at her. "I'll be honest, I haven't had much experience with street art, but this is stunning."

She could feel her face growing warm from his praise. "Well, thanks. I'm glad you like it."

"I love it."

She felt really hot now, and she suspected her face was red. Trying to cover, she closed the sketchpad.

"Just another two to go, then I'm done," she said brightly.

"Why are you embarrassed?" Casey asked.

So much for covering.

"I'm not. I'm just... I don't know. It's hard not to feel self-conscious when people say good things about your work."

"But you know how good you are, right?"

She stared at him, confronted by the question. She remembered the way she'd almost cried in front of Andie McGregor when the other woman praised the quality of her original pitch. Was her sense of her own worth and talent really so fragile that she could be so affected by a few simple words of approval?

It seemed counter-intuitive, given the lengths she'd gone to to throw her hat in the ring for this commission. She'd driven across four states to advocate for herself, practically insisted that they interview her…and yet, deep inside, there was a part of her that was afraid she wasn't up to the challenge she'd set herself.

"I used to think I was pretty hot shit," she said slowly, thinking it through. She gave him a wry, self-effacing smile. "When I was younger and I was going to set the world on fire with my blazing, undeniable talent. Then I met Dane, and I got sucked into his career, and over the years of doing everything I could to be there for him, channeling all my ideas and energy into his work, I lost a sense of who I am as an artist, what's important to me. I guess I'm trying to rediscover that now, but everything still feels a bit shaky. I keep second-guessing myself, interrogating my choices, asking if I'm doing something because I want to do it, or because it's what I've always done when I worked with him, or because it's the opposite of that…" She shook her head. "There's a lot of traffic in my head right now."

Casey studied her face, his expression serious. Then he reached out to brush his thumb along her cheek. "You got this. There's not a doubt in my mind. And the proof of that is right here."

He tapped the sketchpad with two fingers.

"I can feel you in this picture. The emotion in her eyes…that comes from you. That's what people are going to respond to."

She captured his hand, hugely touched by his words. It was a little scary how good it felt to have someone so unequivocally on her side. "Thank you."

"You don't need to thank me for speaking the truth."

She shook her head. "You don't understand." She considered their joined hands for a moment. "For years, I lived off scraps of approval, and told myself it was okay. I put my own ideas and ambitions in deep freeze, and supported someone else because I believed in him. And I never got anything back. It was always a one-way street. So having someone be on my side…that feels pretty revolutionary to me right now."

Her throat was tight, and she had to swallow before she could say anything more.

"Here," Casey said, pulling her close. Her head came to rest on his shoulder as he wrapped her in his arms. She blinked rapidly, trying to get a grip on her runaway emotions.

"I don't want to give that jerk any more time or energy, because he's already taken so much from you. But he's not holding you back anymore, baby. The sky's the limit."

It was the exact right thing to say, and Eva turned her face into his chest and squeezed him tight, breathing in the good, clean smell of him. When she was confident she wasn't going to blubber all over him, she lifted her head.

They stared at each for a long beat, and Eva could see her own feelings echoed in his beautiful green eyes.

"This was supposed to be just fun," she said, because one of them needed to name the elephant in the room.

"I know."

"If I don't get this commission, I have to go back to LA this week."

"I know that, too. Your life is there, mine is here. I get it. But none of that stops me from thinking about you all the time, or wanting to be with you."

Her chest tightened with emotion. "I can't stop thinking about you, either," she admitted.

"Good," he said, then he kissed her, and Eva let herself fall into him, into the magic of being with him, and let everything else drift away.

All her worries, all her doubts, all the pressures and uncertainties would still be there tomorrow. Right now, in Casey's arms, she had everything she needed.

Chapter Eleven

TWO DAYS LATER, Casey scrubbed his face and pushed the laptop away from him on the kitchen table.

He'd just spent three hours poring over their bookkeeping software, juggling expenses as much as he could, but there was only so much he could rob from Peter to pay Paul. Until they sold some stock, things were going to be tight. And since they didn't plan to go to market until later in the year, something had to give.

He needed to talk to his siblings. When Jed had come clean about the trouble the ranch was facing last September, they'd learned he'd been forgoing wages for himself in order to ensure the ranch remained viable. They'd all agreed that that kind of shit was not going to happen again, and they'd all tipped their personal savings into the pot to help ease the situation. Two bad seasons and a run of shitty luck meant that it had barely touched the sides of their problems, though. And now Casey had more bad news to deliver.

Delaying the inevitable wasn't going to make it any easier, so he stood and went in search of his sister. He found her behind the house in the veggie patch their mother established twenty years ago, pulling weeds and straightening stakes.

"Sierra. You got a minute?" he asked.

She shaded her eyes with a gloved hand. "A real minute or is that just a clever ruse to lure me inside?"

"Definitely the second option," he said, and she must have heard the heaviness in his voice because she stood and brushed the dirt off her knees.

She followed him inside and was at his side when he knocked briefly on the study door and pushed it open. They both paused on the threshold at the sight of Jed fumbling hastily with the mouse, quickly closing down a window on the computer screen. Casey only caught a glimpse, but it was enough to tell him what his brother had been doing: Facebook stalking his former girlfriend, Mae Berringer.

Mae had been Jed's girlfriend in senior year at Marietta High, and they'd shared an apartment together for two years when they both went to college at Montana State. Then life as the Carmodys knew it had imploded when their parents died, and everything had gone to hell. Jed had dropped out of college to come home and take over the ranch and look after the rest of them, and Mae had been left behind.

Or something like that. Casey had never really been clear on just what had happened between his brother and the woman he loved, he simply knew that Jed hadn't really looked twice at another woman since.

There was a small silence before Jed cleared his throat.

"What's up?"

"Why don't you just call her?" Sierra asked, bull at the gate as always.

"What are you talking about?" Jed asked, his cheeks

turning a giveaway pink.

"She's talking about Mae. If you're still hung up on her, why don't you just message her?" Casey said.

Generally, his policy was live and let live when it came to his siblings' personal lives, but it was so obvious that his brother was stuck on Mae, someone needed to say something.

"We're not having this conversation," Jed said, his tone clipped.

"What would it hurt? If you've got unfinished business, maybe it would help you move on if you saw her again. And who knows, maybe she's still single, like you. It's worth a shot, isn't it?" Sierra said.

"I said I don't want to talk about it," Jed said.

"Sierra's right. You should call her. Get it out of your system," Casey said.

Sierra nodded enthusiastically. "Or not. Maybe you're still in her system, and you two can pick things—"

"She's engaged to some guy in Helena," Jed blurted, and Casey could see it hurt his brother just to say it out loud.

"Shit. I didn't realize. Sorry," Casey said, feeling like an asshole.

Mind, it had been thirteen years, so it was only natural Mae had moved on. The bigger surprise was probably that she wasn't married with kids already.

"They announced it last week," Jed said heavily. "I was just checking to see if they've set a date."

Casey remembered the night Jed had uncharacteristically encouraged him to ask Eva out. What were the odds that was the day he'd heard Mae's news?

"Have they?" Sierra asked.

"Not yet."

Jed looked so gutted, Casey didn't know what to say.

"Maybe you should still talk to her. For closure," he suggested tentatively.

"You a relationship expert now, are you?" Jed snapped, his face hardening, and Casey was smart enough to know when to back off.

"Nope, not by a long shot. I was just trying to help, that's all."

"Do I look like I need help?" Jed asked.

Casey considered his brother, trying to be objective. Tanned and strong, Jed was a good-looking guy, but there was no denying that the burdens he'd carried from a young age had taken their toll. Lines bracketed his face and eyes, and there was a seriousness to him now that was at odds with the happy-go-lucky person he'd been before their parents died.

But Casey had been different then, too. They all had.

"Fair enough," Casey said, holding up both hands to show he was conceding. "Point taken."

"Did you come in here just to bust my balls or was there something else?" Jed asked.

"I need to talk to you guys about wages," Casey said.

"Sit," Jed said, pointing to the two battered chairs against the wall.

He and Sierra sat and Casey explained how tight things were, how the latest fence repairs had pushed their account at Big Z Hardware back up past a point he wasn't comfortable with, and how he was worried that the reason the automatic waterer had failed was because their reticulation system was so old now, it was close to collapse. Given that it had been installed by their father nearly twenty years ago, it wasn't an unexpected problem—but it was definitely an expensive one if it turned out they needed to replace the whole thing.

"I'm happy not to take a wage," Jed volunteered when Casey was done.

Sierra shook her head. "No. We agreed no one was making that kind of sacrifice again. We'll all take a cut. It's not like we're living it up on caviar and lobster. We can live cheaply enough if we're careful."

"What about your flight hours?" Jed asked.

Sierra shrugged. "So I pull back for a while. I can start clocking hours again when things ease up. And Jack's still throwing me hours when he can, although Gideon's been spending a lot more time in Helena lately."

Casey shifted in his chair. He'd always hated the fact that Gideon Tate's private pilot had taken Sierra under his wing. Jack seemed like a decent enough guy, but Casey was not in love with the idea of his sister being beholden in any way to the man who had walked away without a scratch from the accident that had killed Casey's parents. He knew it was probably irrational—his father's car had skidded in front of Gideon Tate's expensive SUV, not the other way around—but it didn't change the way he felt.

Unfortunately, there was precious little he could do about it when they didn't have the money to pay Sierra real wages, so there was nothing for him to do except suck it up.

For now, anyway.

"Here's what I'm thinking—we all go down to half wages for a while, just until we get some stock to market. And I'll start pressure testing the pipes so we can find out where we stand."

"That suits me. Maybe we should start looking around for a good price on poly pipe, just in case?" Jed suggested. "If we're prepared to suck up a long lead time, we might get a good discount."

"Great idea," Casey said.

"Leave it with me, I'll see what I can hunt down," Sierra said, and neither he nor Jed objected because her Google skills were much better than both of theirs. "Anything else we need to worry about?"

"Nope. Just pray it doesn't rain before we get the alfalfa in," Casey said.

They all nodded grimly, then Sierra stood and pulled her gardening gloves from her back pocket.

"Better get back to the battle of the weeds," she said.

"Wait a second. I wanted to ask you both if you were doing anything tonight?" Casey said.

"When am I ever doing anything?" Jed said.

"I'm around. Why?" Sierra said.

"Eva's got her presentation tomorrow, and I was thinking it might help her to do a dry run in front of the three of us tonight."

Sierra nodded, her expression neutral. "Sure, cool. Happy to help out."

"Ditto," Jed said.

"Thanks, guys. Really appreciate it."

Sierra flicked her hand dismissively to let him know it wasn't a big deal before exiting the study. He followed her, troubled by the subtle undercurrent of tension between them since their late night conversation about Eva.

Sierra hadn't said another word on the subject, and as far as he could tell she'd been just as friendly toward Eva, but there was a certain reserve behind her eyes when she looked at him, as though she was guarding her true thoughts or biting her tongue.

Never in his life did he think he would miss his sister's take-no-prisoners, well-intentioned nosiness, but it was genuinely weird not to have her in his face, asking for details or offering unsolicited advice.

"Sierra," he called, catching her as she was about to exit the house.

"What?"

She had one hand on the doorjamb, the other on the door, her expression expectant as she waited for him to speak. He stared at her, but his mind was stupidly blank. He honestly had no idea what to say to allay her concerns. The truth was, she was probably right—he was probably going to be gutted when Eva went back to her real life in LA. But that wasn't going to stop him being with her in the meantime. Things were too good between them, on every level.

"You should wear a hat. It's hot out," he finally said, and Sierra gave him a look.

"No kidding," she said, then she disappeared through the door.

He slapped his hand against his thigh, frustrated with himself, then headed out to the trailer to deliver his good news. He found Eva sitting outside in her lone camp chair, a frown on her face as she read over what he assumed was a printout of her presentation.

"How's it coming along?" he asked.

"I think it's okay, but I lost objectivity many hours ago. The great thing is that I keep finding new typos that I missed previously, so that's awesome," she said, lifting her face for his kiss.

As always, she tasted amazing to him, and he instantly wanted more. Her lips clung to his when he moved to break the kiss, her hand closing over his shoulder to hold him in place, and he followed her lead as she stretched the moment out.

Her eyes were a smoky, hazy blue when they finally came up for air, and he knew she was thinking of getting him naked and the things she wanted to do to him.

Heat pooled in his crotch, but he made an effort to ignore his libido and concentrate on more important things.

"Do you still want to go over your presentation tonight?"

"Yes, please. I need you to be my guinea pig so you can tell me if it's too long, or too boring, or if I've missed anything out," she said, the frown back between her eyebrows.

"How about using multiple guinea pigs? Jed and Sierra are both happy to help out after dinner."

"Really? That's so nice of them. Are you sure, though? I don't want to stop them from doing something that's actually fun," Eva said, her expression both hopeful and concerned at the same time.

"Jed never has fun, and Sierra had no plans for tonight, so don't sweat it," he assured her.

She gave him a warm look. "Thank you for recruiting

them, even though I am now super nervous about doing my run-through in front of them."

"It's not a big deal," he said.

"It is to me," she said.

He'd be lying if he pretended he didn't get off on the way she was looking at him right now—as though he'd hung the moon and the stars just for her. The truth was, he wanted her to be happy, and there wasn't much he wouldn't do to make it happen.

"What time is your appointment tomorrow?" he asked.

"Two, at the library again."

"I can rearrange a few things so I can drive you into town if you'd like," he offered.

"You don't need to do that. I'll be fine once it's all happening. I just need to get to the point where I can't change anything else. Then I can stop second-guessing myself."

"The offer is there if you want it."

"Thank you. I really appreciate it."

She reached out and tucked a finger behind his belt, using it to pull him closer. Her face was level with his groin and she leaned forward to press a kiss against his fly, her eyes lifting to his naughtily.

"I feel like you deserve a reward for being so supportive and thoughtful."

"Virtue is its own reward. I'm pretty sure they taught us that in Sunday school," he said.

"Oh, okay. So you don't want me to do this, then?" she asked, pulling his fly down and slipping her hand inside his jeans.

Her fingers brushed against his cock through his under-

to jump into this, okay, so I don't chew up too much of your evening."

"Whatever suits you," Casey said.

He dropped a quick kiss onto her mouth, aware of Sierra watching from the couch. Then he crossed to the armchair and sat.

"The floor is yours, Ms. King," he said with the wave of a hand.

"Okay. Here goes nothing."

For the next twenty minutes Eva walked them through her presentation, the nervous quaver in her voice gradually disappearing as she progressed through the material. She showed them a graphic featuring her finished studies overlaid onto a computer model of the grain elevator, and she explained why she'd chosen each image, what aspects of Marietta's history each one represented, why she'd opted for such a vibrant color palette. She drew their attention to the blue-purple bulk of Copper Mountain uniting the past, present, and future of Marietta, and she talked about her idea to approach other towns nearby to create a larger than life art trail of murals across the region.

When she was done she gave a sigh of relief and held up her hands.

"Okay. That's it. Phew. How did I do?"

There was a moment of complete silence, and the bottom dropped out of Casey's stomach as he waited for his brother and sister to react. He'd thought Eva's presentation was great, but Jed was hard to read at the best of times, and Sierra looked nothing short of stunned.

Then Sierra started clapping, the stunned look on her

face morphing into a smile that took up her whole face.

"I don't know what to say. Outstanding. Sold. I want ten. No, make it twenty. I want to build a grain elevator in the yard just so we can look out at those amazing images every day," she said.

Jed was smiling, too, and Casey shot Eva a look, pleased to see she was smiling, and that the color was back in her cheeks.

"It wasn't too long-winded when I was going through the technical bits?" she checked.

"I think it's smart to talk about life-span and mainte-nance the way you did," Jed said. "It's one of the first things I'd be thinking about if I was on the committee. Everyone knows the weather can be brutal here, so it's no good putting up something pretty that's going to be peeling off in a single season."

"Pretty? Please. Those images are heart-stopping," Sierra said. "Can I see them again, please?"

They spent the next twenty minutes critiquing Eva's proposal, and Casey's admiration for her only increased as he watched her genuinely engage with the process. He was almost certain he'd have been telling his brother and sister where to stick it after ten minutes, but Eva simply made notes and asked questions and offered alternative ways of delivering the same information.

As he watched her, a warm sensation filled his chest, pushing against his ribcage. It took him a moment to recognize it—he was proud of her, of the way she was handling herself, of what she'd pulled together.

She was so talented and smart, so capable and thoughtful. On some instinctive level he'd understood she was special the moment he met her, and every second since had only underscored that belief.

She was hyped after the run-through, talking in a stream of consciousness as they walked side by side out to the trailer. He listened and responded and watched her beautiful face and finally admitted to himself that he was more than half in love with her.

Not exactly a huge revelation, but it added an extra layer of complexity to the situation.

"God, listen to me—can't shut me up," Eva said, dumping her stuff on the counter.

"I like listening to you," he said.

She smiled wryly and shook her head. "Do you ever say the wrong thing?"

"Have you met my sister? She'd be happy to give you chapter and verse on my many follies, vices, and faults," he assured her.

She sat on the edge of the bed, still smiling. "Name some of them for me."

"You want me to inform on myself? I'll leave it up to you to discover my feet of clay for yourself."

"Give me just one fault, then. Something I can cling to whenever I start to despair over how perfect you are."

"All right. Let me think," he said, gazing toward the ceiling as though he really needed to interrogate the subject. "Okay. Sometimes, I put my elbows on the table during dinner."

Her smile widened into a grin. "That was pathetic. You know that, right?"

"It's not my fault my faults are so minor."

"I'm not going to tell you any of my faults now," she said.

"Just as well. We don't have all night."

"Oh. Foul. That was brutal," she cried, but she was laughing, and when he joined her on the bed, her arms came around him willingly as they tumbled back together onto the mattress.

"Take it back," she said, her nose only an inch from his.

"Okay, I take it back."

"I think I'm going to need a physical token of your contrition."

"Really. What would that look like?" he asked.

She wrapped her legs around his thigh and humped it shamelessly.

"I'll give you two guesses," she said, and he couldn't keep a straight face any longer.

"What could it possibly be?" he wondered.

The next half hour involved lots of laughter interspersed with liberal quantities of nudity, heavy breathing, and moaning. By the time they were lying tangled and replete beneath the covers, Casey had sore stomach muscles from laughing so much.

"Thank you. I needed that," Eva said, lifting her head from where it was resting on his chest to look him in the eye.

"Anytime. And I mean that."

"I believe you." She lifted a hand to press the tip of his nose playfully. "That offer you made earlier to drive me tomorrow—is that still on the table?"

"Absolutely."

Sierra filled a fresh filter with coffee and slotted it into the coffee maker. "Well, her presentation is really impressive. She's got a good chance."

"Hope so."

Sierra started to say something, then clearly thought better of it. Instead, she simply rested a hand on his shoulder briefly before reaching for a couple of mugs.

"You want bananas with your pancakes, or berries?" she asked.

He spent the morning servicing the sickle-bar mower. They were probably still a good three weeks off harvesting the second cut on their alfalfa crop, but he wanted to be ready for all contingencies. A good run of weather, or some unseasonal rain could change everything. If they lost the harvest…

He didn't want to think about what would happen if they lost the harvest.

At one, he went inside and washed off the grease in the shower and changed into fresh clothes. Then he went to pick up Eva from the trailer.

She was sitting on the step, her head lowered, hands clasped together over the nape of her neck when he found her.

"Hey. You okay?" he asked, lengthening his stride.

"Yes. I think so. Just, you know, a bit shaky." She offered him a wan smile. "I'll be fine. I just want this over with now, so I can be on the other side of it all."

He understood what she meant, and he rested his hand on the center of her back in silent sympathy.

"I love it when you do that," she said quietly. "You've

got good hands."

"We don't need to head into town just yet, but I thought you might want to get there a little early, just to make sure you're on time."

"That's a great idea. Not that Marietta probably gets a lot of traffic jams, right?"

"Had a logging truck turn over on the highway once. Couldn't get into town for hours," he said.

Her eyes widened with alarm and he quickly reassured her.

"That was years ago. We'll be fine."

"Okay. Good."

She stood and dusted the seat of her pants. She was wearing the same tailored black pants she'd worn the first night they were together with a black, silky-looking shirt that had a draped panel across the front that was tied over her hip. Her hair was more refined than usual, smoother and less spiky, and her eyes were carefully made-up, making them look bluer than ever. She looked arty and interesting and stylish, and he felt another surge of pride in her.

"You look great," he told her. "You're going to do great."

She just smiled faintly and shook out her hands. "Let's do this before I literally wet my pants with nervousness."

She was silent on the drive into town, and after a few minutes, he reached across and took her hand in his. It was cold and clammy, just like last night, and he brought it over to rest on his thigh and laid his hand over it.

She gave him a grateful look, the frown easing from between her eyebrows briefly.

"You want the radio? Or we can talk?"

"The radio might be good. I need to get out of my own head."

He flicked the radio on and the sound of Kacey Musgraves filled the truck. He kept shooting glances Eva's way, wishing he could do something to take away her nerves or reassure her.

"The Whiskey Shots should enter that," Eva said suddenly, glancing at him.

"Enter what?" he asked.

He'd been so busy thinking about her he hadn't registered that the song had finished or that the announcer was talking.

"The radio station is running a competition for local bands. I didn't catch all the details," she said.

"Already on it. We'll probably record something this week or next to send in."

"Really? That's great," she said.

He kept his eyes on the road. "The boys are keen. Figured we might as well put our hat in the ring."

Personally, he still didn't see the point in putting their hands up for attention they didn't need or want, but he didn't want to rain on the other guys' parade, either, so he was prepared to go along for the ride.

"Don't be surprised when they love it," she said.

"We'll see."

A few minutes later, they were driving into town and it wasn't long before he was parking the truck in a spot opposite the library.

"Ten minutes to spare," he said, and Eva nodded, her gaze fixed on the dash, the intense little frown once again pleating her forehead.

He was about to say more when a group exited the library, their obvious high spirits drawing his gaze across the road. Too late he saw that Dane formed the nucleus of the group, and he shot a look at Eva to see if she'd noticed. Being rattled by her ex was the last thing she needed right now.

Sure enough, she'd seen them, too, and her mouth pressed into a flat line.

"Looks like they had a good meeting," she said.

"Doesn't mean anything. He probably thought he had a great meeting last time, too, and you'd blown them away so completely they had a complete rethink."

She nodded, but her gaze remained on her ex.

"Want me to walk you in?" he asked.

She blinked, then shook her head. "No. I'd better do this last bit on my own." She shifted so she was facing him more fully. "Thank you for last night, for organizing the run-through, and for making me laugh so hard afterward. I needed that distraction like you wouldn't believe."

He caught her hand and lifted it to his mouth for a brief kiss. "You're amazing. You're going to knock their socks off."

She mustered a smile. "Okay. I'm going to try to hang on to that. I'll see you in half an hour, I guess."

She leaned across to plant a quick kiss on his lips, then she turned and opened the door. Her laptop was in her backpack, along with her handouts, and he passed it to her as she got out of the truck.

"I'll be here," he told her.

"Okay." She took a deep breath. "Putting on my big girl

panties…now. And here I go."

She gave him one final shaky smile, then started across the road.

He could see the nervous tension in her body as she walked—the way her shoulders were too stiff, her gait tight and too fast. Again he wished there was something he could do to convey to her his belief in her talent and tenacity. She was brilliant, and the committee had to see that. They had to.

The next half hour crawled by like molasses. Casey checked the clock on the dash so many times he started to think it must be broken. Eventually he got out and paced beside the truck, unable to sit still any longer.

He imagined Eva in her meeting, walking the committee through her vision. He remembered how good her graphics had looked last night, how impressive her studies were.

Come on, man, this has got to be hers. She's fucking earned it.

He'd never wanted something for another person so fiercely before. It was a little scary, feeling this invested so quickly. Her happiness had very swiftly become his happiness. But there wasn't much he could do to slow down the charging freight train that was his emotions—and he wasn't even sure he wanted to. Yes, this was a crazy ride, but so far, it had been the ride of a lifetime and he hoped the best was yet to come.

If she won the commission, she'd be in Marietta for at least another couple of months. It wasn't long, but it wasn't nothing, either.

It was three-quarters of an hour when she finally

emerged from the library. He could see her relieved smile from across the road and he checked the traffic before dashing across to meet her at the bottom of the steps.

"I didn't throw up on anyone or fart inappropriately," she said as she came to a halt in front of him, "so I figure I mostly got away with it."

He pulled her into a hug, pressing a kiss onto the top of her head. "Well done. You're awesome."

Her arms came around him and she squeezed him fiercely, her fingers digging into his back. "Couldn't have done it without you," she said, her voice muffled by his T-shirt.

He let his hand rest on the nape of her neck, wishing he could say even half of the things going through his head. But it was too soon, and her day had been dramatic enough already.

And if she was leaving town in the near future, him spilling his guts would only make things worse, not better, for both of them.

"What do you want to do now? Grab something to eat? Get drunk? Go somewhere private and fuck like bunnies?" he suggested.

"Those are all pretty good options. Can I say D, all of the above?" she said, lifting her head to laugh up at him.

"Eva. I was hoping you'd still be out here."

They both turned to see Andie and Heath McGregor coming down the library stairs, both of them beaming.

"Hi. Did I forget something?" Eva asked, slipping free from his arms, her face professionally neutral.

Andie looked to Heath, who gestured that she had the floor.

"You blew us away in there," Andie said. "Your drawings, the care and thought you put into your proposal… But the thing that made it a no-brainer for us was your concept of creating an art trail in the region. We need more reasons for people to discover our great little town, and we think you can be a key part of making that happen. So I'm over the moon to tell you that the Marietta Chamber of Commerce would officially like to offer you the commission to create a mural on the Clarke grain elevator."

Eva blinked, her eyes wide. Then a slow smile curved her mouth. She looked at Casey, reaching out to grab one of his hands, her grip tight with excitement. He squeezed back, aware of the burn of emotion at the back of his eyes as he registered her success.

She'd done it. All her hard work had paid off. She'd be staying in town, painting her dream in vivid colors, one hundred feet tall.

"Thank you," Eva said. "I won't let you down, I swear. This mural is going to be amazing."

"We don't doubt it for a second," Heath said. "Congratulations, Eva."

He offered her his hand, and Eva shook it, then Andie enveloped her in a hug, and Casey reached into his back pocket to pull out a handkerchief.

"Thanks," Eva said ruefully as he passed it over so she could dab her eyes dry. "This is such awesome news."

Andie checked her watch. "You know, it's pretty close to the end of the day. I feel like we should go to the Graff and buy something with bubbles to celebrate. What do you say?"

Eva looked to him for his response and he smiled. "Of

course we need to celebrate," he said.

"You don't need to get back to the ranch? I don't want to keep you from your work," she said.

"The mower will still be there tomorrow. Let's go party," he said.

"We'll meet you over there," Heath said. "My truck's gonna get towed if I leave it near the Courthouse."

Casey slipped his arm around Eva's shoulders as they walked back to his truck.

"How do you feel?" he asked.

Her face was glowing when she lifted it to his. "Like this is a dream. Please don't wake me if it is."

"It's not a dream, and you earned this, babe. You worked your ass off for this."

They stopped on the sidewalk beside his truck and she slipped out from beneath his arm.

"You realize this means I'm going to be around for at least another seven or eight weeks? Think you can handle that?"

"What do you think?"

She searched his face, then she smiled and reached for his hand.

"I think we need to go celebrate."

"Sounds like a good idea to me."

EVA WAS STILL feeling a little seedy the following afternoon when she walked the short distance from the trailer to the house.

Last night had been huge. She'd lost track of how many

rounds of drinks she'd bought, and she only had cloudy memories of Casey putting her to bed in the small hours, but she knew that it had been *good* to know that all her hard work and persistence had paid off.

She'd woken to an empty bed and a headache, Casey having slipped out hours earlier to start work for the day. After lying there wallowing in her triumph for a good half hour, she'd made a feeble attempt to think past the cotton wool in her brain and had eventually given herself permission to have the day off.

She'd been running on adrenaline, hope, and fear for weeks now. She could afford to have a rest day.

She used the time to tidy up the trailer and do her laundry, puttering around in a happy daze. Somehow the day had slipped through her fingers, and she'd been surprised to see it was nearly four when Casey dropped to remind her he had band practice tonight.

He'd promised he'd be back in time for dinner, and she kissed him goodbye and waited until the sound of his truck had well and truly faded before heading for the house.

Now she paused on the porch, torn between whether to enter via the kitchen or the front door. All the Carmodys had urged her to make herself at home and take advantage of the kitchen, larger bathroom, and laundry room in the main house whenever she felt the need, but there had been a certain…*distance* in Sierra's attitude toward her lately that made Eva inclined to use the front door today.

It wasn't obvious, and it definitely wasn't malicious, but it was there, and Eva didn't want to step on any toes. Listening to her gut, she knocked on the weather-beaten door and waited.

It didn't take long for it to swing open, revealing Sierra's surprised face.

"Hi. You don't have to knock, you idiot," the other woman said, gesturing for Eva to come inside.

"I didn't want to assume anything," Eva said lightly.

"Don't be silly. If you wanted to do more laundry, I'm just about finished with the machine," Sierra said, heading back into the kitchen.

Eva trailed after her, admiring the other woman's dark wavy hair and long legs. Most of the time Eva didn't have a problem being short, but there was no denying that Sierra had an awesome set of pins that looked nothing short of sensational in well-worn denim.

"Actually, I want to pick your brain, if that's okay. I want to take Casey out for dinner tonight to thank him for being so amazing through this whole crazy process, and I was wondering if you could steer me in the right direction."

"Oh. Okay," Sierra said, her eyebrows meeting in a frown.

"Hopefully it'll only take a moment or two, if you're not too busy," Eva said brightly.

"Sure. Of course. If you want recommendations for places in town, you can't go wrong with Rocco's. Or if you want somewhere fancier, there's always the Graff. I haven't been there for a while, but I've heard good things."

"I wanted to do something a bit more personal," Eva said. "I was thinking of picking up some things from town and doing a sort of picnic-style dinner. So I was hoping for some pointers on what Casey's all-time favorite treats are, and if there's a good picnic spot around here somewhere where I could take him?"

"Sounds very romantic," Sierra said, her frown deepening. Her gaze darted around the kitchen, and she rubbed her palms down the sides of her jeans. "Um. Let me think. Casey loves meatloaf, and he'd crawl over broken glass for pecan pie. Flo could hook you up with both of those at the diner. His favorite drink is Dalton's cider—you can get that in town, too."

She still hadn't made real eye contact and Eva's heart sank.

It definitely hadn't been her imagination—there was something going on with Sierra.

"Hey, we don't have to do this if you don't want to," Eva said. "I don't want to step on any toes or make you uncomfortable."

"I'm not uncomfortable," Sierra said. Then she laughed, the sound odd and tinny and profoundly uneasy.

They were both silent for a moment, then Sierra sighed and reached up to tuck her hair behind her ears.

"Okay. That was a little uncomfortable," she admitted.

"I'm going to go out on a limb and guess that you aren't exactly thrilled about me and Casey being together…?" Eva said.

"No. That's not it," Sierra said quickly. "Well, not exactly. I really like you, Eva. I think you're awesome. And I can see how much Casey likes you, and normally I would be over the moon that he's got such good taste."

"I'm sensing a 'but' coming," Eva said.

"That's because you're going to go back to LA in a few

weeks. I don't know you that well, I have no idea what your life is like, but I do know Casey, and I know his feelings run deep. Like I said to you when we were driving in to see the Shots that night, he doesn't do casual."

"You think I'm using him? Is that what you're trying to say?" Eva asked, feeling a little offended at being cast as the easy-come, easy-go vixen who was going to break Casey's heart.

"Honestly? I have no idea. I hope not." Sierra sighed again. "I guess what I'm trying to say is that if this is just a few weeks of fun for you, part of the whole rural Montana experience, don't make it worse by taking Casey on picnics and feeding him his favorite foods and generally being as romantic as all get-out. Don't make him think this is something it isn't."

"I wouldn't do that to him," Eva said, stung. "I wouldn't play with his feelings like that. You think I don't see him? You think I don't understand how beautiful he is, inside and out? Yes, this started out as a fling. Hell, it was only ever meant to be a one-night stand, but it quickly turned into something else and I am just as deeply invested as Casey is. Very much so."

She was out of breath when she finished, and her eyes were hot, and she looked away, blinking rapidly.

"Shit, Eva, I'm sorry," Sierra said, her face puckered with concern. "I wasn't trying to offend you, I swear. I'm just worried. I never should have said anything."

Eva nodded, still not trusting herself to speak, and Sierra's mouth flattened into an unhappy line.

"I really didn't mean to upset you. Can I give you a hug,

please?" she asked.

Eva nodded again, and Sierra wrapped her arms around her.

"Like I said to Casey, you're probably the coolest person I know and I'm really glad you two are on the same page," Sierra said. "That's all I was really worried about—that Casey was getting too invested in something he shouldn't."

"That doesn't mean it's not going to get messy," Eva said, her voice muffled by the other woman's shoulder. "I have no idea what's going to happen when I have to go back to LA."

"Well, no one really knows anything in life, do they?" Sierra said, letting her arms fall to her sides and stepping back from their embrace. "Anything could happen to anyone. That's no reason not to be with someone, not if it feels right."

"This is the last thing I expected when I came to Marietta," Eva admitted. "The absolute last thing. I swear to you I hadn't even thought about sex for months until I saw your brother."

"Okay, we may have just reached the part of the conversation where I need to tap out before my gag reflex kicks in," Sierra said, and Eva laughed.

"I wasn't about to get graphic, don't worry."

"Good." Sierra considered her for a beat. "Are we cool? Or have I just become the hideously protective sister you're now going to go out of your way to avoid?"

"You're allowed to be protective. I have a sister, and I'd do anything for her. And Syd would totally throat punch Dane if she could. In fact, he should probably worry about accidentally running into her in LA, because I honestly don't know what she might do if she had the chance to physically hurt him."

Sierra snort-laughed. "God, I almost hope it happens."

"Me, too, a little bit. But only if there are no witnesses."

Sierra smiled, then glanced at the clock. "If you're planning on doing this picnic thing tonight, you'd better get your skates on. Casey will be home from band practice in another hour or so."

"Good point."

"Come on," Sierra said, leaning across to grab her car keys. "I'll drive you in to town so you can hit Flo up for Casey's favorites, and I'll show you where there's an awesome picnic spot on the way."

"You're sure? I don't want to steal your afternoon."

"I was just doing laundry. This is much more fun. Come on," Sierra said, heading for the door.

Eva half suspected Sierra's generosity sprang from the impulse to make up for her earlier censure, but Eva had meant it when she'd said she understood where the other woman was coming from. It was actually pretty nice that Sierra loved her brother enough to want to guard him from hurt, and it wasn't as though she'd barged into the trailer and imposed her point of view on Eva.

In fact, Eva suspected if she hadn't pushed the issue, Sierra would have gone on being friendly and lovely, albeit just a degree or two cooler than previously.

So even though she didn't really need an escort, she followed Sierra out into the yard and climbed into her truck and did her bit to put their moment of tension behind them.

Chapter Thirteen

CASEY WAS THE first to arrive at band practice, letting himself into Danny's garage with the spare key before checking his phone. There were no messages, so he figured the others were just running late.

Figuring he might as well get set up, he got out his guitar and plugged it into his amp, then settled on a stool. He'd finessed 'Been Too Long' since their last practice, and he ran through the new chorus and bridge one more time to satisfy himself he'd finally got it right. It sounded good, and he preferred the way the melody built in increments now, slowly expanding until it hit the chorus.

If the guys were willing, it was ready to become part of their lineup.

He checked the time on his phone—the guys were a full ten minutes late now—then warmed up with a hodge-podge of his favorite parts from of an old Oasis song before switching to a Beatles track. He thought about Eva as he played, remembered how tipsy she'd gotten last night, buoyed by winning the commission' and lots of champagne. She'd danced in her seat and laughed too loudly and generally been the life of the party, surprise surprise.

Afterward, Jed had driven them home in Casey's truck. Eva had rested her head on his shoulder the whole way, her hand splayed on his chest over his heart.

He'd put her to bed when they got home, holding her steady while she pulled off her pants before making her brush her teeth. She'd snuggled in to his side when he joined her in bed, kissing his shoulder and chest, her hands roaming hungrily. Minutes later she'd fallen fast asleep, drained by the high emotion of the day, her hand still trapped down the front of his boxer briefs.

He smiled at the memory, amused all over again, thinking about how much he loved being with her, how she just had to look at him or touch his leg or chest or arm and he was *gone*.

"Whoa. What the hell is *that*?"

Casey's hands stilled on the guitar as he glanced over his shoulder to find Rory and Danny standing there, both of them looking like someone had just goosed them.

"Sorry?" he said.

"That song you were just playing. What was it? Please tell me it's one of yours," Rory said, hands pressed together as though in prayer.

Which was when Casey registered he'd been playing the song he'd written about Eva, his fingers automatically picking out the notes while he was thinking about her.

"It's not for the band," he said automatically.

"Why not?" Danny asked.

Casey frowned. "Because. It's not ready. And it's not for public consumption."

Rory made a rude noise. "What? Are you kidding me?

No way can you keep that song under wraps. Play some more for us."

Casey shook his head. "There's no point."

"Play it, Carmody," Danny insisted.

Rolling his eyes, Casey picked out the opening few bars, aware of Danny and Rory nodding along.

"Give me two seconds," Danny said, slipping behind his kit.

He pulled off the dust cover, then the deep, low sound of the bass drum sounded as he picked up the rhythm of the song. Casey could feel it through the soles of his boots and he couldn't stop himself from starting the song again from the top, loving the way the bass underscored the earthy raunch of the song. He was aware of movement out of the corner of the eye, and then Rory was playing, filling out the sound with even more bass. Despite his reservations, he started getting excited.

"What the hell is that?"

Wyatt stood in the doorway, looking like someone had just hit him over the back of the head with a two by four.

"Casey's new song."

"My man," Wyatt said, shaking his head. "That's epic. You are on fire with the songwriting at the moment. Give me a second to get set up."

"It's not for the band," Casey repeated as Wyatt set up his keyboard stand with the efficiency of long practice.

"Why the hell not?" Wyatt asked.

"He still hasn't come up with a good reason," Danny said.

"It's personal," Casey said.

"Not when it's that good, it ain't," Wyatt said.

He settled his keyboard on the stand and fed the power line into the back of the unit.

"Okay, let's do this."

"There's no point," Casey said.

Danny and Rory simply started playing, ignoring him, and Wyatt listened for a few bars to get his ear in before chiming in. Casey shook his head, but they were right, it sounded *good*, the keyboard adding yet another dimension to the song, and he couldn't stop himself from joining in.

"Hit us with the lyrics," Wyatt said after the first run-through, making a gimme gesture with his hands. "We know you've got some, so don't be a holdout, Carmody."

Casey fought the urge to squirm. "Like I said, it's personal."

"All the best songs are. Talk to Clapton about 'Tears in Heaven,'" Wyatt said.

Casey knew the other guys would let it drop if he really put his foot down, but the truth was that the musician in him wanted to hear his song at its best. Already it had taken on a life of its own, and he knew from past experience that it would only get better, because his bandmates were awesome collaborators.

"All right," he said, rubbing the back of his neck. "But I don't want any shit, okay? One word and this is over."

He kept his focus on the neck of his guitar as he started from the top again, steadfastly refusing to meet any of his bandmates' eyes.

"*Skin like velvet, body made for sin, she walks in the door, I forget everything…*"

When he got to the chorus, he caught sight of Wyatt's grin out of the corner of his eye.

Fine. Whatever. He was crazy about Eva, and now they all knew it.

He played the final notes, then set his guitar down and stood to face his friends.

"You've heard it now, so let's do some real work," he said. "Do we still want to change the set list for our next gig?"

Danny shook his head. "Oh, no, my friend, it's not gonna be that easy. You think we're just gonna let that song slip away?"

Rory swapped his bass guitar out for his Rickenbacker electric, his expression thoughtful. "I freaking love the grind in this song, Carmody. Did you ever think about getting some slide in there, really muddy it up with more sustain?"

He demonstrated, playing the bridge, and Casey felt his spine get straighter as he heard what the new sustain did to the song.

"Oh, yeah, baby," Wyatt said, clapping and laughing. "That is *insane*."

Which was when Casey understood that his friends were not going to crucify him for his song celebrating all things Eva. They were engaged by the music, as always, their focus on making it better, giving it The Whiskey Shots signature sound.

"You really want to waste more time on this?" he asked.

"It's not wasted time. This is the best thing you've ever written, Case. And you've written some of our best songs."

Wyatt and Rory were both nodding.

"Seriously?" Casey asked, thrown.

"Oh yeah, man," Wyatt said. "This song gets under your skin. This song is sex and lust and love and all the good things, with a side order of obsession."

Casey laughed, feeling self-conscious. "You trying to tell me something?"

"Hey, we all saw her. We get it," Wyatt said, slapping Casey on the back. "I look forward to playing at your wedding."

Casey flinched. "That's not gonna happen."

"This song disagrees," Wyatt said. He focused on Rory. "The slide rocks. What if we save it for the chorus, really make it pop?"

For the next hour, they worked on the song, workshopping arrangements, shifting things around. Finally Danny played a little drum roll on his snare, finishing with a single hit to the crash cymbal.

"Gentlemen, we are ready to record. Let's do this," he said.

Casey frowned and shook his head. "What? No. What are you talking about?"

The other Shots looked at him as though he'd hit his head and was talking stupid.

"Recording the song for the KUPR competition," Rory said, hands spread as though the answer was obvious.

"I thought we were all putting a song forward and voting?" Casey asked.

Rory shrugged. "We hadn't heard this when we said that. It's memorable. People will get an ear worm after listening to this."

"I'm with Rory. This is the one we should enter," Danny said.

"Ditto," Wyatt said.

Casey blinked and shook his head. "Wait. Hold up a moment. I can't put this song out there like that. No one was ever supposed to hear it."

"Dude," Wyatt said, looking at him over the top of his glasses. "You were always gonna share this song with us. At least be honest with yourself. You know how good it is."

Casey couldn't hold the other man's eye. The truth was, if he'd really wanted to keep Eva's song private, he would never have played a bar of it in this space, let alone spent almost the whole of their weekly practice session polishing it.

But that didn't change the fact that it was a deeply personal song. Anyone who knew him and Eva would know exactly how he felt about her the moment they heard it, and he wasn't sure he was ready to parade his feelings around in public like that yet. And then there was Eva. He had no idea how she'd react to hearing he'd written a song about her. Just the thought of telling her made the back of his neck hot with embarrassment.

Not that he was ashamed of his feelings—he wasn't. But it was early days for them—very early—and he didn't want her to feel pressured. They'd only just acknowledged that this was a lot more than casual sex for both of them.

"What's wrong?" Danny asked.

"Eva doesn't know I wrote this," he admitted.

"Ah," Rory said. "Okay. I guess that's a different issue altogether."

The guys looked at each other, then Danny shrugged.

"Okay, we go with another song. 'Been Too Long' is a great song, too."

"Sure. It's a toe tapper. People will want to dance to it," Wyatt agreed.

"They won't want to fuck to it, but that's okay," Rory said, and they all laughed, the small moment dissipating some of the tension.

Casey could see they were all prepared to move on, and he knew the other song was good. But he also knew that the song he'd written for Eva was special, because it had come from a raw and primal place inside him.

The guys were right—it was their best chance of winning the KUPR competition, and it would feel as though they were sabotaging themselves if they entered anything else.

He pinched the bridge of his nose, barely able to believe what he was about to say.

"Let's record it now, and I'll talk to Eva, see how she feels," he said.

His response was a chorus of hoots and backslaps.

"Yeah, all right, calm down. It's just a song," Casey said, even though he was both amused and warmed by their belief in his music. "And if she's not comfortable, there's nothing you guys can say that's gonna change my mind."

"We got that, loud and clear," Wyatt said.

Danny was already heading for the cupboard at the back of the garage where he kept his recording equipment.

"Let's get it down before he changes his mind, boys."

Shaking his head, Casey set his guitar aside and went to do his bit.

❧

EVA JUMPED UP from where she was waiting on the porch steps the moment she heard the low, familiar sound of Casey's truck. Sure enough, his pickup appeared around the corner of the drive a few seconds later and she couldn't keep the smile off her face as he pulled into the yard.

"Hey," he called out the open window. "Sorry I'm late. Did Sierra hold dinner for us?"

"Nope, I told her not to, because I'm taking you out for dinner," Eva said.

Casey looked confused until she pointed at the picnic basket near the front door.

"Are we going on a picnic?" he asked, looking both bemused and amused.

"We are. Wait for a second while I get the cold stuff from inside," she said, turning on her heel and running up the steps.

By the time she got back, Casey was sliding the picnic basket into the bed of his pickup. She was just in time to catch him lifting the lid to take a peek inside.

"Hey, no previewing. It's a surprise," she said, and he dropped the lid and held his hands up to let her know he'd gotten the message.

She passed him the cooler and the blanket. "Sierra said there's a lantern in the barn that we might want to take, and that you'd know where to find it."

Casey tilted his head. "This is sounding like a very elaborate picnic."

"Cowboy, us city girls don't do things by halves," she said.

"I have noticed that," he said, his gaze sliding over her

tight tank and denim mini skirt.

"Go get the lantern," she said, giving him a little shove on the hip to get him moving. "But save that thought for later."

A couple of minutes later they were cruising down the drive, an old Dolly Parton song playing quietly on the radio.

"Turn left when you hit the highway," she instructed, and he shot her a speculative look.

"I don't get to know where we're going, either?"

"Not until we get there," she said, even though she knew the odds were good he'd guess long before then. He was the local after all, not her.

"International woman of mystery," he said, smiling faintly, but he turned left as she'd asked and followed the rest of her instructions without objection until she told him to pull over on the side of a single-lane gravel road.

"This is the Daltons' land," Casey said, peering out the window at the lines of well-established apple trees marching away from the road.

"I know. Sierra made a call, and we are welcome to enjoy their orchard this evening as long as we take our trash home."

"This is like a military operation. Did you pull all this together today?" he asked, pushing the car door open.

"Sierra helped me," she admitted.

"Of course she did."

Together they walked to the rear of the pickup to collect everything. Eva hefted the cooler and blanket, while Casey took the basket and lantern.

"I assume you know where you're going?" Casey said,

gesturing for her to lead the way.

"I do."

She lifted the cooler through the post and rail fence alongside the road before following it through, and Casey followed suit with the basket. Then they walked through the trees, heading down a gentle slope until the faint sound of water was audible.

"Almost there," she said.

"I know this place. We used to swim here when we were kids," Casey said as they stepped out from beneath the trees and onto a broad swathe of wild grass that sloped gently down to a slow-moving creek.

"Apparently the sunsets are to die for out here," she said.

"We won't have too long to wait," he said, glancing toward the horizon where the sun was already a glowing red ball above the mountains.

"That's why we needed the lantern," she explained.

"Like I said, a military operation."

Together they chose a good spot and she spread the blanket out before Casey set the basket on one corner.

"Okay, now you sit back and enjoy," she insisted.

"I can't let you do all the work."

"Don't know if you've noticed, but I'm not exactly sweating over a hot oven here," she said.

Opening the cooler, she pulled out two bottles of Dalton's Sweet Bite cider.

"Seemed appropriate," she said as she flipped the cap off one of the bottles and passed it over.

"Hey, I love this stuff," Casey said.

She sent up a silent thank you to Sierra for the excellent

intel.

"I know."

She opened the picnic basket next, pulling out two enormous meatloaf hoagies and slices of the Diner's famous pecan pie.

"You got me a meatloaf hoagie?" Casey asked, his delight more than obvious.

"I did. Flo even included extra green tomato relish for you because she said you always ask for more."

Casey gave her a warm look. "Babe. You have knocked it out of the park."

She smiled, ridiculously tickled. "Good. Now you have to endure a few seconds of discomfort because I want to propose a toast."

She lifted her own bottle of cider, the amber glass cool and slippery with condensation.

"To you, Casey Carmody, for being my rock through the past week. Even when we barely knew each other, you looked out for me, and you have been so sweet and kind, organizing for your poor brother and sister to sit through my presentation so I could practice, and driving me to my meeting. And let's not forget that you are the genius who pointed out that this state is literally littered with abandoned grain elevators. Pitching the idea of an art trail is what got me over the line, and I will never, ever forget that that idea came from you," she said. "So this is my way of saying thank you, and letting you know that I appreciate your thoughtfulness and generosity more than I can ever say."

Casey's eyes remained steady on hers throughout her little speech, and she could see he was both touched and a little embarrassed by the acknowledgment.

"Don't make me out to be too much of a saint," he said. "I really didn't do much."

"You cared. You made me feel like what I wanted was important. That's everything to me, Casey," she said, her voice thick with sudden emotion.

"Of course I care. I want you to be happy," he said.

"I know. Ditto. And I'm going to make you very happy once you've finished your hoagie," she promised him.

"Oh yeah?" he said, his expression arrested. Then his gaze cut over her shoulder to consider the privacy of their surrounds.

"The main house is miles away, Sierra tells me," she said.

"It is. A long, long way away."

"That's what I figured." She reached for one of the hoagies and passed it to him. "Eat up, you're going to need your strength."

"Only if you come sit by me," he said, patting the blanket beside him.

She obliged, and they spent the next half hour talking and laughing and marveling at the astonishingly vivid colors of the sun as it set behind the mountains. Maybe it was the fresh air, but Eva couldn't remember the last time she'd eaten such delicious food. Twilight was starting to take hold by the time they'd both washed their pie down with a second bottle of cider and all the summer insects erupted into a noisy chorus.

Eva leaned her side against Casey's and enjoyed the solid strength of him as she breathed in the warm night air.

"I can barely remember what my life in LA is like," she

said dreamily. "Traffic jams and fancy coffee and spin classes and show openings… It almost seems like a different world out here. The sky goes on forever and the air smells like it's newly minted and people smile at you on the street. Did you know that?" She sat up so she could see his face. "I was walking into the diner today and this nice couple I didn't know from a bar of soap commented on what a nice day it was and we talked about the weather for a couple of minutes. That never happens in LA."

"Welcome to Marietta," he said.

She laughed. "Yeah. I'm glad I get to stay longer. With you."

She took a deep breath then, because there was another reason she'd wanted to have this picnic tonight. It seemed to her that she and Casey had both been pussyfooting around their feelings, neither of them prepared to name what was happening between them. And that was *fine*, she didn't want to rush into anything, but she did want to know that they were at least headed in the same direction. She thought they were, but she'd been wrong in these matters before. And the only way to be sure was to use her words, as scary and vulnerable as that might be.

"I don't know if it's occurred to you or not, but if I can get interest from other towns in the region, there's a chance I could be busy here in Montana for a while. Months and months. If it happens fast enough, I might not have to go back to LA at all, maybe."

He was suddenly very still, his gaze very focused.

"That's true. I hadn't thought it through that far. If the art trail ideas gets traction, you'd need to stay local."

"I would. Which, for the record, I would be really happy about, for obvious reasons." Suddenly she felt ridiculously, unaccountably nervous. "I know neither of us signed up for a relationship. I wasn't looking for one, and I can only assume you weren't, either, and maybe I am reading way, way too much into this whole situation, but I just wanted you to know where I was at."

Casey frowned slightly, a bemused smile on his lips. "You know how I feel. I've been pretty obvious I'm crazy about you."

"I know you like fucking me. And you listen to me and laugh at my jokes. I know it's not just about sex." She shrugged, unwilling to put more words in his mouth.

Casey shifted on the rug, and she realized he was pulling his phone from his back pocket.

"Please don't tell me you're about to phone a friend," she said, only half joking.

"I was going to talk to you about this tonight, for different reasons. But this'll answer your questions better than anything I can say."

She frowned, confused, as he tapped the screen, bringing up what looked like a music app. Then he hit play, and a song started to unfurl into the dusky night, a dirty, grinding song with a demanding beat. She looked to Casey, confused, and then his voice came in over the music, singing about a woman with skin like velvet, his voice low and deep and raw.

"Oh, wow," she whispered as it hit her what she was listening to.

He'd written this song for her.

Holy shit.

The lyrics spoke of desire and need, fascination and delight, tenderness and possessiveness, while the twangy guitar and boozy bass evoked dark nights and tangled sheets, whiskey shots and whispered words.

All too soon Casey's soulful voice faded into silence and Eva was left feeling overwhelmed, unable to even begin to process what she'd just heard.

She was aware of Casey watching her, waiting for her response, and she tried to marshal her thoughts.

"I don't know what to say. It's beautiful. And so sexy—you have no idea how much I want to tear your clothes off right now." She stared at him, shaking her head again. "I can't believe you wrote it for me."

"I told you, you drive me crazy," he said. He ducked his head for a beat, and when he lifted it again, she could see the intensity of his emotions in his eyes. "I feel like I wasn't even really alive until I met you. That's how much you light up the world for me."

It was too much. Eva didn't work with words, she channeled her art and emotions through her hands and that was the only way she could possibly convey the depth of her reaction to what he'd just shared with her. Reaching for the hem of her tank top, she stripped it over her head, revealing her black satin bra. A flick of the wrist and it was unclasped and sliding down her arms. She stood, her hands going to the stud on her denim mini. She popped it, then released the zip and shimmied the fabric down over her hips.

"Lie back," she told him, thumbs in the sides of her panties.

Casey hesitated, seemingly transfixed by the sight of her

stepping out of her underwear. She moved in front of him, then placed a hand on his chest and pushed him backward.

"I said lie back."

The night air was warm on her skin, but her breasts were already tight with arousal as she stepped over his prone body so that she stood straddling his hips. Then she sank down onto her knees and pressed her breasts to his chest, her mouth seeking his.

His tongue stroked into her mouth, hot and urgent, his hands coming up to cup her backside. She could feel how hard he was through his jeans and she rubbed herself against him, the sensual friction making her purr with pleasure.

Even though she was aching for more, she stretched the kiss out, loving the feel of his warm arms around her. Only when she couldn't stand it another second did she reach between them to release his jeans. He lifted his hips to help her push them down, passing her a condom. They both watched as she smoothed it down over his thick, hard cock. Then she lowered herself onto him, unable to hold back a gasp at how good and right it felt to have him inside her.

"Can you feel how much I want you?" she asked as she tilted her hips and let him slide out again, almost to the point of losing him.

His eyes glinted in the darkness. "Yes."

"That's what your song did to me. That's what you do to me," she told him.

She plunged back down onto him, grinding herself against his pubic bone.

"Oh, fuck," he groaned. "Sorry, babe, but I can't. Not tonight."

She was about to ask what he meant, but he was already sitting up, his big hands holding her in place as he rolled her under him. And then he was over her and in her, and she was holding on for dear life as he started to pump his hips.

It was so good, and she was so turned on, all she could do was try to remember to breathe as he stroked into her again and again. What he did to her, the way he made her feel, the lust and the care and the kindness…

All the emotions swirling in her head got mixed up with the tension ratcheting her body toward fulfillment and when she came, she was surprised to feel the dampness of tears on her face.

He found his own bliss not long after, and she turned her face to the side as he recovered, hoping he wouldn't notice her tears before she had a chance to wipe them away.

"Hey. Eva… Are you okay?" he said, his voice gentle, his eyes concerned.

So much for him not noticing.

"I'm fine. Sorry. That's never happened to me before."

He propped himself up on his elbows, his face creased with concern, and there was so much worry in his eyes that she forgot about protecting herself.

"I'm just so glad I met you," she said. "That's all. Everything that's happened has been so amazing. I feel incredibly lucky and grateful."

He stared down into her face, his expression intense. "I knew the moment I met you that you were someone special."

They held each other then, their grips tight. There were so many things she wanted to say, but she held them back because it had only been a week, and she was here for another two months at least, and there was time.

Casey kissed her forehead before releasing her, a tender benediction that made her chest get tight. Then she came back to earth and realized true night had fallen while they were locked in each other's arms.

"I'll turn on the lantern," he said.

Eva shivered, surprised by how quickly the heat had gone out of the day. Casey passed over her tank, and she pulled it on without bothering with her bra before reaching for her mini skirt. She was shrugging into the hoodie she'd brought with her when a memory tickled at her.

"You said you were going to talk to me about the song tonight for some other reason…?"

"Right." Casey shot her a look from beneath his eyelashes before concentrating on doing up his jeans.

She cocked her head, realizing this was the first time she'd seen him truly uncomfortable.

"Spit it out, Carmody."

"I wrote that song thinking no one would ever hear it," he said.

"What? No. That would be a crime. It's so good," she said, surprised he'd even consider burying his work.

"Yeah, well, the rest of the Shots agree with you. I wound up playing it for them tonight and they pretty much all voted for it to be the song we enter in the KUPR competition. But I didn't want to do that until I spoke to you. Because it's your song, too."

Eva opened her mouth, ready to urge him to enter the song. Then she thought about the lyrics, about the earthy, raw emotion he'd evoked. Everyone who heard the song and saw them together would know it was about her. She wasn't sure she was ready for that kind of exposure.

On the other hand, it was a compelling, attention-grabbing song. If she heard it on the radio, she'd want to hear it again.

Casey was waiting for her response, his expression so earnest and worried, and she understood his primary concern was for her, not his song, not his band, and suddenly the answer was easy.

"Send it in," she said.

"You're sure?"

"It's a great song. People are going to love it." A thought occurred to her. "What's it called?"

He looked a little sheepish. "'Song for Eva.'"

She laughed, then leaned across and kissed him, hard. "Might as well own it, huh? It's perfect."

Chapter Fourteen

EVA STARTED WORK in earnest the next day. The rental company delivered a cherry picker to the elevator site first thing, and she was finally able to inspect the condition of the weatherboards up close.

There were a few sections that were in worse shape than she'd hoped, but Heath had already put his building team at her disposal to affect any remedial work required. By the end of Friday, the rotten boards had been replaced and she was ready to start removing the old paint with a sandblaster. Again, the rental company delivered her equipment first thing Monday morning and she spent the day working her way down the structure.

It was hard, noisy, dirty work, and even though she wore the most effective protective gear available, she still went home feeling gritty at the end of the day. The next morning, she arrived at the site and stood with her head tilted back at the base of the elevator, marveling at the beautiful, big canvas she had to work with.

This was when shit started getting real, and it was her favorite part. Before she could start laying down the outline for her first portrait, she needed to prime the surface, so her next task would be to get two coats of a sturdy, all-weather paint primer onto the wall.

Walking back to the van, she unpacked her air compressor and spray gun and lugged it back to the cherry picker. Her phone pinged to let her know she'd received a message, and she saw it was from Casey, texting to ask how she felt about him bringing her lunch.

She felt very good about it and let him know as much, smiling when he sent her back a series of ridiculous emojis with love-heart eyes and puckered lips.

Putting her phone away, she moved on to fueling the generator and mixing thinners into the first of the buckets of primer, a necessary task to ensure the paint didn't choke her spray gun. Then she lugged the first bucket into the cherry picker and finished linking the air compressor to the spray unit.

It was hot enough that she'd been avoiding pulling on her well-worn, paint-splattered work overalls until the last moment, but she finally did so before collecting her full-face respirator.

The generator rumbled to life immediately when she hit the go button, and she climbed into the cherry picker's cage and engaged the motor. Slowly she rose through the air until she was mere feet from the top of the structure. Pulling the respirator down over her face, she plugged in her ear buds, and dialed up one of her favorite playlists.

Then she took aim with the spray gun and started laying down swathes of paint across the elevator wall, her movements slow, steady and practiced. By the time it was nearly twelve, she'd worked through more than thirty gallons of paint and half the wall was painted a mottled white.

She hit the button to lower the picker's cage, pleased with her morning's work. The warm breeze was a sweet and welcome relief after sweating under the respirator for hours and she ran a hand over her damp hair and rolled her shoulders. They'd be sore tonight, but that was par for the course when she was at this stage of a job.

She was just stepping out of the picker's cage when the sound of an engine slowing made her look over her shoulder. She was expecting to see Casey, since it was close to lunchtime, but instead she saw a glossy black SUV roll into the parking area. Dane was behind the wheel, his face inscrutable behind a pair of sunglasses.

Well, shit.

She'd thought—hoped—he'd be long gone, since he'd lost the commission. But apparently he hadn't been able to tear himself away without saying goodbye.

She turned her back and closed her eyes for a beat, reminding herself that he was the past and that there was nothing he could say that would hurt or harm her. Then she turned to face him, watching as he climbed out of the SUV.

He glanced at the wall briefly before walking toward her.

"Starting with a shitty spray job, I see," he said. "For the record, I'd have your ass up there doing it again properly if this was my job."

He was so obviously trying to make her second-guess herself and feel inadequate, she couldn't repress a smile. There wasn't anything she didn't know about surface prep, and they both knew it.

"Did you want something?" she asked.

He seemed disconcerted by her smile and it took him a moment to find his groove again.

"I wanted to put you on notice—this is the last commission you'll get from me, okay?" Dane said. "This makes us even. Whatever debt you think you're owed is paid in full and if I find out you're targeting another one of my projects, I'm coming after you with everything I've got."

Eva stared at him, barely able to comprehend what she was hearing. Was he… Was he really trying to make it sound like he let her win this commission as a way of addressing her claims against him?

It was such an arrogant, twisted take on what had really happened that for a moment she didn't know how to process it.

And then she did, and she burst out laughing.

"Consider me on notice," she said.

What a delusional tool. She felt ashamed that she'd once admired him so much she'd put her own ambitions on hold for him.

He snatched off his sunglasses, the better to glare at her, she imagined, but it only made her laugh again.

"You think that this mural will be your moment of triumph, but all people are going to see is a copycat version of me and my work," he said.

The nastiness of his words helped sober her and she considered him for a moment, trying to understand why he was so angry with her. She was the one who'd given him everything and put her own hopes and dreams aside, not him. She was the one who had worshiped at his altar and been so bitterly disappointed to realize their relationship was contingent on that worship. Yes, she'd effectively out-pitched him for a lucrative commission, but she knew what his work schedule was like. Her win wasn't going to hurt him or his career.

"All I ever wanted was for you to respect me the same way that I respected you," she said quietly. "I wanted you to care about my art and my happiness as much as you cared about your own. Was that really asking so much?"

Dane frowned. "Your failure to create is not on me. I didn't make you do anything. You volunteered to work for me. You're the one who took all the admin on—I never asked you to do that. So don't go pretending you're some kind of martyr now."

She could hear the bafflement beneath his anger, and it dawned on her for the first time that he was genuinely incapable of putting himself in her shoes. From his point of view, they'd had a professional and romantic relationship that gave him everything he needed and wanted, and he was angry and confused that she had rocked the boat and asked for more and ultimately walked away when he failed to offer it.

She was the one who had let him down, not the other way round.

Amazing.

Maybe in years to come, he'd be able to extract his ego and his hurt from the situation and see their relationship differently, but she didn't really care. They were over, and there was nothing he had to say that interested her.

What a joy that was to realize—she didn't *care* about him.

What a sweet, blessed release.

She nodded as though she was agreeing with him. "Okay. Safe travels, Dane. Good luck with everything."

Because, really, what else was there to say?

She pulled the respirator off her head and carried it over to the van. Dane followed, an angry presence at her back.

"You think this project is all you need to get to my level? You're deluded," he said.

She turned to face him, unruffled by his rage now she understood where it came from. God, she almost felt sorry for him.

"Dane, please just go. I don't want to stand here throwing words at you. Haven't you got better things to do? Go make art somewhere. Move on. Do things that make you happy. That's what I'm doing."

He stared at her as though she was speaking a language he didn't understand. The sound of another car engine drew her gaze over his shoulder and she saw Casey's pickup pull in beside the rented SUV.

She could see the wariness on Casey's face and the alertness in his body as he got out of the truck and she smiled and waved to let him know she was just fine.

"Who's this?" Dane asked. Then his chin lifted minutely as he recognized Casey. "Right, the cowboy from the bar the other night. You've been busy."

"I totally have," she said, unable to hold back her smile.

Casey came to a halt at her side, his eyes concerned as they scanned her face.

"All good here?" he asked, flicking Dane a cool look.

"Yep. Dane was just going."

Dane eyed Casey as though he was thinking about pushing the issue, but then he simply shrugged a shoulder angrily and turned on his heel to march back to his SUV. Then he slammed the door like a three-year-old and tore out of the lot leaving a plume of dust behind him.

"Happy to chase him down if I need to," Casey said, his eyes narrowed slightly as he watched the SUV speed up the highway.

"You don't need to. I don't give a single hoot what he thinks, does, believes, or says."

She smiled to prove it, and Casey rewarded her with a slow smile in return.

"Good."

She stood on tiptoes to hook her arm around his neck and pull him close for a kiss, savoring his taste and the feel of his body against her own.

"It *is* good. It's very, very good. Now, what did you bring this starving woman for lunch?"

SUNDAY MORNING, CASEY woke to find Eva kissing the back of his neck, her hand working a slow path over his hip toward his groin.

"Morning," she whispered in his ear, and for the next little while she made him forget about everything except how good they were together. Afterward, they showered and headed for the kitchen, where Jed was parked at the table, reading the weekend paper.

"You know you can read that online now, right?" Eva teased him, automatically refilling his coffee cup before pouring coffees for the two of them. "No ink-stained fingers, no paper to recycle."

"I like turning the pages. I'm old fashioned like that," Jed said.

"You're such a cowboy," Eva said.

"Spoken like a true city slicker," Jed retaliated.

Casey slotted bread into the toaster and propped a hip against the counter to wait for it to brown. Sunday was the one day none of them got up early, and he and Eva were due at the McGregors' for a barbecue lunch later in the day. He was looking forward to what would essentially be their first real public outing as a couple, looking forward to letting the world know he was with her and she was with him.

She'd been working long hours since winning the commission, leaving for the site the moment it got light and not coming home until dusk was threatening. He'd always been impressed by her tenacity and creativity, but over the past week he'd learned her capacity for work was truly astonishing. She might come home with sore shoulders and arms each night, but it didn't stop her from attacking each day with renewed vigor and enthusiasm.

It was a genuine honor to pay witness to her passion and craft, and even though she hadn't yet finished painting in the threadbare outline of her triptych, he already knew it was going to be a breathtaking piece of artwork. His woman was a genius, and he freaking loved it.

Now, he smiled as he listened to her tease his brother, enjoying the way she looked in her skinny jeans and plain white T-shirt. She'd been talking about needing a haircut, but he liked the way her hair stood up in messy spikes when she ran her fingers through it.

Hell, who was he kidding? He liked everything about her, from her sassy mouth to her ballsy attitude to her sexy body, and he still couldn't believe she was his.

But she was, and it was the best thing to happen to him in a long time. Maybe even forever.

Despite Andie and Heath insisting they not bring anything to lunch, they drove into town to buy more Dalton's cider and some locally brewed pale ale before heading over to the McGregors' place near Riverbend Park.

Eva let out an audible gasp as they came around the corner in the drive and she got her first look at their house.

"Good Lord."

"Pretty impressive, huh?" Casey said, admiring the jutting roofline of the wood and stone house. Built to take advantage of views over the town, it featured huge windows and sprawled luxuriously across the hillside.

"I'm suddenly really glad I didn't wear my cut-off jeans," Eva said.

"No one would have minded. The McGregors aren't like that," Casey said.

Heath had been a few years ahead of him at school, but he'd played football with him and Andie's brother, Beau Bennett, back in the day. Back then, Heath had been one of the poorest kids in school, living in a one-bedroom apartment with his father.

Clearly, times had changed.

There were several other cars parked in front of the house and they were just getting out of the car when Lily Bennett appeared around the side of the house.

"Andie said to come straight around the back, since we're all set up out here," she said.

"Who is that?" Eva whispered to him as they collected the drinks from the bed of the truck. "She's goddamned stunning."

"That's Lily, Andie's sister-in-law. She's married to Beau, Andie's brother."

"Was she a Victoria's Secret model in a former life?"

"Not that I'm aware of," Casey said, amused.

With her unusual purple-brown eyes and long brown hair, Lily was attractive, there was no denying that, but she didn't do half as much for him as the blond force of nature by his side.

"Lily, this is Eva. Eva, Lily," he said as they joined the other woman.

"Great to meet you, Eva. Andie has been raving about your work for weeks," Lily said.

"Dear God, how tedious for you. Please don't hate me on sight," Eva joked.

Lily laughed as she led them around the side of the house. "Deal. Hope you guys like trout, because the boys went fishing first thing and came back with a cooler full."

"You know I'm from LA, right?" Eva said. "The only fresh thing I'm used to is pollution."

Andie stood from where she was sitting at a long, rough-hewn dining table when she saw them, coming forward to kiss them hello. A wooden pergola soared over the table, the deep green leaves of a grape vine wrapping its beams to create a lush green frame. Large flagstones were underfoot, while Heath and Beau stood at an impressive-looking grill that had been built into the side of the house.

"Great to see you both," Andie said, frowning slightly when Eva offered her the cider. "You guys. I said not to bring anything."

"No one ever means that," Lily scoffed.

"Well, I did," Andie said. She waved a hand at the long benches either side of the table. "Make yourselves at home. The boys are just heating up the grill. Food shouldn't be long."

Eva slipped into conversation with Lily, and Casey drifted over to the grill to hang with Beau and Heath, quickly getting sucked into a discussion about football. Pretty soon there was fish and steak on the grill and Andie was ferrying various salads to the table. Casey went to help and it wasn't long before they were all sitting down around the big table.

"Eva, I have a confession to make," Andie said as she passed the bowl of potato salad off to her left. "I really, really wanted you to win the commission after your first presentation and I had to recuse myself from the final vote."

"Really?" Eva said, surprise on her face.

"You were so good, and I could see how much you wanted it. I may have been a little annoying about advocating for you." Andie slid a sideways look at Heath, who just laughed and shook his head. "But it didn't matter anyway, because the decision was a no-brainer after we saw your full proposal."

"Well, that's very nice to hear, thank you. I'll take this memory out and polish it next time I'm having a bad day," Eva said.

Beau was busy opening a bottle of wine, pouring glasses

for everyone, but when he came to Andie she smiled and shook her head.

"Wine always makes me sleepy in the middle of the day," she said.

Casey was aware of Heath shooting his wife a quick look from the end of the table but didn't think much of it until Lily piped up.

"You have to have some—this is that Australian pinot gris I was telling you about that we discovered," Lily said, grabbing Andie's glass and passing it to Beau to fill. "Honestly, I feel like I've been doing wine all wrong since we found this."

She gave the glass back to Andie, an expectant look on her face, and there was a short pause as everyone waited for Andie to take a sip. But Andie just looked at the wine, a bemused look on her face, before turning to Heath.

"Told you it would be too hard to keep this a secret," she said.

He shrugged. "It was worth a shot."

Lily was wide-eyed by now, her gaze shooting between the two of them. "You are not. Tell me you are not," she said excitedly.

"I'm pregnant," Andie said. "We only found out this week, and it's very early days, only seven weeks, so we weren't going to tell people for a little bit yet."

"Oh, guys, that's so great," Lily said, wrapping her arms around the other woman.

Casey watched Eva offer Heath and Andie her congratulations and it hit him that if things went right between them, this could be them in a few years' time.

He waited to feel freaked out by the idea—it hadn't even been a month, after all—but it never happened. It might still be early days for him and Eva, but there wasn't a doubt in his mind where he wanted their relationship to go: all the way.

He'd never felt this way about another woman before, never felt so sure about his own feelings and what he wanted.

It was a warm, breezy day, and it was no hardship to sit under the McGregors' pergola and eat good food with nice people, the radio playing in the background. They collectively decided to pause before tackling dessert, and Eva turned on the bench seat so she could rest her back against his chest, explaining she needed to concentrate on digesting so she could fit more food in. He savored the warmth and weight of her body against his as he opened another bottle of cider and decided he'd definitely had worse days.

Then Eva jerked upright in his arms, twisting to face him.

"Casey. It's your song. Oh my God, *they're playing your song.*"

She leapt off the seat then, racing across to crank up the volume on the radio. Sure enough, he recognized the sexy, grinding beat of "Song for Eva."

"Is this The Whiskey Shots?" Heath asked, eyebrows raised. "I didn't realize you guys had an album out."

"We don't. KUPR have got a competition on, so we entered," Casey explained distractedly.

"Shh, I'm listening," Andie said, flapping her hands to indicate they should all pipe down.

Eva glanced at him, clearly thrilled. "How cool is this?"

Casey took a long swallow of his cider and tried not to let his sudden nervousness show. It had been one thing to agree with Eva that the song could go public, but he hadn't given much thought to their song getting radio play. Rory had told him it would only happen if they were selected as one of the finalists, and that they'd be notified beforehand. As far as he knew, that hadn't happened, so it wasn't as though he'd had a chance to prepare himself for this moment.

He jiggled his knee beneath the table, trying to not be too obvious as he watched people's reactions to the song. When he was up on stage performing, the audience response was immediate and obvious, but this was a completely new experience for him and he wasn't sure if he was into it or not.

Heath was smiling and nodding along with the beat, and Beau's head was tilted slightly as he listened to the lyrics. Lily was grinning, and Andie kept lifting her eyebrows in response to the lyrics, her fingers tapping the table.

Finally the song faded out and was replaced by the announcer.

"That was The Whiskey Shots, favorite sons of Marietta, singing 'Song For Eva.' The Shots are finalists in KUPR's Undiscovered competition and I'm sure none of you are going to forget that song in a hurry. You'll be hearing from the rest of our finalists over the next hour, so stay tuned for more."

Lily and Andie exchanged a look when they heard the title of the song, then Lily pretended to fan herself and they both laughed.

Beau eyed his wife with an amused expression on his

face.

"Don't go getting any ideas, babe. I don't have a musical bone in my body, so there will not be a 'Song for Lily' anytime soon," he said.

Everyone laughed, and Casey felt Eva's hand slide onto his thigh, the subtle pressure signaling he should stop jiggling his leg. He looked at her and she leaned close so only he could hear.

"Relax. That was amazing. I'm so proud of you," she said.

He smiled faintly, warmed by her support, and made an effort to chill.

"Awesome song, Casey," Heath said. "I think you boys are going to have a hit on your hands."

"Might be hard to do that when we haven't released it as a single," Casey said.

"You should get it out there, then," Andie encouraged. "I would download it for sure."

Lily nodded agreement, and Eva nudged him with her elbow.

"You guys should get onto it right away, make the most of the promo from the radio station to raise your profile."

"I guess we should," Casey said.

The Shots had talked casually about recording some songs so they could sell them online, but they'd never gotten further than talking. Their focus had always been on the music, on writing songs. and playing live. But maybe they were being stupid, not making their songs available for download. None of the other Shots were raking it in through their day jobs, so any money they might generate from sales would certainly be welcomed by all of them. It would certainly come in handy for Casey—he could throw it into the pot to help improve the ranch's financial position.

"So, did you know you guys were finalists?" Lily asked.

Casey shook his head. "They were supposed to let us know, but I guess something must have gotten lost in the translation."

"So that was the first you knew of it?" Lily asked, eyebrows raised.

"That's right."

She laughed. "You have an amazing poker face. You must have been freaking out just now."

"A little bit," he admitted.

They all laughed, and Heath went inside to bring out a decadent-looking red velvet cake for dessert. By the time they'd moved on to coffee, it was heading toward late afternoon and Casey figured they were close to wearing out their welcome.

They said goodbye to Lily and Beau then collected their jackets and sunglasses before following Heath and Andie through their house, walking through an impressive kitchen and an even more impressive living room before they reached the front door.

"Let's do this again," Andie said, kissing them both goodbye on the doorstep. "I had a great time."

"Me, too," Eva said. "Thanks so much for inviting us."

"Let us know when that single of yours goes live, Casey," Heath said, shaking hands.

"Will do," he said.

The pickup's seats were warm from the sun and he

wound the windows down as they started down the drive.

"Oh my God, Casey," Eva said, twisting in her seat to face him. "I have been trying to keep a lid on this ever since your song came on, but I have to do it now."

Dropping her head back, she gave an excited, joyful squeal and he couldn't help but laugh.

"How excited are you on a scale of one to ten?" she asked.

"I don't know. Six? Seven?"

"Are you kidding me? I'm at eleven and it's not even my song. How can you be so cool about it?"

"I don't know. I guess I'm still processing," he said. "I wasn't expecting anything, obviously, so it's kind of a shock."

"A great shock. I was dying to listen to the other finalists but I didn't want to be rude. None of them will be as good as the Shots, though, I guarantee it."

He glanced across at her. "Not sure you're the most objective judge."

"I don't need to be objective to know you're going to win," she said.

He frowned, her words giving substance to the unacknowledged worry that had been sitting in his gut ever since he'd realized the Shots were finalists a couple of hours ago. He'd entered the radio competition because the other guys wanted to, and he'd done so expecting their entry to be lost in a sea of competition. Not because he underrated the Shots, but because he was realistic—life was not a feel-good movie or inspirational meme. Shit happened, and only rarely did dreams make it off the launching pad to fly high.

So he hadn't anticipated the band being finalists, and he definitely hadn't thought about them winning.

Eva caught his hand in hers and gave it a supportive squeeze. He glanced at her, noting how flushed and happy she was for him. He wondered what she'd say if he told her he didn't want the Shots to win, that he dreaded it, in fact.

He was pretty sure she wouldn't get it. She'd driven across four state lines to follow her dreams. She wouldn't understand why it made him sweaty just to think about it.

Because even though the band had agreed they were only entering the competition for the chance at some recording time and the cash prize, Casey wasn't stupid. If new opportunities came out of this, he knew the other guys would be hungry for it.

And he had no idea what he would do if and when that happened.

Chapter Fifteen

I T TOOK EVA a few days to clue in that something was going on with Casey. He was good at covering his feelings, good at presenting a calm face to the world, so it took her a while to realize he was struggling with something.

She kept catching him staring off into space, his face tight with some unexpressed anxiety, but when she tried to get him to talk, he just laughed it off and changed the subject.

She told herself to be patient. She liked to talk her problems out; obviously Casey didn't. Everyone had their own way of dealing with life's curve balls, and no one way was perfect or right. And it wasn't as though he was walking around with a dark cloud hovering over his head—the change in his demeanor was subtle, barely noticeable. It was only because she was so closely, intensely attuned to him that she felt it.

In lieu of Casey's input, she spun her mental wheels trying to second-guess what might be going on in his head. The long days working alone at the grain elevator lent themselves to introspection and she spent many hours considering and discarding options as she continued blocking in her design.

It was possible he was worried about money. She knew from a few references she'd picked up that the ranch's finances were not in great shape. Casey was fiercely committed to the ranch and preserving his parents' legacy, and if the financial situation had become more stressful, it made sense that it might be eating at him.

Her best guess, however, was that his preoccupation had something to do with The Whiskey Shots becoming finalists in the radio competition. She'd been so excited to hear his song played over the radio at Heath and Andie's place that it wasn't until afterward that she'd registered his oddly muted reaction. He'd been pleased, yes, and definitely flattered by everyone's praise and feedback, but he hadn't been *excited*, not in the way she would have been in his shoes. And yes, they were different people, with different ways of responding to different situations, but she'd seen Casey buzzing with adrenaline after a sell-out show. She'd see him vibrating with intensity as he made love to her.

Something had held him back from fully celebrating the moment, and she kept circling back to the conversation they'd had in his bed one night during their first week together.

The Shots are about making music, not chasing fame and all that other bullshit.

That night, he'd claimed he didn't crave success and fame, that he'd never dreamed of filling a stadium or topping the charts. She'd thought at the time that even if he genuinely felt that way—and she had her doubts—he was swimming against the tide, and she was even more convinced of it now. His talent and music were undeniable, and the world was not going to let him stay small and local and undiscovered for long.

Was that what was troubling him? Was he struggling to reconcile his humble ambitions for the band with the reality of their success?

She still had no confirmation of her theory when the night for band practice came around again. She was winding up a call with Andie when Casey stopped by the trailer to check in and let her know what time he'd be home.

"Not a problem, it would be my pleasure," she told Andie, holding up a single finger to let Casey know she wouldn't be long. "I'll see you soon," she said, ending the call and tucking her phone away.

"You didn't need to hang up because of me. I just wanted to say goodbye before I headed off to band practice," he said.

"All good. Andie wants to talk to me about something, so I'm going to head over to her place now," Eva explained.

"Their place is just past Danny's—I can drop you off if you don't mind waiting till I'm done," Casey said.

"It doesn't make sense for you to drop me off then drive back—why don't I drop you off, then I can come by your practice afterward and sneak in some more Whiskey Shot goodness?" she suggested. "Unless girls are not allowed at practice?"

"Girls are definitely allowed, especially when it's you," he said, pulling her close for a kiss.

"Then I'll just grab my stuff and we can hit the road."

Casey waited with a faint smile on his lips while she swapped shoes and changed tops.

"Pretty sure Andie is not going to judge you on your fashion choices," Casey said.

She understood what he meant—Andie had pretty much worn the same outfit of jeans plus T-shirt every time Eva had seen her—but a girl had her pride.

"I would judge me," she said, scooping up the keys to the van. "Let's go."

Casey had to wait while she cleared supplies off the passenger seat in the van, tossing them into the back, and he gave her a look when she started the engine and the fan belt started to squeal.

"How long has it been doing that?" he asked.

"Just started the last couple of days. It'll settle down. Bertha is made of whatever they make the black boxes in planes out of. She will run forever."

Casey made a dubious noise as he put his seat belt on and immediately clutched the grab handle when she started down the drive.

"Yeah, the suspension's not as good off-road as your pickup," she said, noting his move.

"You're telling me. You could sell tickets to this next time the Fair is on," he said, clearly unimpressed. "Babe, you should get this thing checked out. I bet it's barely roadworthy."

"It's fine."

"Not if the shocks are gone. I don't like the idea of you driving around in a substandard car," he said.

"I'll be fine. Bertha hasn't let me down yet," she said.

"That's because you haven't been in an accident. Does this thing even have airbags?" He glanced around, searching for the telltale markings.

She was about to make another joke when she remembered his parents had died in a car accident.

"I get her checked every year, and there are driver and passenger front and side airbags," she said. "I swear to you she's safe. I wouldn't have driven all the way from LA in her if she wasn't."

His worried frown eased a little. "Okay. But I'm going to check your shocks tomorrow after work."

"Be my guest. I will stand by and admire your manly skills. Do you think you could do it with your shirt off? Just for extra fantasy points?"

"I might be able to arrange something. Tell me more about this fantasy of yours."

They flirted their way to Danny's, where Eva let him out and waited while he collected his guitar from the back.

"I don't think this is going to take long. Andie just wanted to talk ideas for the nursery. She's thinking of doing a mural on the wall and ceiling. I think she's allowing herself to get a bit excited now," she explained. "So I might be back sooner, rather than later."

"Just let yourself in, whenever you get here," he said, kissing her through the open car window. "If we're playing, we won't hear a knock."

"Have fun," she said, waving him off.

She waited until he disappeared into the garage, his guitar case in hand, before reversing onto the street. Maybe being with his friends and playing the music he loved would help clear his mind and heart of whatever was troubling him.

Or maybe she was going to have to force the issue and

make him talk to her. It had to be one thing or the other, because she didn't have it in her to let him go on hurting without doing something about it.

RORY, WYATT, AND Danny had all beaten him to practice this week, and the three of them were talking loudly as he entered the garage.

Casey stopped in his tracks. What the hell? If he didn't know better, he'd think he'd walked into the middle of an argument.

"You should have told us, that's all I'm saying," Wyatt said. "I feel like I just got ambushed."

Okay, so maybe he *had* walked into the middle of an argument.

"Look, I don't know what this is about. He just called and wanted to meet with us all, and I figured now was a good time, since we were all going to be here anyway..." Rory was red in the face, his hands busy in the air as he tried to explain himself.

"Someone want to tell me what's going on?" Casey asked.

Wyatt sighed heavily, then waved a hand toward Rory. "Your dog and pony show, Rory. You fill him in."

Rory rolled his eyes. "I got a call yesterday, from a guy out of Nashville called Jimmy Borman. He said he's in Billings for business, and he must have connections in at KUPR, I guess, because he said he heard our song and they passed our contact details on to him. He said he really liked our sound and wanted to talk. I mentioned we had practice

friend.

Rory hadn't acted maliciously. He just wanted what every guy who'd ever been in a band wanted—to make it big. Casey couldn't really blame him. Not so long ago, he'd have been exactly the same.

Danny started playing, the clash and bass of the drums filling the space. Casey settled his guitar strap around his neck and let his hands find the familiar opening chords of one of the Shot's earliest songs, "Small-Town Love." The guys followed his lead, picking up the tune as he started singing.

By the time he was singing the final words of the song the band had found its groove. They'd been playing together for so long now, it was their default, even though there had been angry words tonight and people's noses were out of joint.

Normally they talked about the set list for their next gig at the top of practice sessions so they could smooth out any creases in the songs they planned to play, but Casey just launched straight into the next song, another of their earlier ballads, and again the guys came along for the ride.

Jimmy Borman arrived halfway through, stepping through the garage door and waving a hand to signal they should keep playing. Casey felt himself getting tense, but he willed it away and focused on the music.

It had gotten him through plenty of things, and it would get him through this, too.

"Hey, that was great," Jimmy said when they were done, and Casey turned to give him a quick once-over, trying to get the measure of the man.

He wore expensive-looking jeans and worn boots, and he looked as though he'd had a few too many long lunches, his western-style shirt straining over his belly. His dark hair was touched with gray at the temples, and a thick moustache covered his top lip. Casey guessed he was in his mid- to late-forties, maybe early fifties, and he could see the assessing shrewdness in the other man's eyes as he studied Casey in turn.

"It's Casey, right?" Jimmy said, offering Casey his hand.

"That's right. This is Danny, and that's Wyatt. And I gather you and Rory spoke on the phone."

"We did, we did," Jimmy said, shaking hands all around. "I'm not sure what Rory told you, but I'm glad I got a chance to talk to you boys while I'm in town."

"I told them what you told me—that you liked our sound and wanted to talk," Rory said.

"I don't just like your sound, I *love* it," Jimmy said. "I just about fell out of my chair when my buddy over at KUPR played your single for me. I'm sure you boys know this, but that song is pure gold. Sexy and catchy as hell, it's exactly the kind of crossover music that is charting right now."

Casey was aware of Danny and Wyatt exchanging looks, pleased with the other man's praise.

"Thanks," Casey said, because what else was there to say?

"I was a little surprised you didn't have a few songs up on iTunes for yourselves, to be honest. Your sound is real polished, and they tell me you've got quite the local following."

"We do okay," Wyatt said. "And I guess we just never

got around to recording anything. We've just been concentrating on the music and our gigs."

"The music is going to be what brings the fans, so you made the right call. Before we talk more, do you mind if I listen to you boys a bit? Maybe you could play me three or four of your crowd favorites. And I'd love to hear 'Song For Eva' live," Jimmy said.

"Sure thing, we can do that. Got some beer in the fridge if you want one, too," Casey offered.

"Don't mind if I do," Jimmy said with a grin, rubbing his hands together happily.

Rory fixed Jimmy up with a beer and got him settled on the old sofa that had been pushed into one corner. Plumes of dust puffed up when the producer sat, but Casey figured the other man had endured worse in his life.

They had a quick consult over which four songs to play, then Danny counted them in.

Twenty minutes later, Jimmy set down his empty beer bottle and applauded as the final notes of "Song For Eva" faded away.

"Fantastic. You boys are tight. And Casey, those pipes of yours are golden. Who writes the songs? All of you?"

The guys pointed at Casey. "He's our resident poet," Danny said.

"Well, Casey, congratulations. You've got a great ear and a lot of talent. Every song you played just now has got the potential to top a chart. And I know you don't know me from Adam, but I don't say that lightly. At all." Jimmy shook his head. "I honestly can't believe you boys haven't been scouted already."

THE REBEL AND THE COWBOY

Casey didn't need to look at his bandmates to see they were pumped by the producer's words. Even Wyatt had recovered from his bad mood and was now grinning like a loon.

"So are you out here scouting? Is that what this is about?" Casey asked.

He held his breath, because there was a possibility this guy was just full of hot air, a big talker with nothing of substance to offer. And if that was the case, Casey could stop feeling like he had a steel band wrapped around his chest. The pressure would be off, and life could resume.

"I've got an arrangement with a major agent group where I bring them promising acts whenever I find them. I guess you could call it talent development at large. After I heard 'Song For Eva,' I had a word with them about you guys. They told me if I liked what I saw here tonight, I was authorized to offer you guys a showcase in Nashville."

Not just hot air, then. This guy had something of substance to offer. This was a real opportunity.

"A showcase. What would that look like?" Wyatt asked. "We just play gigs, we're not up on all the fancy industry stuff."

"We fly you in, put you up at a nice hotel, and you play for a select group of people. And then, ideally, someone signs you boys." Jimmy wiggled his eyebrows suggestively.

Rory let his breath out in an audible rush. "Well, I reckon I could choke that down," he said.

"I'm not going to press you guys for an answer tonight, but here's my card," Jimmy said, passing it to Casey. "Talk amongst yourselves and get back to me. And for God's sake don't sign with anyone else before you talk to me again, okay?"

"Don't think you need to worry about that," Danny said dryly.

Jimmy shook his head ruefully. "Yeah, I do. That single of yours is blowing minds. Every time they play it, the switchboard lights up with people asking where they can buy it."

"For real?" Wyatt asked.

"For real. And I probably shouldn't have told you all of that, but it's not like you're not going to hear it from KUPR. Just remember—I was here first," Jimmy said with a wink that should have looked ridiculous but was actually oddly charming.

"We appreciate you coming all the way down to hear us tonight," Casey said, offering the other man his hand.

Jimmy said his goodbyes, and Rory walked him out to his car. The moment they were alone, Wyatt widened his eyes and mouthed half a dozen four-letter words.

"Can you believe that just happened?" he finally said out loud.

"Kind of surreal, huh?" Casey agreed.

"Do you think he's right? Do you think we're going to get other offers?" Danny asked.

"Does it matter if he can get us this showcase thing in Nashville?" Wyatt asked.

They were both vibrating with suppressed excitement, goofy smiles on their faces.

Rory returned, stopping in the doorway to spread his arms wide. "Huh?" he said. "Huh? Who's your daddy now?"

"Yeah, all right, all is forgiven," Wyatt said, grabbing his friend in a headlock and ruffling his hair.

"So should I call him tonight or wait until tomorrow? What do you think, Case?" Rory said once he'd fought his way free and smoothed his hair back down.

"I think you guys need to work that out for yourselves," Casey said. Every word felt like it was squeezed out of his suddenly dry throat. "I can't do a showcase. I can't go off to Nashville to see how this plays out."

"But this isn't us going on some speculative tour, where we grind away in third-rate venues for nickels and dimes. This is them investing in us. This is top labels wanting to sign us. This changes everything," Rory said.

Casey smiled tightly. "Do you know how many albums get released every year? I tried to count them once, stopped when I got into the thousands."

"Yeah, but they don't have your songs and our sound," Rory said.

"We're not that good, Rory," Casey said with a shake of his head. "I know we're riding high right now, with a few good gigs under our belts and getting a bit of smoke blown up our skirts. But all of that can disappear into nothing overnight. And I can't afford to take that kind of risk, not right now."

"So, what, we just tell Jimmy thanks but no thanks?" Rory asked, his tone incredulous.

"You tell him to book a showcase, if that's what the rest of you want. And I'll help you find another singer. The songs are yours, I'll sign them over. But I can't do this, not the way things are with the ranch right now."

Wyatt was already shaking his head. "We're not doing this without you."

"You think we can just replace you? You're our lead singer," Danny said.

"I'll help you find someone else. There are plenty of guys around who'd jump at the chance, especially with an opportunity like this on the table."

Rory was staring at him, his face pale. "You'd really just walk away? You won't even give it a shot?"

Casey could see the anger and disbelief in his friend's face and it made his gut hurt.

"If I walk away from the ranch right now, we're fucked," he said bluntly. "There's no way we can pay someone to do what I do, not with the money we're making at the moment. We've got big debt on top of the mortgage, equipment that needs replacing, a barn that needs a new roof… I can't just walk away from all that and go off to chase some kid's dream in Nashville."

"There must be some way we can make it work," Rory said.

Casey studied the toes of his boots for a beat, trying to find the words that would convince Rory he'd been over this a million times and still wound up at the same place.

"I think Casey's already gone through all the options. Right, Case?" Wyatt asked quietly.

Casey lifted his head, trying to ignore the stinging at the back of his eyes. "I love you guys, I love this band, and I'm sorry to have to let you down like this. But I just can't afford to take a risk right now. Not when my family need me."

He could say more. He could tell them exactly how tight

their finances were. Ranchers everywhere were feeling the pinch, but none of them were working with as little fat as the Carmodys were. One false step, one bout of bad luck, and they could lose everything their parents had fought so hard to create.

Casey wasn't going to be the one who caused the house of cards to fall. He wasn't going to bail out just when his family needed him to be all in. He wouldn't do it to his brothers and sister. He couldn't.

He blinked a couple of times, avoiding eye contact with his bandmates. Then Wyatt's hand landed on his shoulder.

"Buddy. We're not running off to Nashville without you. If you can't be a famous rock star with us, what's the point?" Wyatt said.

"I don't want you guys missing out on something great because of my circumstances," Casey said. "Tell them you'll do a showcase next month, and we'll find someone good to replace me. I'll keep coming to rehearsals, we can do some gigs, bed the new guy in."

Even Rory was shaking his head now. "Case, come on. Be real. You're the heart of this band. Your voice is our sound. And even if it wasn't, I'm not up for replacing you with some asshole off of Craigslist."

"Come on—he might not be an asshole. You're not even giving this guy a chance," Casey said.

No one smiled at his joke.

"We don't want another singer, Casey," Danny said. "We agreed at the start that the Shots were about the music first. I'm not trashing fifteen years of friendship because some guy dangled a carrot in front of us."

"Agreed," Wyatt said.

"Agreed," Rory said.

Casey had to look at his boots again then, because his eyes were burning and his throat was thick with emotion. After a second he managed to get a grip on himself.

"I don't want to be the one holding you guys back."

"You're not. We'll keep playing gigs, doing our thing. Maybe we'll get another shot at some point, and you'll be in a position to take it then," Wyatt said with a shrug.

"Maybe we won't," Casey pointed out. "What if this is it?"

"We're not doing it without you, Casey," Danny said.

There was no arguing with his tone, and Casey looked from face to face and saw that his friends were united in their decision to stand by him, even if it meant turning down what might be a once-in-a-lifetime opportunity.

"I don't know what to say. This wasn't how I thought this would play out," he admitted.

"You think we're that hungry for fame? Fuck you," Wyatt joked. "Even Rory isn't that desperate."

They all laughed, but Casey could feel how hard everyone was working to keep things light.

"Hey. I thought you guys would still be jamming."

Casey turns to see Eva in the doorway, her slim form silhouetted by the outside light.

"Hey," he said, walking over to greet her. He wrapped his arms around her, holding her close, needing to feel her warmth and strength.

She frowned as she looked up into his face. "What's wrong?" she asked quietly.

"Later, okay?" he said, because he knew without a doubt he'd disgrace himself if he told her what had happened now.

"All right," she said, then she squeezed him tight.

He released her reluctantly, turning back to his band-mates.

"We about done for the night?" he asked.

"I reckon so," Danny agreed.

They all greeted Eva, and she helped them pack up, the vibe subdued. He felt like he was holding his breath as they said their goodbyes and made their way out to the van.

Never in his life had he been so glad to leave band prac-tice, and he sat in the passenger seat of Eva's shitty van and pinched the bridge of his nose, trying to get a grip on his thoughts and feelings.

"Will you please tell me what's going on?" Eva asked, her voice thin with worry.

"Let's get out of here first," Casey said.

He wound down the window and let the moist night air flow into the van as she headed for home. It smelled like rain and dirt and he breathed in big lungfuls and tried to get a grip on himself.

Eva drove for a few minutes without talking, then she pulled over on the side of the road and killed the engine.

"Talk to me, Casey Carmody," she ordered.

He tilted his head back against the headrest and exhaled loudly. "I don't even know where to begin."

"What happened? Did you guys have a fight or some-thing?" she asked.

"No. Not a fight." He sighed. "Rory was contacted by this big-shot Nashville producer today, and he invited the guy to practice without telling any of us."

"Oh boy."

"Yeah, it didn't go over well, but then this guy shows up and it turns out he's really connected and he told us he loves our sound and loves 'Song for Eva' and wants to hear more. So we play for him, and he says more good things and offers us a showcase in Nashville."

"This all sounds not so terrible so far. What's a show-case?"

"It's a private gig, with lots of industry heavyweights. Competing labels, managers, whatever. In theory, if they like what they hear, we get offered a recording contract."

Eva's face was intent as she listened, taking it all in.

"Okay. That all sounds pretty exciting."

He sighed again. He hadn't told her about the ranch's money problems, although he suspected she'd picked up a few clues here and there. Still, he hated having to explain again. It all felt too raw still.

"I can't go running off to Nashville. Not with the way things are with the ranch right now. Money is tight. Really tight. We can't afford to replace my labor."

Eva frowned. "But—"

"No buts. This is just the way it is."

"You wouldn't need that much time off to go to Nash-ville. What, a week? Would that really break the bank?" she asked. "I'd be happy to help out, as long as you didn't need me to ride a horse or lasso anything."

She smiled, inviting him to be amused at her expense, but he was too tense.

"It's not just about the showcase. They'll want us to record an album. That could take weeks. Before they release anything, they'd want us to tour, probably sign us up to support some big name act. They'd want us to *commit*, Eva, and I can't do that. I'm already committed to the ranch."

"Okay, I understand what you're saying. But surely there's some wiggle room in this? Surely you and Jesse and Sierra and Jed could work something out so you could make this work?"

Casey shook his head. "I'm not putting that on them."

"Sorry?"

"I'm not asking my brothers and sister to drive themselves into the ground so I can go off and play rock star." It came out sounding harsher than he meant it to and he shook his head. "Sorry. It's just that I've thought about all this a lot and there's no way to make it work."

She stared at him, and he could see the wheels turning, knew she was still busily trying to find a solution that meant he could have his cake and eat it, too.

"Obviously I don't know Jed and Sierra as well as you, and I don't know Jesse at all, but I think they'd be really pissed if they learned you'd turned down an opportunity like this because of them," she said.

"Like I said, I'm not putting that on them."

She opened her mouth to say more, and Casey leaned across to kiss her.

"I love that you want to fix this for me, babe, but it is what it is."

She frowned. "So, what did the guys do when you told them all of this?"

"I offered to help them find a new lead singer—"

"*Casey.*"

"—and they told me they didn't want to do it without me."

She didn't say anything, but she didn't need to.

"I know. They'll probably hate me for it eventually," he said. "So I probably just destroyed The Whiskey Shots. It's been a great night."

He heard a click, then Eva was shrugging out of her seat belt and climbing across the center console to sit in his lap. She wrapped her arms around him and pressed her cheek to his, her arms tight around his shoulders. He pressed his face into the soft skin where her neck became her shoulder and breathed in the smell of her—perfume and laundry detergent and Eva.

Neither of them said anything for a long moment, then she lifted her head and caught his face in her hands. Her gaze was solemn as she looked at him.

"Don't go killing your chickens before they're hatched," she said. "Those boys love you, and you make beautiful music together. It's not the end of anything, not by a long shot."

He nodded, even though he wasn't convinced. She might be right. He hoped she was. He wasn't sure what he'd do without the band. It had become an integral part of his life, as important to him as the ranch and his family and the woman in his arms.

A car drove past then, the flare of its headlights a shock after the quiet darkness, and Eva disengaged herself from him and slid back behind the wheel. The van squealed to life, its fan belt making his ears ache before it settled down and she pulled back out onto the highway.

She didn't say anything more, and he was grateful for the silence. Not that his own thoughts were a treat right now, but he was all talked out.

It wasn't long before she was bumping along the drive and turning into the yard. She stepped on the brakes hard when she saw an unfamiliar truck and trailer where she normally parked.

"Visitors?" she asked, glancing across at him.

Casey stared at his brother's rig and tried to be pleased when all he wanted to do was go to bed with the woman beside him and lose himself in the softness of her body.

"It's Jesse and CJ," he said.

Then he reached for the door handle and put his game face on, because there wasn't anything else he could do.

Chapter Sixteen

Eva watched Casey climb out of her van, her chest aching with worry for him. It was so obvious to her that Casey belonged on a stage, singing his heart out. The way he came to life up there, the songs he wrote… He was a musician, through and through. And yes, he might be a cowboy, too, but that didn't mean he had to sacrifice one for the other.

That was the way Casey saw it, though, and Eva didn't have enough knowledge of the sort of financial hole the ranch was in to begin to counterarguments he'd obviously spent days, if not weeks, brooding over.

The people who held that knowledge were his family, and she knew in her heart that Sienna and Jed would fight tooth and nail to ensure Casey could follow his dream.

But he wasn't going to give them the chance to do that. He wasn't going to share his good news with them, he was just going to stifle it and bury it and go on being the hard-working, dedicated brother they knew and loved.

It was noble and infuriating and so misguided—and Eva had no idea how to talk sense to him. He'd all but shut her down just now when she'd tried to provide alternative ways of looking at the situation. She understood where that came from—he'd steeled himself to do what had to be done, and he didn't want to go over ground he'd already covered a hundred times in his own mind. But if he wouldn't talk to her or let himself consider another way of looking at his situation, how was she supposed to help him see sense?

She had no idea, but if she didn't hustle, she was going to be walking into the house alone. Casey was already halfway up the porch steps and she slid out of the van and walk-ran across the yard to catch up with him.

"Is this normal, your brother dropping in like this with no notice?" she asked as Casey reached for the front door handle.

"Hasn't happened before. Hope everything's all right."

The voices emanating from the kitchen told them where the action was at, and the moment they entered, it was clear that things were not all right. An athletic-looking woman Eva assumed was CJ was seated at the kitchen table, her left arm in a sling, a dark-haired cowboy hovering over her solicitously. Eva would have known him as a Carmody anywhere—he had the same green eyes, dark hair and cheekbones as his brothers while also possessing a lean edginess that marked him apart from them.

"Casey," CJ said when she spotted them, standing and instantly making Eva feel like a malnourished eight-year-old.

The woman was an Amazon warrior come to life, with broad shoulders and toned legs shown off to perfection by tight jeans, and her smile was broad and infectious as she pulled Casey into a one-armed hug.

"Save me from your brother. He's driving me crazy," she

271

said, shooting an affectionate look over her shoulder.

Jesse smiled faintly and shook his head. "The doctor said to rest. If I have to stand over you with a bullhorn and a whip, that's what's going to happen."

CJ's focus shifted to Eva, her brown eyes warm with interest. "You're Eva, right? I'm CJ. Great to meet you."

The other woman's handshake was firm and strong.

"You, too. I've heard a lot about you guys," Eva said as Jesse stepped forward to shake her hand as well.

"Good to meet you, Eva."

"Okay, I'll ask, since no one is volunteering. What happened to your arm?" Casey asked.

"Broke my wrist. It's not a big deal," CJ said.

Casey looked to Jesse.

"Got crushed against the rail in the chute," Jesse explained. "Still gave the nod, though."

There was reluctant respect in his tone.

"Wait—are you saying you broke your wrist and then still went on to ride a bronco?" Eva asked, sure she was misunderstanding.

"It didn't really hurt until afterward," CJ said with a pragmatic shrug.

"That's why we came home," Jesse said dryly. "I cannot keep this woman still. I figured she'd have less chance of doing something risky if we were back here."

"Does that mean you're missing some dates on the tour?" Casey asked.

Jesse nodded. "Shouldn't hurt us in the standings. As of last weekend, we both qualified for Vegas."

"Hey, that's fantastic," Casey said, slapping his brother

on the back. "Congratulations, CJ. Pretty kick-ass, making finals in your first year on the pro circuit."

"Took me three," Jesse said. There was quiet pride and unashamed affection in his eyes as he looked at his partner.

It was more than enough to make Eva fall instantly in like with this new Carmody brother. She had first-hand experience that not a lot of men were prepared to share the limelight with their partners, especially when they were in the same field. But here was a man openly and generously supporting his woman, even though she was his actual competitor.

"Getting into the finals is one thing, bringing home the title is another," CJ said. "That's why I'm going to be following doctor's orders so I make a full recovery."

"So why did I catch you trying to hitch the trailer this morning?" Jesse asked.

"With my right hand," CJ clarified.

"I'm going to buy a dictionary in town tomorrow so you can look up the word 'rest,'" Jesse said.

"You do that, cowboy," CJ said with a cheeky glint in her eye.

The hurried slam of the front door and the sound of fast-moving boots announced Sierra's arrival, and she skidded to a halt in the doorway.

"Why are you here? Is everything okay? Oh my God, what did you do to your arm?" she asked.

Jed appeared behind her, taking in the scene with his usual quiet calm.

"Broken or sprained?" he asked simply when he caught CJ's eye.

"Broken. But not badly," CJ said. "Good to see you, Jed."

They hugged, then Sierra flung her arms around the other woman.

"Do I want to know how this happened?" she asked when she stepped back from the embrace.

"Probably not," Jesse said. "Nice to see you, too."

Sierra rolled her eyes and gave her brother a big hug. "Yeah, yeah. I saw you there. I was getting around to saying hello. CJ gets priority because she's injured. And a superhero."

Eva glanced at Casey to see how he was taking all this. He was at the counter, slightly removed from the others, arms crossed over his chest. His mouth was smiling, but his eyes weren't and she had to fight the urge to go to him and wrap her arms around him.

"You guys eaten?" he said. "Eva and I were going to make mac and cheese for dinner if you want in?"

"I could eat a horse and cart," CJ admitted.

"I'm gonna take that as a yes," Casey said easily.

Eva joined him, ferrying ingredients from the pantry and fridge to the counter before filling up the largest pot with hot water and setting it on to boil.

The next hour flew by as the Carmodys caught up with each other's news. Eva sat beside Casey at the table and listened to the laughter and tried to give back as good as she got, but the whole time she was aware of how tightly Casey was holding himself. She felt *bruised* for him, and more than anything she wanted right the wrongs in his world, but it wasn't in her power to do that.

In wasn't in her power to do much of anything, really, except be there to listen and offer comfort as needed.

That was the hard part about loving someone—feeling their pain, and being unable to do anything about it.

She went very still as she registered the thought. Then she looked at the man sitting next her, noting the way he was focused on his sister as she said something, a small almost-smile on his lips. His dark hair was touched with golden brown on the tips from all his time outdoors, his skin tanned by the sun.

He was beautiful, and talented, and so bighearted and sweet.

Of course she loved him. She'd been falling in love with him from the moment she met him, and every day since she'd fallen a little harder, a little deeper.

He caught her looking at him and raised his eyebrows. She gave a little shake of her head to indicate it wasn't anything important, and he slipped his arm around her shoulders and dropped a kiss onto her lips.

When she tuned back into the conversation, she saw that Jesse was watching them from across the table.

She understood his curiosity—she was curious about him and CJ, too. These people were Casey's family, important to him, and, by extension, important to her.

Jed was the first person to call it quits for the night, and it quickly became an exodus after that as people registered how late it had gotten. Eva said her good nights and slipped into the bathroom to brush her teeth, then padded barefoot to Casey's room.

She found him sitting on the end of his bed, his head

lowered. He'd taken his shirt off but hadn't gotten any further with undressing and her heart turned over in her chest at how sad and burdened he looked. He lifted his head the moment he heard her, throwing her a tired smile over his shoulder, but, like the rest of his brave-facing tonight, she knew his heart wasn't in it.

Kicking off her shoes, she climbed on the bed and tucked herself in behind him, wrapping her arms and legs around him and resting her cheek against his back.

He accepted her comfort for a beat before moving subtly away.

"Better get in the bathroom before someone else beats me to it," he said.

She let him go, waiting until he'd closed the door behind him before undressing and climbing into his bed. She lay staring at the ceiling, going over the night's events in her mind.

There had to be a solution to this problem. There had to be.

The door swung open a few minutes later as Casey returned, and she watched him strip off his jeans and fold them neatly before placing them on the chair in the corner. She smiled to herself over how neat he was, so different from her, then scooted over as he joined her in the bed. He reached out to turn off the bedside light, and she waited for him to turn to her in the darkness.

He didn't disappoint, pulling her into his arms. She went willingly, her touch gentle as she caressed his shoulders and back. Neither of them said anything, the only sound their increasingly labored breathing as they teased and stroked one another.

Maybe it was her imagination, but it seemed there was an added urgency to Casey's lovemaking when he finally slid inside her. She gave herself over to his rhythm, giving him what he needed, and it wasn't long before she was clutching his hips and shuddering into climax.

Afterward, he curled his body around hers and pressed a kiss to the nape of her neck. She tried to muster the courage to talk about the band again, now that it was just the two of them in the darkness, but she had no new arguments to make. After a while she felt his body relax behind her, and eventually she drifted toward sleep herself.

Maybe tomorrow would bring new insights.

SHE WOKE TO the sound of boots in the hall and discovered she was alone in the bed. The clock told her it was just past dawn, and she sat up and yawned. She wanted to see Casey before he left the house for the day, so she threw back the covers and dressed in a hurry. She regretted not stopping to check her hair when she reached the kitchen—everyone was there already, empty breakfast plates in front of them, coffee cups in hand. She mustered a smile and ran a self-conscious hand over her no-doubt messy hair.

"Let me guess—you're all early risers," she joked.

"Saved some bacon for you but you'll have to cook your own eggs," Sierra said.

"I'll do it," Casey said, pushing back his chair.

He was wearing one of her favorite tops, a forest-green T-shirt that matched his eyes and he kissed her good morning on his way to the stove.

Breakfast conversation was focused on the day's chores, but the discussion quickly deteriorated into a good-natured argument between Jesse and CJ over whether she was allowed to pitch in, even in a small way.

Eva smiled into her coffee and tried not to laugh too obviously when CJ got Jesse with a good zinger. She was so distracted she was taken by surprise when Casey announced he was heading into town to pick up supplies from the hardware store. Gulping down her coffee, she shoved back her chair and grabbed her plate to take it to the sink.

"I'll walk you to your car," she said.

Casey waited by the door for her, and she exited ahead of him. He shot her a questioning look as he joined her on the porch.

"All good?"

"I just wanted to have a quick word with you. The offer from this Jimmy guy—Rory hasn't rejected it yet, has he?"

She could tell by the way his expression blanked that he didn't welcome her question.

"I don't know. We didn't discuss those kinds of details. I assume Rory will tell the guy we're not interested."

His gaze slid away as he talked, and he lifted a hand to rub the back of his neck. He obviously hated that the band was passing up an opportunity because of him.

"Why don't you tell him to hold fire until you've all had a bit of a chance to think?"

"Time isn't going to change anything. Not from my point of view."

"I know you feel that way now, but maybe something

will come up."

He rested his hand on her shoulder and ducked his head to kiss her forehead. "I appreciate the thought, but nothing's going to change, babe. I've made my decision. The guys made theirs. Do I think they'll resent me at some point because I cost them their big break? Yes. Can I make them take the showcase without me? No." He lifted his hands to signal his helplessness.

"But—"

He kissed her forehead again and turned away. "I need to get to the store, get this order in."

She bit her lip as he strode away from her, effectively cutting off their conversation. Talk about stubborn.

The sound of the kitchen door opening behind her made her turn and she gave Jesse a smile as she slipped past him on her way back into the house. She did her bit to clean up, then got ready for the day and drove to the elevator.

She was so sick of her own thoughts by then that she plugged in her earbuds and cranked up her hip-hop playlist. She allowed herself a short break for lunch, sitting in the open doorway of the van, then she got back to it. By midafternoon she'd completed the final section of the outline and she rode the cherry picker to the ground and walked to the edge of the highway so she could get some perspective on her work.

Her three portraits soared above her—stark, strong black on a white background. There was so much to do yet, so much shadow and highlight and color required to bring her vision fully to life, but she could see she'd gotten the bones right. She'd laid a good foundation, and it was only going to get better from here.

She dusted her hands off as she walked back to the van, ready to move on to the next phase, excited by her work. Not for the first time, she was grateful that the committee had taken a chance on her and allowed her to do what she loved on the side of this defunct structure. She was honored by their faith in her, and she was going to make something beautiful for them to be proud of.

She was smiling as she changed the cartridge in her respirator, and then it hit her—this feeling she was experiencing right now, the privilege she had of creating for a living, was something Casey was denying himself. He was so talented, and performing gave him so much joy, yet he was going to turn his back on the chance to turn his passion into a career and share his gift with the world.

It was *wrong*. Why shouldn't he be allowed to pursue his dreams? Then she remembered their conversation about hitting it big, and realized Casey was so bound up in duty he wouldn't even acknowledge that creating music for a living *was* his dream. He'd carved out a small space for music in his life and refused to let himself imagine or want anything beyond that. He was allowed only so much of what he loved, but no more, because otherwise he'd be letting his family down.

It hurt her to think of him denying his true self in the name of duty. She didn't believe for a second that his family would want him to do so. Jesse was living his best life on the pro rodeo circuit, and Sierra was pursuing her ambition to be a helicopter pilot—why wasn't Casey allowed to chase his own dreams? It made no sense to her. In fact, she was certain that if his siblings knew what was going on, they would be offended and upset that Casey was making this sacrifice on their behalf without even giving them the opportunity to find a way to make it work.

Standing in the hot afternoon sun, resolve hardened inside her.

She loved Casey too much to watch him sacrifice his own happiness.

Sliding the van door shut, she walked around to the driver's side and climbed inside. Her hands were trembling as she put the key into the ignition, because she knew there was a very strong possibility that Casey would view what she was about to do as a betrayal.

She really, really hoped that wasn't the case. But she honestly didn't see what else she could do. She'd tried talking to him, and he'd shut her down. There was no reason to believe that was going to change.

Her jaw set, she put the van in gear and headed for the ranch to do what needed to be done.

Chapter Seventeen

CASEY CAME BACK from town mid-morning with wire to fix another break Jed had found in one of the fences. The two of them rode out together to make the repair, and it was late afternoon by the time they got back.

His thoughts turned to the band and last night's events as he took care of his and Jed's horses while his brother went inside to make some business calls. He'd worked hard all day not to dwell on a situation that wasn't going to change anytime soon, and mostly he'd been successful.

But as he rubbed the horses down, he couldn't help remembering the look on Rory's face last night. He and Rory had gone all through school together, from elementary to senior high. They'd been on the football team together; they'd jammed together in the very early days when neither of them could really play.

He'd never seen his friend look so disappointed and defeated, and it killed Casey that he was the one who'd made him that way.

Can't please everyone.

He knew it was true, but it didn't make it any easier.

Sick of himself, he pulled the stall door closed behind

him. He didn't think of himself as a brooder, and he wasn't in the market to become one, so he very deliberately pushed the subject out of his head and went in search of a shower.

He let himself into the house and was halfway across the living room when Jesse caught him.

"Case. You got a minute?" Jesse stood in the wide doorway to the kitchen, a cup of coffee in hand.

"Sure. What's up?"

Jesse gestured for him to come join him in the kitchen and Casey entered to find Jed and Sierra seated at the table. Jed was frowning, and Sierra was sitting back in her seat, arms crossed over her chest, looking about as pissed as he'd ever seen her.

"Grab a seat," Jesse said, taking one himself.

Casey considered his siblings, not liking the tension in the air. "What's going on?"

"You're crazy, that's what's going on," Sierra said, her eyes bright with anger.

"Sierra," Jed said sharply.

"Why didn't you tell us The Whiskey Shots were offered a showcase in Nashville?" Jesse asked.

Casey flinched. How the hell did they know about the showcase? Had one of the guys called the house and blabbed?

And then it hit him: Eva.

Eva had told them.

"Casey?" Jesse prompted, a frown on his face now.

"Because it wasn't relevant," Casey said.

"How can you stand there and say that?" Sierra asked. "And how dare you turn down an opportunity like that without talking to us about it first."

"It's my decision. My band. Therefore it's none of your business," Casey said. He could hear the defensiveness in his own voice and hated it.

He had no reason to feel defensive. Angry, yes, but not defensive.

"No way is it not our business," Sierra fired back. "Not when your reason for saying no is us. In what parallel universe do you think we would ever ask you to sacrifice your music for the ranch?"

"What Sierra is trying to say is that you don't have to do this, Case," Jesse said. "We can find a way to make this work."

"How?" Casey demanded. "How are we going to replace my labor? Getting a ranch hand in alone would set us back minimum of two thousand a month. We've been on half wages for weeks now. So, what, are you guys going to drop to nothing to pay for an outsider? How about all the repairs I take care of? You want to start paying a real mechanic to take them on while I dick around in Nashville chasing a pipe dream? Do you have any idea what that would add to our bottom line? We're barely making interest payments as it is, and I am not going to be the one who pushes us over the edge."

"I don't know how yet," Jesse said with infuriating calm. "But there has to be a way. Case, you are way too talented to walk away from this chance."

"You think I haven't gone over all the options? The only reason this place is still treading water is because we all agreed to take minimal wages. We've got no fat left. None," Casey said, his neck stiff and hot with anger. "This is Mom and Dad's place, and I will burn my fucking guitar before I let it go under. So this subject is officially done, okay? And I don't want to hear another fucking word."

He strode to the door, opening it so hard it hit the near-by cupboard. Then he was outside, his boots loud on the wooden porch boards as he powered toward the front steps. He was halfway down them when he saw Eva walking toward the house. He saw her take in his anger, saw the wariness and regret flash across her face, but it was too late, he was already barreling toward her, driven by hurt and anger.

"You had no right to talk about my business," he said. "If I'd wanted them to know, I would have told them."

"I know you're angry. I know you probably think I betrayed you—"

"I don't *think*, I know," he interjected.

"—but I couldn't let you sacrifice yourself like that," she said.

"Excuse me? *You* couldn't? Who the fuck are you to make my decisions for me?"

She flinched, visibly paling. "I care about you. A lot. I want you to be happy. You're an artist, Casey. You were born to make music, to perform. You shouldn't have to sacrifice your dreams."

"I told you I'm not interested in fame and all that bull-shit. Just because you want to see your name up in lights doesn't mean I'm the same, Eva. I'm happy with my life just the way it is."

"So you don't want to tour? You don't want to stand on a stage in front of thousands of people and feel the love as they listen to your music? Can you really look me in the eye and say that?"

Her blue eyes blazed into his, demanding the truth.

"At least be honest with yourself, if not with me," she said.

Anger exploded in his brain. "You don't get it, do you? Life isn't always about getting what you want. Most of us don't have the luxury of indulging our dreams."

He was yelling now, couldn't seem to stop himself. Eva's eyes were shiny with tears as she clenched her hands in front of her, the knuckles white with tension.

"I know you're angry with me. I know I shouldn't have broken your trust, but Casey, I have been where you are now. I put my dreams on hold for five years because I was being a team player, and it nearly broke me. I couldn't bear to see you do that to yourself when it doesn't have to be that way."

Casey raked his hands through his hair, his whole body shaking with the force of his feelings. "At the risk of repeating myself, who the fuck are you to take that choice away from me? Did I ask you to fix my life? Did I ask you to give me the benefit of your almighty wisdom?"

"I did it because I care," she said simply, her voice thick with emotion.

"If this is what you caring looks like, spare me," he said. "Give me a big fucking pass."

"Casey." Sierra's voice was sharp with censure, the single word ringing out like a gunshot, and he glanced over his shoulder to see her standing at the top of the porch steps.

"Stay out of this," he warned her.

"You need to calm down," his sister told him.

"Back. Off." He spun to face her, grinding the words out through his teeth.

When he turned back, Eva was disappearing around the corner of the barn, her stride long and urgent. He moved to go after her, still vibrating with the righteous fury of her betrayal, but Sierra was there, putting herself bodily in his path.

"You've said enough, don't you think?" she said.

He glared at his sister, but she simply glared right back, daring him to take it further. After a long beat, he took a step back.

"How can you be so smart and so dumb at the same time?" she said.

"You tell me."

Turning on his heel, he headed for the barn. His roan gelding, Meteor, lifted his head as Casey grabbed a bridle from the tack room and came into the stall.

A handful of minutes later he was riding away from the house, the wind in his face and the devil at his back.

Eva straightened the duvet cover on the bed with shaking hands, smoothing the fabric out. Then she turned and started stacking her research books.

The busywork gave her something to do, which was very important because if she stopped fussing she was going to cry. She could feel the tears sitting at the back of her eyes, but she didn't want to give in to them.

Wasn't sure she deserved to give in to them.

Because Casey was right—she *had* taken away his choice. She'd done so in full knowledge that it was not what he wanted. She'd acted arrogantly, telling herself she knew better than him, telling herself it was for a good cause, that she was making his dream possible. Or at least giving him the best chance of making it possible.

Did I ask you to fix my life?

The memory of his words—his anger—made her stomach lurch and she had to pause and press a hand to her mouth.

He'd always been so sweet and gentle and funny with her, and being on the receiving end of his rare anger had been so much worse than she'd anticipated.

If this is what you caring looks like, spare me. Give me a big fucking pass.

She'd thought she was ready to face the repercussions of her actions. She'd thought she was prepared to face whatever was coming her way when Casey found out she'd spoken to his family against his wishes.

Turned out she'd been wrong, because she couldn't seem to stop shaking.

"Knock knock, just me," a voice said from the open doorway and Eva turned to see Sierra standing there, her face creased with concern.

"You okay?" Casey's sister asked, and Eva tried to smile.

"I've had better days."

"He'll come round. He just took off on Meteor. Give him some time to blow off some steam and he'll be back, ready to grovel for being an asshole."

"He had every right to be angry. He was right, I had no

business interfering."

"Of course it was your business. You care for him and he was about to do a really stupid thing," Sierra said.

"He told me directly that he didn't want to burden you guys with this. And I took that decision away from him."

"Good. I refuse to let you feel bad about this, Eva. You did the right thing."

Eva shrugged a shoulder, unconvinced but unwilling to argue the point.

"Why don't you come up to the house and hang with me and CJ?" Sierra suggested.

"Thanks, but I don't really feel like company."

"Well, I'm happy to hang out here. We can drink beer and talk about the lack of eligible men in town for me to jump on."

Eva smiled, mostly because she knew she was supposed to.

"I think I'm just going to finish tidying up the trailer. It's my thing when I'm stressed—I clean. For some reason it helps."

"Well, in that case, feel free to come up to the house when you are done because we have some closets that seriously need sorting."

Sierra stepped forward and gave Eva a fierce hug.

"Please don't regret what you did. I couldn't have lived with myself if I knew that Casey had sacrificed so much for us. You did the right thing."

Eva took comfort from the other woman's embrace and had to blink away tears as they disengaged.

"Come up to the house the moment you get sick of organizing your underwear by color, okay?"

"Will do. And thanks for worrying about me."

"You and CJ are my girls."

Once Eva was alone she let out a sigh and rubbed her face with her hands.

She felt a little better, which had been Sierra's goal. Bless her.

She went back to tidying, rolling computer cables, folding her clothes, and organizing her meager stock of groceries. Then she scrubbed the bathroom and wiped down all the surfaces in the kitchen.

Casey had been gone for a couple of hours by then, and she'd run out of things to tidy. She glanced in the direction of the house, but she really didn't feel like company. Instead, she took a beer from the fridge and sat on the top step to wait, sure that he would come to her once his temper had cooled, as Sierra had predicted.

She drank the beer and went over and over their fight in her mind, wishing she'd handled it differently, regretting not telling Casey what she'd done so he didn't feel ambushed by his siblings. Every time she recalled his final words, she felt the burn of tears but she refused to give in to them.

She was starting to get stiff from sitting, and she stood and rubbed her arms. It was heading toward twilight, and she went into the trailer and pulled on a hoodie. Then she checked the time.

It had been three hours since Casey left on his ride. He must have returned by now. She turned toward the door, then turned back, uncertain. Then she made a frustrated noise at her own indecision and bounded down the steps in a burst of energy. She made her way around the side of the barn to discover the big double doors still open to the yard. She went inside and saw immediately that Meteor was in his stall.

She walked slowly back out into the yard. Casey was back, and he hadn't come to see her. So much for him blowing off steam and coming to grovel.

She was eyeing the house, trying to decide what her next move should be, when the front door opened and Casey stepped out. He paused when he saw her, then shifted his focus to his truck as he descended the porch steps. She started forward, expecting him to meet her halfway, but he walked past her to his truck, opening the door to collect some paperwork from the passenger seat.

Eva raised her eyebrows, shaken all over again by his coldness.

She swallowed nervously as he shut the truck door and turned toward the house.

"So, that's it? We're not going to even talk about this?" she asked.

He glanced at her and she could see he was still very angry with her—so angry—and it made something deep inside her curl up in a ball.

"That's not a good idea right now," he said, his tone tight and clipped.

She nodded, taking a step backward to signal she wasn't going to push the issue. He walked away, tension in every line of his body. She stood watching until he shut the door behind him, then she stood a little longer, her hands pressed against the sides of her legs as though she needed to take strength from the solidity of her own body.

She hadn't expected instant forgiveness, but she had expected him to at least be willing to talk to her, to look at her. His coldness felt like a cosmic slap, and it took her a moment to work out why—Dane had been like that often after their fights, hanging on to his anger and punishing her with coldness and distance.

Sometimes it had taken a day or two before he treated her like a person he actually liked again. At first she'd done everything she could to appease him, but toward the end of their relationship she'd simply endured, retreating into herself, the two of them orbiting around each other like satellites in the house they'd shared.

I can't do this again.

It was a stupid thought, irrational in the extreme, because Casey wasn't Dane. Not in any way, shape or form.

And yet this feeling was so familiar, probably because it had been just months since she packed her bags and escaped from her ex's cold anger.

This is why smart people don't jump straight from one relationship to another.

A shiver ran down her spine and she hugged herself against the cool of the growing twilight. Then she realized she'd been standing like a sentinel in the yard for too long, and she made her way back to the trailer. She looked around at the newly neatened space and admitted to herself she was not going to be able to spend the night here.

It was too close to Casey, and she knew she'd spend half the night lying awake, willing him to come to her to make things right and resisting the urge to go to him to try to do the same.

Been there, done that with her ex, and she wasn't up for a replay of more of the same. She was opting out, breaking the cycle.

She flipped up the lid on her laptop and did a quick search. Multiple options for flights home to LA appeared in her browser window, all of them departing from Bozeman or Billings the following morning. She could easily drive to Bozeman tonight, find a cheap motel room, and fly home for a few days with her sister. She could afford it now she had the commission, and she'd more than earned a couple of days off. Syd would offer her good food and advice, and Eva could get her head straight before she came back.

And if Casey wasn't ready to talk to her then…well, then she had an answer to the question she was too scared to face right now.

CASEY WAS SITTING on the end of his bed picking quietly at his guitar when Sierra tapped on the open door.

He glanced up at her, but didn't say a word. If she was here to harangue him some more, he wasn't up for it.

"We've been talking. We think we've sorted out a way to make this work. It will mean CJ and Jesse do some extra miles to come home more often between rodeos, but it's doable," Sierra said.

"How does the two of them pitching in between rodeos replace my full-time hours?"

"For starters, there are two of them and one of you. You might be awesome, but you're not that good. As long as we juggle things around and schedule labor-heavy jobs for when they are here, there's no reason why we can't hold the fort here for a few weeks."

"And what happens if they want us to go on tour? I could be gone for half a year or more."

"Well, let's hope we have that problem, because I assume they'll be paying you and you can tip some money into the pot to help top up your wages to commercial rates so we can replace you properly. Cara's younger brother is going to be looking for work once he finishes school. He might be a possibility."

Casey shook his head.

"Why are you so resistant to this?" Sierra asked, coming over and sitting next to him on the bed.

Since he'd been hoping to end their conversation sooner rather than later, he frowned at her.

"Because this place needs all hands on deck right now or we might lose it. I'm not taking any chances with Mom and Dad's legacy."

"So, what, you just hunker down here with your nose to the grindstone and think about what could have been for the rest of your life, resenting the rest of us and this place because you gave up what you really wanted?"

"It wouldn't be like that," he said stubbornly.

"Tell that to Jed."

Casey stared at his sister, and she raised her eyebrows, daring him to disagree with her.

But he couldn't do it, because it was true. Jed had sacrificed his dreams when their parents died. He'd walked away from his education and lost the love of his life to ensure their family stayed together and to safeguard their parents' legacy.

He'd never thrown it in anyone's face, but they all knew this was not the life Jed would have chosen for himself—if he had a choice. But he hadn't.

And Casey did.

His sister had just offered it to him—his family were willing to find work-arounds to set him free. They wanted him to go to Nashville with The Whiskey Shots to see how far his music could take him. They wanted him to fly high.

He looked away from his sister's searching gaze, unable to hold her eye any longer.

"Talk to me," she said gently, and he could hear the love and understanding in her voice.

He rubbed the flat of his hand along the guitar strings, feeling the metallic rasp against his palm. Why was it so hard to speak the truth?

"I never let myself think I could have it," he admitted. "I never let my imagination get that far."

He felt a little dizzy saying it out loud, as though he was letting go of the safety rail and edging closer to the precipice.

"You know, one of my teachers said something to me not long after Mom and Dad died," Sierra said. "She told me that losing your parents young teaches you that life is cruel and unfair. Maybe we all learned that lesson a little too well, because we Carmodys seem to really suck at going after the things we want in life. The things that make us happy."

He thought about it for a moment and realized there was a lot of truth in his sister's words. No matter what happened in his life, there was always a little voice in the back of his head telling him to play it cool and not get too excited.

Almost as though he was afraid to want things in case he didn't get them.

The one big exception to that was Eva. He'd wanted her, and he'd reached for her with both hands.

He slanted a look at his sister. "You really think we can make it work?"

"By hook or by crook. With CJ and my smarts, we can work it out."

"You are such a smartass."

"Like I said—smart."

He glanced down at his guitar again and for the first time since Jimmy Borman had made his offer, he allowed himself to imagine what it might be like to accept it. To go to Nashville with his songs and play for people who had the power to launch The Whiskey Shots out into the world.

His heart shifted in his chest, and his stomach dipped as an electric thrill ran up the back of his neck.

It would be *wild*, to be able to do that. It would be incredible.

It was such new territory for him, he felt dizzy again. But maybe that was okay. Maybe that was what letting go of the safety rail was all about.

Hard on the heels of the thought came another:

"I need to talk to Eva," he said, surging to his feet.

"Big time," Sierra agreed.

Passing her his guitar, he strode out of the room.

CJ, Jed, and Jesse were talking quietly in the living room when he entered. Their conversation stopped abruptly as he headed for the front door with purpose. He took the front steps two at a time, his stride long as he took the path beside the barn to the trailer.

With every step he could feel his brain clearing, his chest loosening. He owed Eva an apology. Yes, she'd taken matters into her own hands, but he'd crashed down on her so hard. Too hard. He'd projected all his frustration and resentment onto her, making her the repository of all his unhappiness.

She hadn't created his circumstances. She hadn't killed his parents or fucked up the ranch's finances. She'd simply tried to find a way to allow him to play his music.

And he'd punished her for it like an asshole.

The lights were out in the trailer. The thought of her lying in the dark, miserable and alone made him want to punch himself in the face. He tapped on the door, calling out to let her know it was him.

"It's me. Can I come in?"

It felt important to ask tonight, even though they'd sped past door knocks and permissions weeks ago.

Silence greeted him, and Casey frowned. Some instinct made him push the door open and he sensed the trailer was vacant before he flicked on the light.

The bed was empty, and the doorway to the bathroom was open. She was gone. He stared at the stack of her research books and the neat bedding and registered that something was missing: her suitcase.

Spinning on his heel, he leapt down the steps in a single bound and broke into a run, only stopping when he reached the yard.

Sure enough, Big Bertha was gone, the place the van had occupied achingly empty. He'd been so preoccupied when he passed through a minute ago that he hadn't registered its absence.

Light spilled into the night as the front door open and Sierra emerged, phone in hand.

"Casey—she's heading home to LA. I just saw my phone. I'm so sorry—she texted an hour ago to let me know she's going to Bozeman for the night so she can fly out first thing tomorrow."

For a moment he didn't know what to do or think. He'd monstered the woman he loved so thoroughly she was leaving town. The thought ricocheted around his mind, rooting his feet to the ground.

Then his brain came back online.

"Text and ask where she's staying," he said.

"I already tried. She hasn't replied," Sierra said.

CJ, Jesse, and Jed were ranged behind her in the door-way, silhouetted by the living room light.

"How many motels are there in Bozeman?" Casey asked Jesse.

Jesse spent his life on the road, if anyone had off-the-cuff knowledge, it was him.

"I don't know. Five, maybe six," his brother answered.

Casey charged up the steps and his family parted to allow him to dart back into the house. He scooped up his truck keys and his own phone, then rocketed out the door again.

"What are you going to do, try all of them?" Jed asked.

"If I have to." He caught Sierra's eye. "Text me if you hear from her, okay?"

"Of course."

"Drive safely, Casey," CJ called as he slid into the pickup.

He lifted a hand in acknowledgment and started the engine with an impatient rev. The moment he was rolling down the driveway, he hit the button on his hands-free to call Eva.

The phone rang and rang before finally cutting across to voicemail. He'd been so fixated on wanting her to pick up, he didn't know what to say.

"It's Casey. Call me when you get this, okay? I'm really—"

A beep sounded to let him know he was out of time and the phone cut to the dial tone. He swore and thumped his fist against the steering wheel. He started to call her again, then realized he didn't want to apologize over voicemail.

The conversation they needed to have was not going to be conducted via recording.

The decision helped settle him, and he adjusted his grip on the steering wheel as he approached the grain elevator on the way into town. It would take him an hour to get to Bozeman, and maybe another to check all the motels. He'd find her. He had to.

The moon was on its way to full, and the white background Eva had sprayed on the wall of the elevator glowed an eerie pearl white against the dark night sky as he approached. He was so busy noticing she'd finished blocking in the outline of her three portraits that he almost didn't register the battered black van parked at the base of the building.

Then he did, and relief and gratitude slammed through him.

Braking hard, he pulled into the gravel lot and cut the

engine.

He saw the pale blur of Eva's face as she turned to see who it was. She was standing at the foot of the elevator, arms crossed tightly over her body.

He walked toward her, hating how wary she looked.

He'd done that to her, and it freaking killed him to have her look at him with uncertainty in her eyes.

He stopped in front of her, close but not too close, fighting the urge to simply pull her into his arms.

"Sierra said you were headed for Bozeman. And flying home to LA tomorrow," he said.

"I was. But I changed my mind."

"I was about to chase you up there," he confessed.

"Good. I stayed because I realized that I'm not a runner. I'm a fighter. And you and I are worth fighting for, Casey Carmody."

He took an involuntary step closer, unable to stay away.

"I'm sorry. I overreacted," he said. "I Hulked out on you because I wasn't being honest with myself and I was too scared of wanting something I couldn't have. I was an asshole, and you deserve better, and I'd really, really like the chance to make it up to you."

Her face was intent, her gaze scanning his face as she absorbed his words.

"I was an asshole, too," she said. "You were right, I was out of line, making decisions for you. I should have kept talking to you. I should have trusted in you and us instead of going all white knight and trying to save you from yourself."

"I don't know, it turns out I might have needed saving," he said. "And I can be pretty stubborn when I have my head up my ass, my sister tells me. It may have been so far up there, I wouldn't have been able to hear what you were saying."

Her mouth lifted at the corners and her face softened. She looked so beautiful to him in that moment, so precious and special, and he couldn't stop himself from giving voice to the words that had been living in his heart for weeks now.

"I love you," he said. "I'm crazy about you. I fucking worship you, Eva King. I have a feeling my life is about to become a really wild ride, but I don't want any of it without you by my side."

It wasn't going to be easy. They were going to be pulled in different directions by her art and his music, but he was confident they could make it work—if she wanted to.

If she was all-in the way he was all-in.

For a heartbeat, the world seemed to hang in the balance—then her eyes lit up, and he saw her answer before she said a word.

"I love you, too. So freaking much."

She launched herself at him, her body slamming into his as she lifted her head for his kiss. Her lips were cool, but her mouth was hot, and she tasted like a hundred different types of sin and a thousand promises all at once. He wrapped his arms around her, holding her as close as was humanly possible, absorbing her goodness and rightness and feeling like the luckiest man on the planet.

He'd almost messed up the best thing that had ever happened to him and he would never, ever make the same mistake again, because she was his one and only, the woman he wanted to spend the rest of his life with.

He knew it in the same way that he knew the sky was blue and grass was green. It was a fact, simple and immutable.

They kissed and clung to each other for long minutes, both of them unwilling to let the other go. Then the bright, annoying ring of his phone cut through the stillness, forcing him to lift his head.

His rear pocket was vibrating, and he pulled out his phone to see Sierra was calling. He showed Eva the screen, and she smiled as he took the call.

"Call off the hounds. I found her," he said.

"What? How? I thought she was going home?" Sierra squawked.

Eva leaned close so she could be heard.

"I am home," she said, her eyes warm on his, and he felt the truth of her words in his blood and bones.

His sister's triumphant hoot almost deafened them both.

"All right, calm down. You'll hurt yourself," he told her.

"I don't care. Congratulations, kids. I knew you'd work it out."

"No, you didn't," Casey said, rolling his eyes at Eva because he knew it would make her smile.

"I totally did. I'm the optimist in the family, remember?" Sierra said.

"All right, optimist, I'm going now. The woman I love and I are having a Moment."

"Oh, Casey, I knew she was—"

He ended the call, and Eva laughed.

"She's going to kill you for that."

"I'll die happy, because I have you."

Then he kissed her again and started backing her toward her van.

"Really?" she asked in between kisses.

"We've done it worse places," he said.

She glanced over her shoulder at her beaten-up van. Then she shrugged.

"What the hell, we'll make it work."

Epilogue

TWO MONTHS LATER

"IT'S TOO HOT for everyone to be standing around outside," Eva said. "I think we should do this another time. Andie's pregnant—she doesn't need to be out in this. It's crazy."

Casey watched as she fussed with her jacket, brushing lint from the lapels before tweaking the cuffs. He'd seen her nervous plenty of times, but this was taking it to a new level.

Stepping forward, he gently batted her hands away and smoothed her lapels himself. Then he buttoned the single button and put his hands on her shoulders.

"It's only eighty. Andie will be just fine. And, babe, you look great. You always look great."

"I don't care how I look," she scoffed.

She'd changed outfits four times, but he did his best not to laugh.

"This is happening, whether you like it or not. People want to celebrate what you've done. They're proud, and you should be, too," he said.

Officially, Eva had finished work on the grain elevator three weeks ago, but the wheels of local government moved slowly, and they were only now getting around to holding a ribbon-cutting ceremony. Ever since she'd been notified, Eva had been like a cat on a hot tin roof, but today her skittishness had reached new heights.

"It seems like a lot of fuss when people can just drive out to the site and see the grain elevator for themselves. They don't need to open it. It's stupid."

Her gaze was wandering over his shoulder as she talked, and she kept tugging on the bottom of her jacket like a kid trying to adjust to her first school uniform.

"Here's the deal," he said. "You turned an eyesore into a piece of art and people want to give you the kudos you deserve. Why is that so hard for you to accept?"

"I don't know."

"The moment you get there you're going to be fine. You know that, right?"

She shrugged, looking genuinely miserable, and he pulled her into his arms.

"Why is this so hard for you?" he asked quietly.

She was silent for a moment, and he could feel her thinking.

"I don't know. I feel…exposed. I don't need to be applauded. I just want to get on to the next project."

"Well, Belgrade don't want you for another two weeks, and you won't be able to start on Gardiner until after winter, so you're going to have to just suck up this moment of glory."

So far, Eva had only signed up two more communities for her Montana art trail project, aided and abetted by Jane McCullough from the Chamber of Commerce, but Casey was confident there would be more. Once prospective towns saw the kind of traffic Eva's work generated, they would want in. He was certain of it.

Eva's hands curled into the fabric of his shirt, then she pushed herself away from his chest, a resigned expression on her face.

"Okay. Obviously you're right and I can't get out of this, so let's just do it."

He was pretty sure he'd never seen anyone look so unhappy about being lauded, but he figured she'd come around to the experience once she was basking in the warmth of the crowd. She'd spent so long on the sidelines, she wasn't used to being center stage. What she didn't fully comprehend yet, he suspected, was that she was a superstar, and the art trail she was in the process of creating was going to make her career.

He was confident she'd work it out eventually, however, and he was glad he'd be around to see it happen, because he loved her more than life itself and watching her succeed made him happier than he ever thought he could be.

His family were waiting patiently in the living room, all dressed in their Sunday best. CJ and Jesse had made a special trip home to be here this weekend. It would be the first of many, since the Shots were due in Nashville in a week's time to record their first album, and they'd be picking up the slack on the ranch while Casey was gone.

None of them knew how long he'd be absent yet— Jimmy Borman had said "how long is a piece of string" when Casey had asked for hard and fast dates—but they'd sorted out a number of contingency plans and Casey was as confident as he could be that his absence wouldn't be the deciding factor in the Carmody ranch's survival.

"We ready to hit the road?" Jed asked.

"I believe we are," Casey said, and Eva nodded with grim determination.

"Let's get this over with," she said.

CJ laughed. "Clearly, we do not need to worry about Eva getting a big head over all of this attention. Good to know."

"I'll be happy if we can just get her there," Casey said.

"Are we doing this or not?" Eva asked, not appreciating being the butt of the joke.

He led her out to his truck, the others following in his wake. Jesse's pickup trailed them during the short drive to the grain elevator, where they had to park in the housing development due to the elevator's lot already being full.

"Why are there so many people?" Eva asked anxiously as they walked back to the site.

"Because what you created is literally breathtaking," Casey said, waving a hand toward the mighty structural canvas that towered above them.

Every time he saw it he got chills. Eva's finished portraits were emotional, evocative, and stirring, and he knew he wasn't the only one who was filled with pride for their small community whenever he stood and contemplated the past, present, and future of Marietta as depicted in the mural. Somehow she'd captured the grit and determination, the connection to the land, the hope for the future that had helped forge a home for generations in the shadow of Copper Mountain, and he still marveled that the petite woman beside him could have created this epic piece all on her own.

"It's astonishing, Eva," Sierra said, awe in her voice. "Every time I'm here, I see something new."

Their arrival created a small stir, and a couple of people broke into spontaneous applause when they saw Eva. A few locals came forward to pat her shoulder and congratulate her personally, and then Jane and Andie were there, drawing her forward to where a large red ribbon had been installed across the width of the mural and a small dais offered speakers a few feet of elevation.

"There she is, the woman of the hour," Andie said.

She was wearing a pair of elegant tailored pants and a blue shirt, and Casey could detect the gentlest of baby bumps starting to round her belly. Pregnancy clearly agreed with her—he was pretty sure he'd never seen her looking so well and happy.

He stood beside Eva as they quickly explained how it was all going to proceed, then Jane patted Eva on the shoulder and stepped up onto the small dais.

"Excuse me, everyone, can I have your attention, please?" she called, and gradually the crowd quietened.

"Thank you. And thank you for coming today for this very special occasion. I think I speak for all of us when I say that we are proud and honored to be the first town to boast an Eva King mural."

She had to pause then because the crowd broke into spontaneous applause. Casey slid his arm around Eva's shoulders and felt her tremble in reaction.

"You okay?" he asked quietly.

"Yes. Thank you for making me come." Her eyes were

swimming when she looked at him and he kissed her briefly.

"You deserve this," he said simply. "Get used to it."

She smiled and nodded, and when it was her turn to step up to the dais she spoke confidently and emotionally, thanking the people of Marietta for trusting her with their stories and having faith in her work. Then it was the Mayor's turn, and he talked for far too long, to the point where people were shuffling their feet and starting to talk among themselves.

Finally it was time to cut the ribbon, and Eva stood with the Mayor and smiled for countless photos before the Mayor wielded the scissors with showy flair, slicing the red satin ribbon in half decisively.

Everyone wanted to talk to Eva afterward, and it was a full hour before they were walking back to his truck. Andie and Heath were having another lunch at their place to celebrate the opening, and he pointed his truck in the direction of Riverbend Park as they left the housing development.

"That's done. Thank God. Your turn next," Eva said, unbuttoning her jacket.

"We'll see," he said, because even though the Shots had landed a recording contract after the showcase they'd played a month ago, nothing was guaranteed in the music industry.

"Jimmy thinks you guys are going to be a hit," Eva reminded him.

"That's Jimmy's job, though, right?" Casey said dryly.

As Jimmy had predicted, they'd had approaches from other record labels and management groups off the back of the exposure the radio competition had given to "Song For

Eva," but the band had chosen to go ahead with the showcase in Nashville because they'd felt as though it offered the broadest opportunity. They'd had no less than three recording companies wanting to talk that night, and Jimmy's advice had helped them sort the wheat from the chaff. Casey would be lying if he said he wasn't excited about the opportunities opening up for the band, but he wasn't about to be swept off his feet by any of it, either.

"I don't need Jimmy's prediction, because I've got my own. I know how good you are. I've seen the way audiences respond to your music."

She sounded so sure, so certain and it made him sit a little straighter. Eva's faith was a gift, a force to be reckoned with, and he thanked the universe that she was on his side every day.

He glanced across at her, struck by the realization that all the good things happening in his life right now were a direct result of the day he'd walked out of the barn and been introduced to a sexy, challenging blonde with bright blue eyes and attitude to spare.

She'd opened up his world and his heart, made him believe in broader horizons, and taught him to fly.

She made him stronger. She made him smarter. She made him braver, and he hoped he did the same for her.

Reaching across the console, he took her hand in his.

"I love you, Eva King," he said.

Her hand gripped his, strong and tenacious. "Back at you, Casey Carmody. I love you so much it hurts."

"Tell me where it hurts and I'll kiss it better," he said.

Her smile was slow and more than a little provocative.

"It actually hurts in a few places. I'll point them out to you later."

"You do that," he said.

Then he concentrated on the road ahead.

The End

If you enjoyed this book, please leave a review at your favorite online retailer! Even if it's just a sentence or two it makes all the difference.

Thanks for reading *The Rebel and the Cowboy* by Sarah Mayberry!

Discover your next romance at TulePublishing.com.

If you enjoyed *The Rebel and the Cowboy,* you'll love the next book in….

The Carmody Brothers series

Book 1: *The Cowboy Meets His Match*

Book 2: *The Rebel and the Cowboy*

Book 3: *More Than a Cowboy*

Available now at your favorite online retailer!

About the Author

Sarah Mayberry is the award winning, best selling author of more than 30 books. She lives by the bay in Melbourne with her husband and a small, furry Cavoodle called Max. When she isn't writing romance, Sarah writes scripts for television as well as working on other film and TV projects. She loves to cook, knows she should tend to her garden more, and considers curling up with a good book the height of luxury.

Visit her website at www.sarahmayberry.com.

Thank you for reading

The Rebel and the Cowboy

If you enjoyed this book, you can find more from all our great authors at TulePublishing.com, or from your favorite online retailer.

TULE
PUBLISHING

Printed in Great Britain
by Amazon